Time & Again

WANDA JENNINGS

BOOK TEN OF THE MAGNOLIA MANOR SERIES

Printed in the United States of America
First Printed October 2025

Published by:
Between Friends Publishing,
1080 GA Hwy 96, Suite #100,
Warner Robins, Georgia 31088

ISBN: 978-1-956544-76-3

To Brandy G., the very epitome of Maude Winifred Cooper. Your portrayal of Maude Cooper onstage brought her to life in a way that words alone never could. This book is for you, in honor of the spirit, strength, and life you breathed into her onstage. Thank you for loving Maude as much as I do. Your friendship means everything to me, and I adore you.

Chapter One

When you live long enough to outlive your two best friends, some might say that that's time enough. Maude Cooper and Opal Tyler had been best friends since they were in elementary school. With almost eighty years of friendship under their belt, there were plenty of adventures to reminisce about as the machines beeped quietly. The last five days had not been easy, but they had been peaceful. Maude did all of the talking, perhaps for the first time in her decades of friendship with Opal who was generally the chattier one of the bunch. They had been friends through it all, through life's ups and downs and history's milestones. Though nothing could ever prepare any friendship for what Maude was once again going through. Maude Cooper sat in the hospital room long after the last machine had quieted down. There was a peaceful silence in the room. Opal could have been sleeping, except her chest no longer rose and fell in rhythm. There had been no struggle, no fight. Opal had gone peacefully a few minutes before seven o'clock that evening.

Five days earlier Opal had entered the hospital after yet another stroke. Only this time she didn't regain her ability to walk or talk. She smiled peacefully in the hospital bed whenever someone visited, which was frequent, but for the first time in her life she was quiet. That was what had unsettled Maude the most. Over the past few years Opal had had a few different strokes. Even in the months after an episode when Opal would sometimes talk nonsense, at least she spoke. This silence was eerie and made Maude think that Opal wouldn't be coming out of this particular episode. When Opal slipped into a coma the evening before she passed away, Maude knew the time had come. Opal and Ruby would be reunited and they'd both just have to wait on Maude for whenever that time came.

"I guess I better call the kids," Maude said to no one in particular. She knew she needed to let the hospital staff do their job and let Opal be moved. The funeral home would be called and Maude would sit down with the men there to discuss the details over the next few days. That was another obligation of outliving your best friends; you had to make sure that their final wishes were followed.

The kids referred to Mavis Montgomery and Wilbur Reynolds-Montgomery, no actual relation to her, but they were family no matter what. Wilbur and Mavis had been with Opal and Maude all morning at the hospital, and when they left mid-afternoon, they both had a feeling that they wouldn't be back. They had been expecting the news all day now, but Maude knew it would be a difficult conversation to have regardless. They had already buried Ruby just five years ago, and now another Stone Sister was gone. Maude, Ruby, and Opal as teenagers had nicknamed themselves the Stone Sisters, after their beloved hometown of Rhinestone. It didn't hurt that Ruby and Opal shared their names with precious gemstones. Now it was up to Maude to continue their legacy and make sure that everyone continued on in their absence.

Wilbur picked up the phone that evening with a heavy heart. Somehow in his gut he knew that Opal was gone. It was Opal who had first discovered him as a ragtag preteen in the forest as he escaped one of his alcoholic father's rants in the fall of 1986. His angelic mother had died from cancer when he was a toddler and he had no memory of her, but his father held out til the spring of 1987 before he met his end. He had quickly been adopted by the Montgomery family, Jameson and Ruby Montgomery, and he never wanted for anything from that moment on. They were already raising their young granddaughter, Mavis, after her mother passed away. They were the family sent from heaven above and he was forever grateful. Maude and Opal had become a part of his life back then, too. He never could have imagined that his chance encounter with Opal Tyler would have changed his life for the better. Opal would always be one of his personal heroes.

"Wilbur, it's me, Maude," Maude said the moment Wilbur answered his cell phone. He had told her time and again that her contact was saved in his phone and he knew who was calling, but this wasn't the time to go over that again. "I guess you know why I'm calling."

"Yes ma'am, I'm afraid I do. How are you?" he asked gently. He half hoped that his gut was wrong and that Maude would say that Opal had sat up in the bed and began reciting the Gettysburg Address, but she didn't. "I'm alright," Maude said. "I already miss her."

"I do, too," Wilbur said. "Do you want me to call Mavis?"

"I'll call her," Maude said. "I need to get out of this hospital and get some fresh air. I'll call Mavis and then everyone else."

"What can I do? You know I'm here to help however I can," Wilbur added.

"I know. You've always been a good boy," Maude said. "I'd like for you and Mavis to come with me tomorrow down to the funeral home. I don't know what time yet. I'll let you know."

"Yes ma'am, I'll pick you both up and we'll get through this together," Wilbur nodded. He hung up with Maude and knew that Mavis would be calling him the minute that she heard the news. He better tell Emily before Mavis called her, too.

Emily was in the kitchen working on a puzzle that was proving to be rather difficult. As soon as she saw Wilbur round the corner, she stood up and walked towards him. "It's Opal, isn't it?" she asked. He nodded and melted into her embrace. Emily had only known Opal Tyler for a little more than a year, but she like everyone else in the world was completely enamored with the spry older woman. "I'm so sorry, Wil. Opal is the most amazing woman there ever was. Do we need to get ready to go to the hospital?"

Wilbur shook his head. "There's nothing to be done right now. These next few days are going to be busy."

"I better call my grandparents," Emily said. "The church will want to get involved." She kissed Wilbur on the cheek and walked into the bedroom to call her grandmother, Beulah, who had known Opal for over sixty years.

True to his assumption, Mavis called a few minutes later. She was crying softly and Wilbur felt a surge of affection for his sister. "Wilbur, I'm coming over. I can't be here alone, I'm just too sad. And what about Maude? She shouldn't be alone either. Maybe we need to have one giant sleepover."

Wilbur could tell that Mavis was already in her car and would be pulling up in his driveway in less than two minutes if she took the back road through the woods from Magnolia Manor to his cabin. "I'll have your hot chocolate waiting," Wilbur said. "See you in a minute."

Emily peeked her head out of the bedroom and asked, "Is that Mavis? I'll get the guest room ready."

Mavis, Wilbur, and Emily sat around the small dining room table that evening drinking hot chocolate and picking at their chocolate chip cookies while they reminisced. Wilbur finally managed to talk Mavis out of the idea of surprising Maude with a sleepover at her house. "She needs to be alone for a bit to process this. We'll see her in the morning," he said gently.

No one slept well that night across Rhinestone. Opal Tyler was an institution in this town and many others across the southeast. Those who loved her and knew her best wouldn't be surprised if the whole world entered into a state of mourning. Wilbur told Emily and Mavis that he was going out early to pick up breakfast, but first he stopped at Opal's house to check on things. The bees were buzzing as they hurried to and fro from the hives to the nearby flowers that spread out in every direction. He walked around the grounds and soaked in the rays from early morning sunshine that seemed even brighter than it had been all week. The birds were chirping loudly all around as they pecked at the earth for insects. "I figured I'd find you here sooner or later," Maude said. She had walked over from her house that had been next door since the early seventies. She hugged Wilbur tightly and asked if he had had breakfast yet.

"Not yet," he shrugged. "I was going to run by the Starlight Cafe and pick up something. Want to ride over with me?" He was surprised when Maude shook her head. "I need to gather up some things before we meet with the funeral home later this morning. I told them we would be there around ten."

"Ok. Then I'll swing by around nine-thirty with Mavis," Wilbur replied. He hugged the frail older woman again and watched as she walked back towards her house. She was surprisingly spry for her age and lifestyle choices. She followed a high sugar and carb diet, never exercised, and would still ride a motorcycle if the law would allow it. She had more speeding tickets than most people had teeth. After he picked up a few sausage biscuits and a breakfast casserole from the local diner, he swung by his house and made coffee for the two women who were just now waking up. Emily had offered to call out of work, but Wilbur assured her that he and Mavis would be fine. After she showered, ate breakfast, and finished getting ready, she was off to her office in Junction while Wilbur and Mavis headed to Maude's house.

"It feels strange that the world is still spinning and people are still going on with their daily lives," Mavis said. "I felt the same way after Big Mama passed, too. I guess time really does go on."

Wilbur nodded. "I feel the same way."

Maude was waiting on her front porch when Mavis and Wilbur pulled into her gravel driveway. "She looks so sad," Mavis whispered. Wilbur put the truck in drive and watched as the older woman eased down the front steps and walked towards his truck. Mavis had slipped into the backseat so Maude could ride in the front. Wilbur helped Maude inside and closed the door carefully once she was inside.

Peterson and Sons Funeral Home was well respected by the people of Rhinestone. It was the same funeral home that Ruby had chosen for her own funeral. She had been satisfied with the way that they had handled Jameson's service years before hers. Elijah Peterson had bought the funeral parlor from Mortimer Raven in 1995 and renamed it Peterson and Sons after Mortimer passed away in early 2000. It was only fitting that Opal used them as well. However, Wilbur and Mavis quickly learned that Opal had other plans.

"She wanted to be cremated," Maude shrugged. "She said she doesn't want to be put in a box and buried underground. I have express directions on what I'm to do with her ashes." Maude held up an envelope that had a folded piece of paper inside it.

"She has a plot at Deerlane Cemetery," Mr. Peterson mentioned.

"Well, she don't want it," Maude said. Mavis and Wilbur could hear the edge of agitation in her voice.

"We can donate it to someone else," Mavis suggested.

"We can absolutely do that if you're sure she won't use it," Mr. Peterson replied.

Maude cocked her eyes at Wilbur. "Did I not say she wouldn't be using it?" Wilbur knew he needed to head this off before it went too crazy. "We will discuss donating it for sure," Wilbur nodded. "I think what we need to work out now is when we can do her celebration of life." Opal had insisted that it be a celebration and not a day of mourning. She had always been the most joyous, spontaneous person in life and they wanted to make sure her funeral was the same. "We're expecting quite a turnout," Wilbur continued.

They agreed to hold Opal's ceremony on Friday afternoon. Beaver Crossing Holy Church for the Faithful wasn't big enough to hold the crowd that they were expecting, so the funeral home agreed to open up all of their rooms, and if weather permitted, have an overflow outside. Mavis would be doing the slideshow, Wilbur would coordinate the food, and Maude said she'd get the word out. "Would you like to look at the options for urns?" Mr. Peterson asked, but Maude shook her head vigorously. "Is there a problem, Ms. Cooper? Will we be using the plot after all?"

Maude rolled her eyes so hard that Mavis was afraid they'd be stuck that way. "She's already got an urn," Maude retorted.

"Of course she does," Peterson nodded. "Why didn't I think of that?"

As they walked out of the funeral home, Maude shook her head. "I don't think he realizes how many people will come on Friday," she grumbled.

Mavis was already on her social media announcing the date and time for Opal's ceremony. While Wilbur helped Maude back into the truck, Mavis took a phone call by the large live oak tree. She waltzed back to the truck a few minutes later smiling broadly. "That was William from the news. They're going to run a story on Opal tomorrow. I was giving him the details of the service."

"Wow, Mavis, that's incredible," Wilbur smiled.

"That is nice. Opal would love it. She always liked being on the television," Maude nodded. She pulled out a small notebook from her purse and crossed off a few line items on the first page. "Now we gotta figure out where the rest of Opal's stuff is."

"What do you mean?" Wilbur asked.

"She didn't give me much to go with," Maude shrugged.

"I'm confused," Mavis added.

"Let's get some lunch and I'll show you what she left me," Maude said. She directed Wilbur to her favorite pizza shop just off the highway. It felt like yesterday when he was first meeting Emily and her grandmother at this same spot for their first date, coined a play date by Opal and Maude. It would be hard going anywhere in Rhinestone where no memories of Opal, Ruby, or Jameson lingered.

Mavis ordered a large pepperoni pizza for Wilbur and Maude to share, and a calzone with extra mozzarella cheese, pepperoni, and peppers for her. Wilbur and Mavis waited for Maude to get comfortable in the booth before asking her again what she was referring to. Maude opened the envelope and pulled out a piece of paper with Opal's iconic penmanship visible through the folds. "Maybe y'all can figure it out," Maude shrugged.

Mavis took the piece of paper and gently unfolded it. Tears sprang to her eyes as she held it up to her nose. "It smells like her," she whispered.

Wilbur nodded and patted Mavis on the back. "It really does. It smells like lavender. Where did you find this?" he asked Maude.

"Opal gave it to me two weeks ago. She told me not to open it until it was time," Maude shrugged. "I knew what she meant. You don't stay friends with Opal Tyler for nearly eighty years and not know what she means. Anyways," she sighed. "I opened it last night when I got home and well, you'll see."

Mavis and Wilbur passed the letter back and forth for a full ten minutes. "I'm, well, I'm confused," Mavis finally said. Wilbur merely grinned. "It's a puzzle. She always loved puzzles."

"She really did. And she loved irritating me more than anything," Maude grimaced. "She'd stay up all night to put a puzzle together, but I never did. I hate this kind of thing."

"It's just another adventure for y'all to do together!" Mavis exclaimed.

"So, if I'm reading this correctly, and I may not be," Wilbur mused. "She's leading you on an adventure to find her will?"

"That's what I gathered," Maude shrugged.

"Wow," Wilbur chuckled.

"That's one way to put it. I'm too old for this mess," Maude huffed. Normally Opal was the one who pointed out Maude's increasing age, but since she was no longer around to do that, Maude had to bring it up herself.

"Well, how can we help?" Wilbur asked.

"I don't even know where to begin," Maude said. Wilbur swore he saw a tear in her eye, but he knew better than to ask. He quickly racked his brain and thought of the times over the years where he had seen Maude be visibly upset over something. It wasn't often. He hoped this scavenger hunt wouldn't be the thing to send her over the edge once and for all. "And here's the first clue," Maude said. She opened the envelope and handed Wilbur a small piece of paper with a riddle.

Chapter Two

Maude,

If you're reading this, you know what it means. I hope you haven't read it too early; you were never one to follow instructions. I won't get all philosophical on you, but you know me, I couldn't just go without leaving behind a little sparkle.

You were always the Watson to my Holmes, the sass to my class, and the only person in town who could ever outbid me at an estate auction. So I've left you something, but you're going to have to work for it. I've hidden my will and a few other secrets I've never shared behind a trail of riddles, clues, and memories.

Follow each one, and at the end, you'll find more than just dusty old paperwork. Have Mavis and Wilbur tag along, just for old time's sake.

Your first clue waits in the place where we last laughed until we cried.

With all my love,
Opal

P.S. Wear sensible shoes and don't forget to pack your snacks, you know you work better on a full stomach.

Clue 1:
In velvet chairs and china neat,
Where secrets spill with sugar sweet,
A rose once wilted, now it blooms,
Seek the table near the back room.

Chapter Three

"So, where do we go?" Mavis asked. "What does that mean? Where did you find the first clue?"

"That was easy," Maude said. "It was taped under the rocking chair on her porch. We sat out there just last month and laughed and laughed. I don't even remember why we were laughing. But there this note was taped with a pound of tape, I swear."

Wilbur read the clue over and over again trying to discern its meaning. "Well, it's leading us to a back room. The back room suggests a place, maybe a business. Or is she talking about her house?"

Maude shook her head. "It can't be her house. Opal's back room doesn't have a table in it. It's where she stores everything she brews and cans. There's two shelves full of stuff, but no table."

"Ok, then a business, maybe," he pondered. "Is there a coffeehouse y'all liked to go to?"

Maude scrunched up her nose and thought for a second. "Is she talking about that durned place she liked to go to?" Maude asked.

"I don't know," Mavis squeaked. "Maybe! Let's go and see!"

"Mavis, we can't barge into a random business and start looking in all their cabinets," Wilbur chuckled. "We need a plan."

"We don't need a plan," Mavis and Maude said together. Maude had already swallowed the last bite of her pizza slice and began gathering up the letter and paper that held their first clue.

"Now wait a minute," Wilbur countered. "If it is whatever place you're talking about, we need to figure out the rest of the clue. There's something about a rose. What could that mean? Does this place have fresh flowers anywhere? Is it a flower shop?"

Maude merely shrugged.

"Oh, come on, Wilbur. Let's go see. This is so exciting," Mavis interjected.

"Mavis, I don't even know what place she's talking about," he whispered underneath his breath.

"My hearing ain't that bad, Wilbur," Maude laughed. "I don't know the name of it. Opal loved to go there and I'd take her and drop her off. She had friends everywhere. She tried to get me to go. Maybe I should have gone in there more often. Maybe I should have."

"Don't do that," Mavis quieted her. "This isn't the journey for regrets and could have should haves. This is exciting and meant to be fun."

"I know how to get there," Maude nodded. "It's downtown near her old salon and that small bookstore they opened next to Eddie's old flower shop."

"Wait a minute," Mavis exclaimed. "Do you mean the new Rhinestone Tea Room?"

"It ain't exactly new," Maude countered.

"It's new for Rhinestone!" Mavis replied. "Anything that's opened in the past year is new. I'm so glad Rhinestone is finally thriving again. I was worried there for a bit."

"Have you been there?" Wilbur asked.

Mavis nodded. "Opal and I went last month! Oh my heavens, do you think she left the clue then? I wasn't paying enough attention! That little shop is so cute! They even sell some of Opal's brews there!"

"That could very well be it then," Wilbur smiled. He checked his watch and looked up to see Maude paying the bill. "What are we waiting for?" Maude asked. "Time's a wasting."

Wilbur and Mavis followed Maude outside to Wilbur's truck. It was about a fifteen or so minute drive to downtown Rhinestone. When Mavis and Wilbur were kids, the downtown area was booming, but slowly over the years the businesses either dried up or moved to other towns like Junction. Within the last two or three years, many new independent shops began to open up and the downtown area in Rhinestone was again revitalizing right in front of their eyes.

"The Rhinestone Tea Room?" Wilbur asked as he parallel parked in front of the hand painted sign. "I've never heard of this place."

"That doesn't surprise me," Mavis giggled. "You aren't fancy like Opal and I."

"I bet we won't find a glass of iced sweet tea in there," Maude frowned.

Wilbur held the door open for the two women and followed behind them. His eyes took a second to adjust to the dim lighting. There was a wooden counter with a smiling woman waiting to greet them. "Welcome to the Tea Room," she smiled.

Maude sneezed loudly and rubbed her eyes. "Now where would Opal hide whatever it is?"

"Can I brew you something special today?" the woman asked.

"We're looking for something," Maude grumbled.

"Wonderful. What wonderful brews can I interest you in today? I could also read your tea leaves for you when you're ready," the woman continued.

"That sounds lovely," Mavis shrieked. "Wilbur, come over here." Wilbur was caught between following Mavis to the counter and tracking Maude as she darted around the small shop looking under each of the three tables, chairs, and every teacup she could reach.

"What brings you here today?" the woman asked. "Hello, I'm Lauryn." She stared at Wilbur and batted her eyes, but he was too busy watching Maude to notice. They would be lucky if they made it out of this quaint shop without Maude breaking anything.

"We're on a scavenger hunt," Mavis said breathlessly. "We think our first clue led us here."

"How marvelous," Lauryn breathed. She suddenly looked up to see Maude standing on top of one of the tables trying to reach a shelf of teacups. Wilbur had also noticed and hurried over to help Maude down before the entire shelf tumbled over. "Let's take it easy," he mumbled, knowing full well that Maude had never taken anything easy a day in her life.

"What's the first clue?" Lauryn asked. Mavis handed her the small piece of paper and watched as recognition dawned on her face. "Our back room has velvet chairs and a china cabinet full of our most delicate teacups." As soon as she said that, Maude perked up and looked around. "Maybe it isn't the safest room for your friend over there," Lauryn whispered to Mavis.

"Why don't we wait out here?" Wilbur suggested. He led Maude to a table that was clear of anything breakable and sat down across from her. "Y'all go and look in that back room, but please hurry, Mavis. I don't know how long I can give you." He gestured towards Maude who was staring him down.

Mavis scurried to the back room with the employee right behind her. "This is so exciting! Nothing ever exciting happens here!" Lauryn crooned. Mavis looked around the contents of the small back room. There were the velvet chairs and china cabinet that held beautiful ornate teacups and saucers. This had to be the place. "What are we looking for again?" Lauryn asked.

"Where secrets spill with sugar sweet," Mavis read from the card. "People like to chat and gossip when they sip tea together. And then it mentions a rose. Is there a rose in this room? Maybe a fake one because a rose can't last forever. Hmm."

"Our rose patterned china is over here on this shelf," Lauryn explained. She pulled a tiny key from her pocket and unlocked the cabinet. Five beautiful teacups and saucers were arranged in a perfect order along the top shelf. Each cup had an identical pale pink rose pattern on it.

"These are beautiful!" Mavis breathed. "There's nothing on the cups that I can see though."

"What about this?" Lauryn asked. She gently lifted each cup and saucer off the shelf to see the linen that was underneath acting as a barrier between the shelf and the cups.

"What is that?" Mavis asked.

"Some sort of runner, I think. It's silk. Hold on, let's see," Lauryn replied. She laid the silk linen on the table nearest her and gasped. "It's a rose in bloom! And there's something stitched underneath it!"

"You've got to be kidding me!" Mavis exclaimed. Sure enough, there was golden stitching underneath the runner, hidden from the eyes of anyone who sat there and didn't turn it over. Opal Tyler's name was stitched perfectly for them both to read. "And here's a note!" Lauryn gasped. She handed the piece of paper to Mavis who read it eagerly. "History whispers in sepia tone, portraits watch, forever alone. Find the lady in the feathered hat. She always knew just where I sat."

"What does that mean?" Lauryn asked, incredulously.

Mavis merely shrugged. "I guess it's our next clue! Let's go show Wilbur and Maude." Before Lauryn could object, Mavis quickly jerked the runner off the shelf, much to Lauryn's surprise. Lauryn straightened up the backroom and then followed Mavis to the front near the counter where Wilbur was talking to Maude. Mavis handed Wilbur the runner and note and watched as he read it. "This doesn't make any sense to me," he chuckled. He handed it to Maude who took the runner gingerly. "Opal made this," she said quietly. "I'd recognize her stitching anywhere."

"What does the clue mean?" Mavis asked as Maude ran her fingers over the lettering.

"She's leading us to that place where she donated that ugly old lady," Maude whispered.

Mavis looked at Wilbur who looked equally as perplexed. "I still don't understand," Mavis breathed to Wilbur. "What place and what old lady?"

"Is Opal a criminal?" Lauryn asked. "Because you can't just throw out old ladies or donate them or whatever the note is saying. That is odd for sure."

Before anyone could respond, the front door opened and a customer walked in, thus capturing Lauryn's attention. "I mean, she's right," Mavis said. "What old lady are we talking about?"

"That picture she painted," Maude said. This didn't help clarify anything to Wilbur or Mavis as Opal had been an avid painter for as long as either of them had ever known her. "You know the one I'm talking about. She's wearing a blue hat and is smiling. The hat has a big old feather in it."

Mavis nor Wilbur had any clue about any portrait of a mysterious lady. "Where is this portrait at?" Wilbur asked. He hoped that with pointed questions he could direct Maude in a more certain direction. "At the historical society," Maude said. The historical society was located in one of Rhinestone's oldest buildings one street away from the tea shop.

Mavis hurried to the counter and thanked Lauryn for her time and let her know that she'd be back in soon for some tea. "Bye Mavis! Bye Wilbur. Come back anytime!" Lauryn called out to them as they scurried out.

"Shall we drive over to the historical society?" Wilbur asked. He knew it wasn't far, but he didn't want to force Maude to walk in the heat of the day.

"It ain't far," Maude huffed. She took off down the sidewalk with a surprising amount of gusto. Wilbur and Mavis hurried off behind her. Without a sound, Maude ducked down a narrow alleyway that had trash cans and a stray cat eating what looked like a set of fish bones on the ground. "Shouldn't we stay on the sidewalk?" Mavis asked cautiously, but Maude ignored her. Thankfully, the alley wasn't long or dangerous, though the feral cat did hiss when Maude almost stepped on his tail.

"This is it," Maude said as they walked to the front of the ancient brick building on the corner a few minutes later.

"I don't think I've ever been in here," Mavis said. She peered through the large glass window, but the lights were off inside. There didn't seem to be anyone inside either. "It's closed. What do we do now?"

"I have a key somewhere," Maude said. She rummaged around in her purse that had been slung over her shoulder.

"A key for what?" Mavis asked.

"The front door of this here place," Maude frowned. "It's in here somewhere." She dumped her purse on the sidewalk and began sifting through the contents.

"Why on earth do you have a key to the historical society?" Mavis asked. She looked at Wilbur but he didn't have any idea why Maude Cooper of all people would possess a key that could unlock all of Rhinestone's history.

"Found it!" Maude huffed. She handed Wilbur a ring full of keys and looked at him as he stared back dumbfound. "Which key is it?" he asked. There were easily thirty different keys of various sizes on the ring.

"How the hell should I know," Maude shrugged.

"Why do you have so many keys?" Mavis asked.

"You never know when you might need one," Maude said.

"Right," Wilbur nodded, even though that hadn't answered any of their questions. "Well, are we even allowed inside? Assuming we find the correct key of course."

"The key is on there," Maude said. "If we have a key, we ain't breaking in. Though I could do that, too." She handed Wilbur what he realized was a small lock picking set. "Why do you have this?" he gasped.

"Wilbur, sometimes it's best to not ask questions. Now are you going to unlock the door or not?" Maude replied.

Wilbur looked to Mavis for help, but she merely smirked. "Ok, here goes nothing," he shrugged. He studied the keys on the ring after looking at the shape of the lock and determined that half of the keys could potentially be the right one. Who knew if the correct key was even on the ring at all, but he had to try. Otherwise Maude would attempt to pick the lock and who knows what kind of alarms would be set off. "Oh sheesh, what if there's an alarm that we trigger?" he asked.

"Then we hurry up and get what we came for and leave," Maude said. She had forgotten that these two kids were not on her same level. "Wilbur, hand me those keys. I'll do it myself." She took the ring of keys back and began the process of figuring out what key would work. After five minutes of trying, she finally found the one she needed. "Here we go," she announced to a sweating Wilbur and Mavis. It was far too warm outside to be standing directly in the sun while she fiddled with the keys. She marched inside and looked around for a light switch. "I can't believe I forgot my flashlight."

"I don't hear an alarm, do you?" Mavis whispered. "Oh no! What if it's a silent alarm? Harlan's going to swoop in and arrest us."

"I think it's fine," Wilbur said, looking around. He didn't see any panels on the wall suggesting that the old historical society had an alarm system in place. The lights came on overhead and Wilbur saw Maude waiting for them on the other side of the room. "The art exhibit is over yonder past where we had the Ladies Auxiliary meetings back when."

Maude led them to a room that was full of portraits and photographs on the walls. There were columns that held objects in glass cases with gold plaques underneath showcasing artifacts from Rhinestone's beloved history. "Here's the old lady," Maude pointed out. Wilbur and Mavis hurried over to a framed portrait on the wall that was roughly the size of a standard piece of paper. "She isn't ugly," Mavis laughed. "She's unique."

"Who is she?" Wilbur asked.

"The plaque says she's the wife of the founder of Rhinestone. Let's see, her name is Petunia. Opal painted her just a few years ago. How neat!" Mavis exclaimed. "The clue has something to do with her." She looked intently at the painting and read the plaque a few more times.

"Oh hell, do I have to do everything?" Maude grumbled. She grabbed the painting and pulled it off the wall. She flipped it over and ignored the shocked gasps from behind her.

Chapter Four

"You can't do that!" Mavis gasped.

"I just did," Maude shrugged. "I know what I'm doing. See, look here. It's another one of those note thingies." Sure enough, there was a small envelope taped to the back of the portrait. Maude ripped it off and hastily hung the portrait back where it belonged. She opened the envelope and handed the note inside to Mavis to read.

"Tick-tock, the hands do spin, but memories are stored within. We broke this clock that summer night, its pendulum swings with hidden light," Mavis read. "Ok, so it's a clock. Well that's not helpful. I bet there's thousands of clocks this could be."

"You know exactly what clock it is," Maude shook her head, but Wilbur and Mavis both looked perplexed. "You've both seen it a million times at my house," Maude continued.

"The clock at your house?" Wilbur asked. "The one by your front door right when you walk inside?"

"That's the one," Maude nodded. "It has to be. Ruby, Opal, and I broke that clock one summer when we tried to move it down the hall. Jameson tried to fix it, but it's never worked since. I could have taken it to someone to repair, but I kind of liked it better. I always hated the noise." Now that Wilbur thought about it, he had never heard the clock make a noise, and he had spent so much time at Maude's over the years. He had never paid too much attention to the old clock. "Well don't just stand there, let's get on to my house," Maude said. There was a sudden gleam in her eye that hadn't quite been there lately.

"Well, hold your horses, we have to lock up here first and make sure everything's where it's supposed to be," Wilbur said as Maude rushed past him. She tossed him the key ring full of keys. "Ok, I'll make sure that everything is locked," he chuckled. He motioned for Mavis to follow after Maude while he locked the front door. Mavis and Maude couldn't get very far without him. He had the keys to his truck, or at least he thought he did.

Wilbur locked the front door of the building and jogged to catch up with Maude and Mavis who had vanished while he searched the key ring for the right key. He felt around his waist and reached in his pocket for his truck keys, but they weren't there. He hadn't unclipped the truck keys from his belt loop, and he hoped they hadn't fallen off along their walk to the historical building. He cut down the alleyway that Maude had shown them earlier and made his way back to the tea shop where his truck was parked. To his surprise, Maude and Mavis were in his truck and the truck was running.

"About time you got here," Maude said as Wilbur climbed in the driver's seat.

"How did you get my keys?" Wilbur asked.

He looked at Maude who was grinning in the passenger seat. "Wilbur, this ain't my first rodeo. One day I'll teach you my ways."

Mavis collapsed in a fit of laughter. "Oh Wilbur, she was quicker than lightning. She unclipped them and scooted on back to the truck before you even blinked. I swear she has more energy than me and you combined."

Wilbur knew that to be true. He drove to Maude's house and waited as Maude unlocked her front door. There was the antique grandfather clock that he had seen so many times. Mavis read the note again and frowned, "The clue doesn't say anything about where the next clue could be hidden. We can't take this old thing apart!"

"Simmer down," Wilbur chimed in. "We'll figure it out." He turned towards Maude who was standing a few feet away. "Where did this clock come from?"

"It was my aunt Winifred's," Maude explained. "When she passed away, my father brought it to my house. One summer I was cleaning out some stuff and wanted it moved. I didn't realize how heavy it was. Opal, Ruby, and I tried to slide it, but it toppled over," she smirked. "Jameson had to come over and the four of us managed to get it back standing. He tinkered with it for a bit, but never could get it to make noise again, which was fine with me."

As she spoke, Wilbur got down on his hands and knees and inspected the old clock. There were a few scuffs and scrapes along the back where he assumed it had fallen when the three women had attempted to move it. He ran his hand underneath the base of the clock where there was an ornate ridge and felt around. "I think there's something under here," he said. "Do you have a flashlight?"

Maude nodded and walked to her kitchen where she knew a flashlight should be. She handed it over to Wilbur and he laid flat on the ground to get a better look. He shined the light underneath and nodded. "There's an envelope under here. Let me see if I can fish it out."

He swiped his hand a few times underneath the base of the clock and managed to push the envelope out. Mavis leaned down and picked it up. She shook the dust off and opened it carefully. Wilbur stood up and brushed off his pants. "For what it's worth, I think I could fix it if you ever decide that you want it to work again," he told Maude.

"Thank you," she smiled. She turned quickly to Mavis who was waiting to read the next clue aloud.

"Where roses climb and wisteria twine, my favorite bench marks the line. Sit and listen with your heart, beneath you'll find a clue to the next part," Mavis read. "And look, here's a key!"

"Not another one," Wilbur laughed.

"This is an odd looking key," Mavis said. She passed it over to Maude who frowned.

"I don't recognize this key," Maude said. "Wilbur?"

Wilbur held it in his hand and shook his head. "I don't recognize it either."

"It has to be something outside because where

roses and wisteria climb," Mavis mused. "Oh my heavens, it's the Manor. Magnolia Manor. Roses and wisteria! Wilbur, it's gotta be that old gate in Big Mama's back garden where that concrete bench is. Big Daddy built that arbor and everything. But wait," she fretted. "There can't be an envelope still under that bench out there in the elements."

"It's worth a shot," Wilbur said. He turned towards Maude who was reading the note with the clue. "What do you say?"

"It has to be that old bench. Opal loved to sit out there and listen to the birds and bugs and whatever else she listened to out in nature," Maude nodded.

"Alright, let's head over to the Manor," Wilbur said. He looked at the clock on the wall and noticed that it was nearing supper time. He was surprised that Maude hadn't mentioned food by now. Emily should be getting off work soon. He checked his phone and saw that he had two missed calls from Emily. "Hold on, let me call Emily back." He stepped outside to the porch and called his wife.

"Hey!" Emily said. "Is everything ok?"

"I'm sorry," Wilbur said. He quickly caught Emily up on the events of his day and could tell that she was excited. She said she would meet them all over at the Manor and bring over something for them all to eat for supper. Wilbur was the luckiest man in the world to be married to the women of his dreams, who just so happened to adore his family as much as he did. He walked back inside and caught Mavis and Maude up on the plan. "Let's get a move on then," Maude nodded. She wasn't sure how many clues there would be in this saga. Knowing Opal, it could go on for ages.

Emily wasn't at the Manor when Wilbur, Mavis, and Maude arrived, so they hurried to the back garden that Ruby had so painstakingly tended to in her day. The garden gate was more for decoration than anything as there wasn't a lock on it. "Then what is this key for?" Mavis asked as she looked around. She had taken great care of the grounds after her grandmother had passed away. There in the center of the rose garden was a handmade wooden arbor carved by Jameson with roses and wisteria winding around it, with a concrete bench underneath. They searched and didn't see an envelope anywhere. "It has to be here somewhere," Mavis pondered. "Ok, so the bench is beneath the arbor, but there's nothing written or inscribed on the bench."

"What about under the bench?" Wilbur asked. He looked underneath and didn't see anything there either.

"You got a shovel?" Maude asked.

"Great idea!" Wilbur said. He hurried to the garden shed and found what he was looking for. Leave it to Opal Tyler to bury the next clue. It didn't take him long to discover a tin box hidden in the dirt beneath the bench. "How clever!" he chuckled. He blew the dirt off the metal box and handed it to Maude. "I bet I know what that key is for," he smiled.

Maude inserted the key and heard the click as the lock opened. She lifted the lid of the box and found the desired envelope. "Here, Mavis, you do the honors," she instructed. She handed the envelope to Mavis and waited for her to open it.

"Voices rise where vows were said, and secrets lie where prayers were led. Under the pew where you once tripped, a paper waits, its edges ripped," Mavis read carefully. "It has to be the church!"

"I thought I heard y'all out here," Emily called out as she came around the corner. "I hope you're hungry. I picked up some fried chicken, mashed potatoes, green beans, biscuits, and peach cobbler."

Over supper, Mavis told Emily all about their adventures and lamented that it was getting too late to continue on their adventure. "Maybe I can come with you tomorrow!" Emily suggested.

"Good idea," Maude nodded. She drained her glass of sweet tea and eyed the pan of peach cobbler that was sitting on the counter.

"Who all wants peach cobbler?" Mavis asked. She already knew the answer. Peach cobbler was a fan favorite amongst them all. She ladled out the cobbler into bowls and topped each portion with a generous scoop of vanilla ice cream. For an added garnish, she drizzled caramel sauce on top and passed the bowls around to everyone. When supper was over, Wilbur took Maude back home and promised to be over at her house in the morning with Emily and Mavis in tow. When he returned to the Manor, he found Emily and Mavis at the kitchen table with boxes of photographs and photo albums spread out. "There are so many perfect photographs for the slideshow. I don't know how to choose!" Mavis whined.

"Put as many as you want," Wilbur said. "The slideshow can be two hours long. In fact, we may need it to be. I have a feeling that this is going to be a very popular service." He sat down and helped the women sort through photos for the rest of the evening. By the time he and Emily left a few minutes before midnight, he carried a stack of photos that Mavis had given him that he had long forgotten. His favorites were the photos of when he first came to the Montgomery family at age twelve with young Mavis and Ruby, Jameson, Opal, and Maude in their prime. Emily taped them to the refrigerator until she could pick up new photo frames for them.

Mavis was ready early the next morning when Wilbur and Emily pulled up to the Manor. Emily had taken off from work that morning, but was scheduled to go back to the office after lunch. They picked up Maude who was sitting on her porch waiting for them. She had a shovel, the tin box that now held all the envelopes, and her infamous bag that Wilbur was certain held whatever else they may need. "I brought some flashlights this time," Maude said as she climbed into the truck. "I shouldn't have forgotten them yesterday, but I won't forget again."

"What else have you got in that bag?" Emily asked.

"Stuff," Maude replied.

"Probably that ring full of keys," Wilbur added.

"Exactly," Maude nodded. "I added that key to the box to it so we're ready just in case."

"To the church!" Emily hollered.

"To the church!" Mavis echoed.

"It's going to be a long day," Maude grumbled. She had not slept well last night and was up before the roosters crowed at the farmhouse down the lane. She wasn't certain why she had tossed and turned all night, but she had her ideas. This was the first time in her entire life that she was without Ruby and Opal both. It had started to wear on her. She was dreading Opal's celebration of life service, not because she didn't want to celebrate Opal, but because it just didn't feel right celebrating one of the most incredible women on earth without her there.

"Where exactly at Beaver Crossing is the next clue hidden?" Emily asked.

"Voices rise where vows were said, and secrets lie where prayers were led. Under the pew where you once tripped, a paper waits, its edges ripped," Mavis repeated. She had memorized the clue from the day before. "That sounds like it's inside the church."

"Where did you trip?" Emily asked Maude.

"How am I supposed to remember that?" Maude asked. "We'll have to check all the pews."

"Is the church unlocked?" Emily asked.

"I'm sure she has a key," Wilbur laughed.

"I do," Maude nodded. She pulled out the infamous key ring and began to look at the various keys. "Here it is." She held up and nodded for dramatic effect.

When they pulled up to Beaver Crossing, Maude hopped out of the front seat of the truck with ease. Mavis and Emily clamored after her while Wilbur took his time. He was fine letting the three women take point on this scavenger hunt. It did his heart good to see them so excited over something. Leave it to Opal to give them all one last gift in her departure.

Maude had the church opened in no time. Reverend Simmons burst forth from his office with a panicked look on his face. "Oh, it's just you!" he gasped. "I thought we were getting robbed."

"You need to get out more," Maude scoffed. "We're not here to rob anybody. We're looking for something. It shouldn't take long."

Reverend Simmons smiled nervously and went back inside his office. The less he knew about the antics of the Montgomery family and Maude, the better. They were always up to something, though he did have a soft spot for Mavis. She had been one of the best things to ever happen in his life. Her skills as a life coach and therapist when he first became a pastor had been life changing. Without her help, he would never have become the successful man he was today.

"Y'all take that side and Mavis and I will take this side," Maude directed them all to their positions. She was like a general commanding her troops. After a few minutes of searching, Mavis squealed loudly. "I found it!"

Emily rushed over and was nearly knocked over by Maude who barreled over to Mavis at the same time. "You tripped here?" Emily asked Maude.

"Probably," Maude shrugged.

"It was taped underneath this pew," Mavis

giggled. "Here, you do the honors." She handed the envelope to Maude who opened it carefully.

Chapter Five

The envelope contained another clue written in Opal's handwriting, as well as a torn and aged black and white photograph of three young women standing in front of a familiar creek. "Look at this," Maude chuckled. "I haven't seen this picture in sixty years." She passed it around to Mavis, Emily, and Wilbur to look at. "Is that you, Opal, and Ruby?" Emily asked.

Maude nodded. "In our much younger days. Right here in fact. That old creek sure looked bigger back then."

"Look how young y'all were!" Mavis crooned. "Y'all were so beautiful!"

"Were?" Maude scoffed. She opened the envelope that contained the next clue. "I'm no longer here, don't fret or frown, but come to where I laid down. The queen of hearts, the southern belle, left her last note where lilies dwell," Maude read. She snickered loudly. "Queen of hearts? Southern belle? She always could throw down a rhyme."

"Well, what does that mean?" Emily asked.

"The old coot's talking about her bedroom!" Maude chuckled. "Her bedspread is lilies. Has to be that."

"Oh goodness," Emily laughed. "I love her turn of phrase."

"Well, shall we head that way?" Wilbur asked. Mavis and Emily had already walked towards the front doors of the church, but Maude had lingered by the front baptismal. "Y'all go on outside," Wilbur whispered to Emily and Mavis. "I'll wait for her." He handed Emily the keys to his truck and walked quietly down the middle aisle between the rows of pews.

"It's oddly quiet in here," Maude said as he approached.

"It sure is," Wilbur nodded. He sat down on the front pew and wondered if Maude would sit down or be ready to go. "I remember when we got this baptismal back in the early seventies," Maude continued. "It's changed over the years, but it's really thanks to Opal and Ruby and them that the church got it in the first place. That and the new fellowship hall and the podium and the, well, I could go on and on."

"They left a wonderful legacy," Wilbur nodded. Maude sat down next to him and sighed. "I miss them," she whispered.

"I do, too," Wilbur agreed. He missed them all more than anything. Jameson, Ruby, and Opal were the foundations of who he was as a man, as a husband, a brother, and a friend. He couldn't imagine where he would be in life had he not encountered them when he was a child.

"Opal always said it wasn't like people left forever. She went on and on about some spiritual mess about being in the wind and seeing signs in birds and butterflies. I don't know. Maybe she was right," Maude said.

"She was often right about a lot of things," Wilbur nodded. "I don't think the world will ever be the same without her." Maude nodded and reached over and squeezed his hand. "I guess we better go wrangle those two," she smiled.

Wilbur nodded and helped Maude stand up and walked next to her towards the front doors. He saw Reverend Simmons peek around the door to his office. Wilbur waved goodbye to him and saw the look of relief flood his face as Maude exited the church.

Maude was quiet on the ride to Opal's house. There was a definite somber mood in the truck as they pulled into Opal's driveway. Maude unlocked the front door and together they walked inside to Opal's living room. Everything was in its perfect place. Nothing seemed out of order. It was almost like Opal was merely out of town on vacation and would be coming back home soon. Yet there was a stillness in the air that had never quite been there before at Opal's house. Her home had always been one filled with warmth and energy. As Maude had said about the church, it was oddly quiet. The record player was still. Wilbur glanced at the last record Opal had been playing and smiled. The Otis Redding album was well loved. He decided to see if it would still play, and to his delight, it did. "Sittin' on the Dock of the Bay" floated throughout the living room. Emily began to sing along, which was something that Opal herself would have done.

"It feels like she's still here," Mavis smiled

tearfully.

"She is," Emily nodded. She sat down next to Mavis on the couch and hugged her sister-in-law tightly. "Maude, I think you should get the next clue. We don't all need to disturb Opal's room. We'll wait here for you." Wilbur nodded and joined them on the couch.

Maude knew Emily was right. Not that Opal would care who was in her room, but she felt like this was the last clue and she should be the one to find it. She walked down the short hallway towards Opal's bedroom and gently pushed open the door. Opal's room was immaculate and her bed was made perfectly. Leave it to Opal to make her bed before entering the hospital. Maude read the note again and decided to look underneath the yellow pillowcase with embroidered lilies on the front. There was another envelope with Opal's handwriting waiting underneath.

If you've made it here, you've followed my breadcrumbs through my last adventure, and I couldn't be prouder. Inside the box is my last will and testament, yes, the official one. There's also something else: a scrapbook I never let anyone see. It's filled with memories, love, and things I never said aloud. Keep it close. Thank you for being the friends and family of a lifetime.

Opal

Maude reached under the other pillow on the bed and found the box and scrapbook that Opal had referred to. The book was thick and she was immediately overcome with emotion. Ruby had always been the one to record their memories and adventures. She had no idea what to expect from this scrapbook. She sat down on the bed and decided to open the box first. Folded neatly inside was Opal's will and other various documents. Four envelopes were stacked at the very bottom, each with a different name written on the front: Maude, Wilbur, Mavis, and Emily. "Please don't let this be any more clues," Maude whispered.

Maude put the envelopes and paperwork back in the box, but decided to keep the scrapbook a secret for now. She had no idea what kind of memories and adventures were recorded inside. She wasn't in the head space to take a deep dive into that book at the moment, so she slid the scrapbook back under the pillow and gathered the box under her arm. Mavis, Wilbur, and Emily were waiting for her on the couch. She handed Wilbur the box and said, "Well, here it is."

Wilbur opened the box carefully and nodded. He pulled out Opal's will and saw the bundle of paperwork. Then he saw the envelopes. "There's one for each of us," he said.

Maude nodded and gestured for him to hand them out. He handed Emily and Mavis their envelopes and then took his. They were all identical on the outside with their names on the front. Maude had her envelope still clutched in her hand. They all took turns looking at each other, wondering what to do next. "Do we open them all at once or wait till later?" pondered Emily. Mavis anxiously looked up and said, "I don't think I can wait." Maude nodded and told her to go ahead and open it. Mavis stood up and walked to the kitchen so that she could be alone. Emily decided to open her envelope right there on the couch. After a few moments, Wilbur kissed Emily on top of the head and said he would step out on the porch to read his. They could hear Mavis crying softly in the kitchen.

Maude wanted to wait until she was back home in the privacy of her own home before she read her note. She looked over and saw that a tear were trickling down Emily's face as she held her hand over her heart. Opal knew how to evoke motion, that was for sure. Instead of reading her own note, she decided to sit down in Opal's recliner and wait for everyone to finish. "There will never be another woman like her," Emily said quietly from her perch on the couch. She had her legs tucked up underneath her as she sat against the big throw pillows Opal had decorated her couch with. "I better go check on Wil." Emily slipped quietly out of the room and opened the front door. Maude caught a glimpse of Wilbur sitting on the porch swing before Emily closed the door behind her.

Maude was left alone in the living room of her best friend, a room she had been in hundreds not thousands of times over the years. It had never felt so empty before. She noticed the framed photo of her, Ruby, and Opal from one of their adventures in Italy in 1960. She held the frame in her hands and wondered what on earth was going to happen with all of Opal's things that she had carefully collected and displayed over her eighty plus years. She didn't hear Mavis come in behind her and sit down on the couch. "What do we do now?" Mavis whispered.

Maude looked up and saw Mavis who still had tears running down her face. She stood up and enveloped Mavis in a big hug. She wasn't sure what to say, because truthfully she didn't have an answer. Maude certainly never thought she'd be in this spot. Opal was healthy and had always taken such great care of herself physically and mentally. "We deal with this the best we know how. We're all in this together," Maude said soothingly. "First, we get some lunch and then call the funeral home and make sure they're ready for Friday."

"We have over two hundred RSVPS so far," Mavis nodded. "I hope they're prepared."

Wilbur and Emily walked back inside at that moment. "How about we get some lunch together and then let Em get to work. She's got a big meeting this afternoon." Emily kissed Wilbur on the cheek and sat down next to Mavis on the couch. "In honor of Opal, let's go to the salad shop in Junction," Emily suggested. She half expected Maude to grumble, but instead of countering, Maude nodded.

"I could go for some rabbit food," Maude agreed to everyone's surprise.

"Then it's settled," Wilbur smiled. "Mavis, I'll take you home and then Em and I will go change clothes at our house. If you'd like, I'll swing back by the Manor and get you and then we can pick up Maude at her house. Emily will need her car to drive back and forth to work."

They all nodded and agreed to hurry at their respective homes. By the time Wilbur picked up Mavis at the Manor an hour later, she looked like a different person than she had that morning. "Opal loved the color yellow, so I knew this new dress would be perfect," she smiled.

"It looks great," Wilbur nodded. The drive to Maude's house was full of stories from their childhood that revolved around the silly antics of Opal and how much she adored them. Maude was waiting on her front porch for them to arrive. She had not changed clothes, but her hair was styled and she carried a thick envelope under one arm and a large box under the other.

"We have some things to discuss after lunch," Maude announced as she climbed into Wilbur's truck. "If y'all have some time to discuss them."

"Another scavenger hunt?" Wilbur teased.

"I hope not," Maude shook her head. "I've got her will and last wishes. Wilbur, I assume you already know what I'm talking about."

"Yes ma'am, I do," Wilbur nodded. He had known he was to be the executor of Opal's will for the last few years, though he did not know what her will contained. He had never read through it, and he had never wanted to up until this point. He was thankful that Opal trusted him well enough to carry out her last wishes. She was the loveliest godmother there could ever be. Even though he was in his forties, she would always be his first hero.

Maude had to admit that the salad shop

was delicious. The owner behind the counter loaded her salad up with fried chicken, so much so that she could barely taste the leafy green lettuce underneath the thick layer of homemade buttermilk ranch dressing. Once Emily hugged them all goodbye, Maude suggested they walk across the street to the donut shop that she loved. They had eaten there many times over the years since it was so close to the hospital where Ruby and Opal had both spent so much time. Once they were seated at a table with donuts spread between them, Maude opened the envelope that contained Opal's will. She handed it to Wilbur for him to read over.

"Well, what do you think?" Maude asked him as he finished the short but sweet last wants of Opal. "I've already called Tally, her attorney, and he says it's all done up neatly. We can meet with him if there's any issues once the death certificates are ready."

"It looks to be all tied up nicely," Wilbur nodded. He looked at Mavis and read the part that mentioned her aloud. "Oh, Opal," Mavis smiled. "She was too good to me then and now."

"Y'all both know that if there's anything else you want, just tell me. I don't want to fight over anything, and I know we never would. Mavis, I want you to have her coffee table if you want it. And Wilbur, I want you to have that bench and outdoor shelves that you and Jameson made when you was a boy," Maude directed. Wilbur and Mavis both nodded and thanked her.

"I called the funeral home to keep them

abreast of the head count. I don't think they knew what they were getting into, but they know now," Mavis chuckled.

"They called me right before y'all pulled up," Maude nodded. "I need to drop that urn thing off to them before we head back to Rhinestone."

"Is that what was in that box?" Mavis asked. Maude nodded and added, "Wait til you see what it looks like." She asked Wilbur to retrieve the box from his truck, and when he brought it inside, she instructed him to open it.

Opal had selected an urn unlike any traditional vessel; its sleek, classical jar shape cloaked in riotous waves of color looked as though it was painted by the wind itself. Swirls of fiery red, golden yellow, deep cobalt blue, and vibrant violet rippled across its ceramic form, occasionally melding into streaks of emerald green and soft pink. Each hue seemed to dance into the next, reminiscent of a living tie dye or a modern abstract painting, yet infused with an energy all its own. "I believe she made it herself many years ago," Maude pondered.

The surface, glossy and smooth, caught the light from the donut shop's displays in a magical swirl of reflections. The lid, gently domed and perfectly matched, completed the form as if it were one continuous artwork rather than a two piece container. "This sure is something," Wilbur said. "It's beautiful and unique. I love it."

"Me too," Maude nodded. "Me too."

Chapter Six

"And y'all, I think I'm going to finally join that book club in Junction that started a few weeks ago. Opal told me that I should get back to doing the things I love like reading," Mavis said as she clutched Opal's first edition copy of Gone With the Wind with Margaret Mitchell's autograph scrawled across the title page. "She said it could be life changing."

Wilbur and Emily sat across the table from Mavis in the kitchen of Magnolia Manor that Friday morning eating homemade biscuits and jam. "That's a great idea, Mavis!" Emily exclaimed. "I'm reading a wonderful thriller right now. I'll let you borrow it when I'm done."

When they were done eating, Wilbur cleaned the table while Mavis finished getting ready. Emily went upstairs to help Mavis pick out some last minute jewelry to complement her black dress. No one was particularly looking forward to Opal's funeral that afternoon, but they knew it would be a joyous occasion, a way to celebrate the life and love of one of the most brilliant and wonderful people to ever live.

Mavis and Emily both wore black dresses, though Mavis had added a sunflower broach to her outfit to brighten it up. Emily added a sunflower to her long hair to finish the look off. Wilbur wore his black suit with a white button-down shirt, but like Mavis and Emily, he wanted to add something significant to his outfit. Emily had found him a tie with a sunflower print on it. They had no idea what Maude was going to wear. None of them could remember the last time they had seen Maude Cooper in a dress, so when she walked out of her front door wearing a lilac colored pantsuit, Wilbur breathed a sigh of relief. Seeing Maude in a dress was not something that he thought they could handle. A lilac pantsuit was very appropriate for the event. Opal would never want all of them to wear all black, but none of them felt comfortable wearing tie-dye suits or dresses to match her urn. They were sure there would be people in all kinds of outfits there to honor Opal at the service though.

When they arrived at the funeral home two hours before Opal's visitation was supposed to begin, they were thrilled to see that the funeral home had indeed been listening. They had decorated the front doors with sunflowers and ferns. Mona Bridges opened the front door to wave Wilbur, Maude, and Mavis inside. "You're early!" she exclaimed. "I'm almost done putting the finishing touches on the podium."

"This was all you?" Mavis exclaimed.

"I loved Opal Tyler fiercely," Mona smiled. "She was the original flower child and I'm doing my best to keep that legacy going. Wait til you see the inside. I hope I did her proud."

"Oh Mona," Mavis declared. "It's so perfect!" Mona had taken bundles of sunflowers and daisies from her flower farm and decorated the funeral home in its entirety.

"Opal helped me so much by teaching me the proper ways to garden, it felt fitting to give back to her in this way. I'm going to run home and change clothes and then I'll be back," Mona said. She hugged Mavis and Emily and rushed outside to her truck.

The sky had a nice cloud cover with the sun peeking out. It was the perfect weather for this celebration of life. There wasn't much for anyone to do, as the funeral home and Mona had taken care of everything. Opal's vibrant urn was on display on an ornate white column at the foot of a small stage with a podium behind it. Mavis' slideshow was just over two hours long, and they all smiled and wiped a few tears as they watched the pictures slide in and out of the presentation. Reverend Simmons arrived and began doing his calming exercises to steady his nerves for the big event. Wilbur went over his notes for his part of the ceremony. Maude was set to say a few things, but no one knew what exactly she was planning on talking about. Mavis was going to sing a hymn to close out the service after Drew Washington sang Opal's requested song.

As predicted, hundreds of people filtered in and out of the funeral home over the two hour long visitation. Everyone had such beautiful things to say about Opal. As expected, there was not room for everyone in the chapel area, so it became standing room only as Reverend Simmons took the stage. He opened the service with a prayer and turned it over to Drew Washington, a pastor in Junction and friend of Opal's for the past forty years.

"Welcome everyone. What a privilege it has been to know Ms. Opal Clementine Tyler. We gather here today to remember, honor, and celebrate the life of a woman whose presence was a blessing to everyone who knew her. I have stood behind this pulpit many times, and I have spoken many words over the years, but today the words come not just from the Good Book, but from a full heart full of memory, full of gratitude, and full of love for Opal, who was not just a pillar of Rhinestone, but its very heart. Opal was born with a spark. The kind that didn't just light up a room, but lit the path for others. She had a grace that didn't come from polished manners or fine clothes, though Lord knows she wore her Sunday best even on a Tuesday, but from the kindness in her eyes, the wit of her tongue, and the strength in her spine. She believed in goodness. She believed in second chances. And she believed with unshakable certainty that love could mend what the world had broken. Whether she was tending her roses, baking one of her famous lemon chess pies, or sitting on the porch with a cup of tea and a knowing smile, Opal offered herself to this town again and again in quiet, tireless acts of grace. Now, I remember one Sunday, not long after the storm that nearly tore through the heart of our county, and some of our hearts with it, I saw her standing at the front of the sanctuary of my church. No words. Just standing. And in that moment, I swear, it was like the Lord Himself was reminding us: "Be still, and know that I am God." Opal had that gift of stillness that held strength, and a resilient silence that held wisdom. She loved fiercely. She forgave freely. And though she never raised her voice, her life spoke louder than most of us ever will. To those of us left behind, her absence will feel like a room with no lamp. A porch with no rocking chair. A song without its last note. But let us not forget: the seeds she planted in each of us, seeds of compassion, courage, and faith, will continue to bloom. Opal always said, "This life is just the front porch to forever." Well, I believe she's stepped through that door now, into a glory that no earthly storm can shake. And I can just picture her there with her arms wide, eyes bright, perhaps humming one of her hymns, as she finally takes her place among the saints. So let us weep, yes, for we will miss her dearly. But let us also rejoice, for we were lucky enough to walk beside an angel right here on earth," Drew finished. There was not a dry eye in the place.

"How am I supposed to follow that?" Wilbur chuckled a few moments later. He stood behind the podium and gathered his notes before him. "Hello, everyone. For those of you who don't know me, I'm Wilbur Reynolds-Montgomery, though if you knew Opal, you probably knew me, too. I've had decades to try and put into words what Opal Tyler meant to me, and I still can't quite get there, but I'll do my best. The first time I met

Opal, I was around twelve years old, hiding in the woods with bruises on my ribs and blood on my lip. It was the fall of 1985. I remember the sound of her footsteps on dry leaves, slow and steady like she already knew I was there. She knelt down, not scared, not angry, just calm, and started talking to me like we were old friends.

And that's what she gave me that day: friendship. A family. Because of her kindness, I found a home with her and Maude and the Montgomery family. They gave me love, something I hadn't known before. They gave me purpose. Opal didn't just pull me out of those woods. She pulled me out of darkness. She didn't ask me for anything, not even an explanation. She never treated me like I was broken, only like I was worth loving. And Lord, how she loved. That woman loved with a fierceness like I had never seen in such a small gentle body. I remember once, when I was about sixteen and full of vinegar, I told her I didn't believe in God. I said, "If there's a God, why'd He let my dad hit me?" She didn't argue. She just said, "Maybe so you'd end up right here where love could find you." That stayed with me. I've spent most of my life trying to live in a way that makes her proud. I still fall short, but every time I hold the door for someone, or check on a neighbor, or put on a clean shirt even when the day's been hell, I hear her in my ear: "That's it, Wil. Keep going." Opal Clementine Tyler didn't just save my life, she gave me life. The kind worth living. And though my heart is breaking today, I know what she'd say if she saw me standing here with tears in my eyes.

She'd say, "Now don't go turning into a puddle, Wilbur. There's work to be done. There's joy to be lived. I will, Opal. I promise. You were more than a godmother to me, you were my compass, my constant, my miracle. I love you forever."

Emily and Mavis were a puddle of tears by the time Wilbur finished. Most of the people in the crowd were, too. Wilbur didn't often talk about his childhood or allow himself to get too caught up in those kinds of memories. He had had a rough start to life with the death of his mother when he was a toddler and grew up under the strong arm of his abusive father who struggled with drugs and alcohol. He often thought of his life truly beginning once he joined the Montgomery family at Magnolia Manor, thanks to Opal. There were things he would never speak about aloud that would be buried with him, and other secrets that he didn't even fully know or understand that belonged to the Stone Sisters and his father. That night his father died under the magnolia tree at Magnolia Manor were full of fuzzy and complicated details that he had never wanted to fully know. All that mattered was that he was finally safe. The county took the small parcel of land his father owned and bulldozed the house. A beautiful bed and breakfast owned by the Nelson family had resided there for some twenty years now.

Drew Washington stood back up and sang a beautiful rendition of "What a Wonderful World." The entire time during the speeches and songs, Mavis' slideshow played beautifully in the background. "Now, Opal's lifelong best friend, Maude Cooper, would like to say a few words," Drew added. He walked down to the first pew and offered his arm to Maude who gladly accepted his help. He led her to the podium and adjusted the microphone for her.

"Thanks, Drew. Ok, well, most of y'all know me. It wasn't often that you saw one of us without the other. Me, Opal, and Ruby were thicker than thieves. And I mean that like we were best friends because ain't none of us ever been thieves in our whole lives. Anyway, well, I suppose I knew this day would come. But knowing don't make it easier. For those of you who don't know me, I'm Maude Cooper. And for nearly eighty years, I had the great fortune, no, the blessing, of calling Opal Tyler my best friend. She, Ruby Montgomery, and I were known as the Stone Sisters, though we weren't kin by blood. Folks called us that 'cause we were solid, unshakable. You knock one of us down, the other two would show up with pie, peroxide, and possibly a shovel. We met when we were kids. Opal had these starched socks and a lunch pail with her name on it. She shared her sandwich with me that first day, and I knew right then she was someone special. Someone soft, but not weak. Kind, but no pushover. She had a backbone made of cedar and a heart that never ran out of room. We three stuck together through everything: school dances, heartbreaks, wars, weddings, babies, funerals. That's what sisters do. And believe me, we were sisters. Now Ruby went on ahead of us a few years back, and when she did, Opal told me, "I'm not ready to be the last one standing." And I remember holding her hand and saying, "Well, we're not done yet." But now, here I am. The last of the Stone Sisters. I won't lie to you, it feels mighty strange, like a three-legged stool that's lost two legs. But even as my heart aches, I feel them with me. I feel Ruby's laugh in the breeze. I feel Opal's wisdom in every hush between hymns. You know, Opal had a way of seeing people. Really seeing them. Their fears, their gifts, their goodness, even when they couldn't see it themselves. I saw her do it again and again, from brokenhearted teenagers to grumpy old men to scared little boys hiding in the woods. She'd gather folks up like stray kittens and never ask for anything in return but the promise that they'd be kind to the next lost soul. And don't get me started on the stray cats she found throughout the years. And the snakes, and bees, and chickens. That was Opal. A woman who made gentleness a force of nature. Who believed in the healing power of peach cobbler and prayer. Who could hold her own with mayors and misfits alike, and often at the same table. She was our north star. And now, she's gone home. I like to think she's with Ruby now, probably sipping tea and shaking her head at me for rambling in front of y'all like this. But I also think she'd be proud. Proud to see this room so full of people she loved. Proud that her legacy is love, plain and simple. So I'll carry on. I'll keep showing up to Sunday service, tending her roses, and telling her stories. I'll live the rest of my days in a way that honors her, and Ruby, and the bond we forged when we were still braiding each other's hair and dreaming about the future. And I'll hold fast to this: when my time comes, they'll be there, Opal and Ruby, and so many others, all the saints and sinners, waiting just past the veil. And we'll be the Stone Sisters again forever," Maude trailed off. "Ok, that's all I've got."

Drew hurried up to the podium and helped Maude back to her seat in between Mavis and Wilbur. "Thank you, Ms. Cooper. That was lovely and so fitting," Drew said. "Now, Mavis, would you like to sing our closing hymn, then I'll pray and we can all be dismissed to enjoy the beautiful weather outside." He smiled at Mavis who took the microphone and sang Opal's favorite hymn. Drew closed the service in prayer and urged the crowd to spend time together either outside or inside.

"That was perfect," Mavis said as she hugged her brother tightly. "I think Opal and Big Mama would be so proud."

"I know they are," Maude said as she sat down in the pew in front of Opal's urn. "I know it."

Chapter Seven

Instead of meeting back at someone's house, the after service potluck was held outside under the grove of pecan trees behind the funeral home. It was the perfect way to honor a person who was known for bringing people together. As the evening wound down, people began to filter back to their cars. There were so many flowers and plants that Mavis tried sending them home with various mourners. Even after three fourths of them were gladly taken, they were still left with too many to fit in their various vehicles. Mona had done a splendid job decorating for Opal's service. Wilbur and Emily took some to their house, Mavis and Maude both took some home, too, but there were still quite a few left over.

"Can we take some to Big Mama and Big Daddy?" Mavis asked.

"I'd like that," Maude nodded.

The bed of Wilbur's truck was loaded down with various plants and flower arrangements. While Emily went back to work the following Monday, Wilbur, Mavis, and Maude decided to go down to Deerlane Cemetery and sort through the various arrangements. They convened at the graves of Ruby and Jameson Montgomery.

Mavis set identical flower arrangements on their headstones and sat down to spend some time with them. Maude grabbed an arrangement of silk flowers and walked a few rows over to the grave of Nadine Waters, her lifelong frenemy. She and Nadine had also known each other since they were children, and they lived to aggravate each other throughout the years, though in the years before Nadine's passing, the two of them had cultivated a truce that had turned into a beautiful friendship. Maude laid the white silk flowers at the base of Nadine's headstone and looked around. The cemetery was full of Rhinestone's best. There were graves that held past mayors, soldiers, pastors, lawyers, doctors, teachers, drifters, children; people of all ages. There was so much history within the gates of Deerlane.

Maude took another arrangement and placed it on the grave of Mortimer Raven, the longtime coroner and funeral home director who was one of Opal's great loves in her younger days. Out of the corner of her eye she saw Wilbur carrying two flower arrangements towards the back of the cemetery. She had a feeling she knew where he was headed. Mavis was now sitting at the foot of her mother's monument, so Maude slipped away quietly from Mortimer's grave and followed Wilbur. She found him staring at his father's headstone that had been placed next to his late mother's grave site. Wilbur felt her drawing near and smiled as she edged up next to him. "I feel like I never really knew him," Wilbur said softly. He laid the flowers on the two gravestones and looked back at Maude.

"I'm grateful he gave you life," Maude said. "Not everyone deserves to be a parent, Wilbur. I'm glad he gave you to us." She hugged the tall man tightly and together they walked back to where Mavis was still sitting. She leaned over and hugged Mavis. "I'm glad Melly gave us you, too," Maude said. "You think we got a few more spaces to put some of these?" Maude gestured to the pile of flowers. "Patsy, Ellen, and Lucille are over yonder."

Wilbur and Mavis helped Maude divvy out the rest of the flowers between some of Rhinestone's elite. The morning sun began to beat down on them as they walked back to Wilbur's truck. The plan today was to begin to go through Opal's household items. Maude had inherited the house and land, but she had a home and land of her own. It pained her to think about selling it, but she wasn't sure what else she could do with it. "I just wish I could hand pick my new neighbor," Maude had said the night before when they were making plans.

They spent the afternoon going through Opal's garden shed and storage room that she had specifically asked Wilbur to take home with him. They weren't sure what all they would find, but it was mostly pleasant surprises. Wilbur made sure to relocate the small rat snake he found hiding in the garden shed before Maude came over to help him sort through the tools.

Opal had a beautiful antique lawnmower and more garden tools than he knew what to do with. After letting Mavis go through some stuff he thought she would like to have, he called Mona to come over and look and see if she wanted anything. She was over the moon at the thought of taking home some of Opal's gardening equipment. Conversation soon turned to what was going to become of Opal's house. "I bet someone will snatch it up quickly. Who doesn't want to move to Rhinestone!" Mona exclaimed.

Maude nodded and changed the subject back to Opal's storage room that was attached to her kitchen pantry. Once the garden shed was emptied, they moved onto cleaning out the storage room. Opal kept a very neat house, so they weren't expecting much clutter in there. When Wilbur opened the door he laughed out loud. "Well, I'll be!" he chuckled. "What in the world has she got in here?"

There were dozens of clear bins labeled on a shelf. As he looked them over, he was astounded to find that they were all full of various plant and flower seeds. One was full of pumpkin seeds, another full of sunflower seeds. "Tomatoes, potatoes, some kind of pepper, cucumber, squash, wow!" Mavis exclaimed. "She has a whole lifetime of seeds in here."

"A vault of seeds!" Wilbur exclaimed. "This is incredible."

This was also the room that Opal kept all her natural cleaning products that she made. As Wilbur continued to look, he found a filing cabinet with every single recipe she had ever crafted for her "Color Me Crazy" hair dye and hair product line.

Opal had a remedy or recipe for almost anything that could be thought of.

After his truck was loaded down with garden tools, equipment, the filing cabinet, and boxes of seeds, he bid the women farewell and met Emily back at their house. Emily was in the kitchen adding the finishing touches to some lasagna she was baking for supper that evening. Wilbur was excited to unload all of his spoils and Emily was equally thrilled to see all of Opal's things going to good use. Wilbur put the tools and gardening equipment in his state of the art barn and organized the remainder of the seeds that he had kept after Mona and Mavis had taken what they wanted. He loved that Opal's legacy was still spreading all throughout Rhinestone. Opal had always been very proud of her garden, and now those plants would continue on for generations.

He placed the filing cabinet with all of Opal's hard work in the small office near the guest room. He showed Emily the recipes and files that Opal had given him. "What's this?" she asked. She tugged on a loose piece of paper that was near the back of the stack. "Oh my goodness! Wilbur! I think it's her bucket list!" She handed Wilbur the page that had been written in Opal's handwriting. It was full of notes and little drawings on the front and back. "More than half of her dreams were accomplished. I wish she had been able to finish this list. It's a long one!" Emily said. "Wow! Look at all these memories!"

"I need to call Maude," Wilbur said. "I wonder if she knew about this list."

Emily read over the list while Wilbur called Maude who answered on the third ring. "I knew she had one, but I ain't ever seen it," Maude said on the other end of the phone. "I'd love to see it one day."

"Let's all have dinner tomorrow evening!" Emily suggested. "I'll cook over here and we can go over it. What does she think?"

Wilbur relayed Emily's message to Maude who readily agreed. "Y'all let Mavis girl know. I'll be there around five." She hung up the phone before Wilbur could tell her that Emily didn't get off until five in Junction and dinner wouldn't be ready till closer to seven o'clock. "I guess I'll have to entertain her for those two hours," he chuckled. He quickly called Mavis and filled her in on the plan. Mavis promised to bring the dessert.

True to her word, Maude arrived at the cabin a few minutes after five o'clock. Mavis scurried in a few minutes later with a plate of chocolate chip cookies. They all gathered around the table the next evening to eat supper. As soon as the dishes were cleared, Wilbur produced the bucket list and handed it to Maude. "I bet wrestling alligators is on that list!" Mavis exclaimed that next night, but Maude shook her head vigorously. "Opal would never put that on there because she would be afraid that someone would hurt the alligators," she countered.

"Fair enough," Wilbur nodded.

"I had an alligator purse once," Maude said. "Opal threw it into the river and said it needed to go back with nature." Mavis and Wilbur both giggled like they were little kids. They could picture Opal doing that exact thing.

"What does it say?" Mavis interjected. "Oh! There's so many things crossed off already. Good for her."

"But there's a lot left, too," Emily pointed out. "See a leprechaun in Ireland. Watch the bison run in Yellowstone National Park. See the Eiffel Tower in Paris. See a Shakespearean play at the Globe Theatre in London. Eat tamales in Mexico City. Take a hot air balloon ride. Those are amazing things for a bucket list. I wish she would have been able to do it all."

"It doesn't feel right that so many are still left," Wilbur nodded.

"Then let's finish it!" Mavis exclaimed. "Come on, Maude! You're the perfect one to finish it. We'll all help!"

"Now I don't know about that," Maude countered. There are some pretty wild things on this list. Opal had already drug her into some pretty wild adventures while she was alive, but leave it to Opal to continue that streak well beyond the grave.

It could be a lot of fun," Emily pushed. Mavis nodded enthusiastically beside her.

"Wilbur?" Maude asked. "What have we gotten ourselves into?"

Wilbur laughed and said, "What a life we get to live. Is that a yes?" He already knew Maude wouldn't say no to a way to honor her best friend, and who could say no to Emily and Mavis when they got so excited about things!

"Alright, I'll do it," Maude nodded. "But on my terms. I get to choose which ones I do first and if I don't make it out alive, y'all finish it." Wilbur caught a glimmer of mischief in her eyes and saw the corners of her mouth twitch into a soft smile. "Oh, Opal, what have you gotten me into now?"

They spent the next hour making copies of Opal's list in Emily's small home office and reviewing what adventures would be the easiest to accomplish and which ones would take quite a bit of planning. "This is going to be so much fun," Emily smiled as she snuggled up with Bear, the beautiful chocolate Labrador, on the couch.

"How in the hell does one see a leprechaun in Ireland?" Maude wondered. "I can absolutely get behind drinking a beer or two in Germany though."

"What tattoo are you going to get?" Emily asked.

"She already has one," Mavis giggled.

"That doesn't count!" Emily replied.

"Sure it does!" Maude countered. "Right?" She looked at Wilbur and gestured to her back where her tattoo was. Mavis nor Wilbur had ever seen it in person, but they had seen a picture or two over the years from Opal who found it to be hilarious. Maude had gotten very drunk on vacation in Memphis when she, Ruby, and Opal had gone to the public opening of Graceland in 1982. Maude had been fit to be tied the next day when she saw the consequence of her wild night.

"I don't know," Wilbur laughed. "You know, I'm honestly surprised that Opal never got a real tattoo over the years. Maybe she just forgot to cross that off by mistake."

Maude shook her head. "No, she never did get one. Unless it was in between her toes or inside her mouth," Maude shrugged. "People get those, you know!"

"How do we know how many states she has left to visit?" Mavis asked. She was making notes on her copy of the list. Wilbur leaned over and saw that she had circled a few different items that interested her. "Whale watching and all the European adventures?" Wilbur asked.

Mavis grinned and asked him which ones interested him. "I wouldn't mind not doing the race car one," he smiled. Wilbur didn't like anything that would make him feel dizzy. Mavis leaned over and whispered, "With Maude driving, we've all probably already done that one."

While Mavis and Wilbur whispered and giggled, Maude had taken out a small notebook and began writing furiously. "I think I got it figured out," she said between her gritted teeth. "Opal's been to forty states."

"How do you know that?" Mavis asked.

"I've known her for over eighty years," Maude shrugged. "Best I can figure is she's still got Alaska, Washington, Oregon, Wyoming, Utah, Idaho, Montana, South and North Dakota, Minnesota left to go to. I'll have to do some more research before I know for sure though. How does that factor in with the rest of this list?"

"The Rocky Mountain train, Yellowstone, whale watching, the northern lights, and white water rafting could take care of many in that general area," Emily pointed out. "You could plan it all out and maybe cross off quite a few on one trip."

"And in Europe you can knock off a bunch more," Mavis nodded. Wilbur got the feeling that Mavis and Emily were already silently planning their own adventures as they accompanied Maude on certain adventures. That suited him just fine. He was more of a homebody and would stay in Rhinestone and take care of things while they flitted across the globe.

"I still don't understand the leprechaun one," Maude said. "I ain't saying they aren't real, because Opal swore she met Bigfoot or whatever she called him one time."

"She met one or saw one?" Emily asked.

"Said she met him and he was a real nice fella," Maude shrugged.

"Bigfoot speaks English?" Mavis gasped.

"She didn't say," Maude answered. "Opal spoke seven hundred languages as it is, so who the hell knows." While seven hundred was a stretch, Opal did speak many different languages. Wilbur knew she was fluent in Spanish, French, Italian, and German. Ruby had always said that Opal could fit in anywhere, like she had an ear for languages the way some prodigies had a special talent for music. She was like a human translation machine at times.

Chapter Eight

Over the next few days, Mavis helped Maude make a plan to tackle the remaining items on Opal's unfinished bucket list. Mavis was thrilled that she could once again use her travel agent skills, and this time it would benefit her. She always had the itch to travel and experience new things.

Wilbur could hear Mavis before he saw her coming across the yard into the ShangriLa that he was working on. The cabinets of Ruby's old trailer that Jameson had set up to house her collections and overflow had begun to deteriorate. Wilbur was sure that he could repair most of the wear and tear, but setting aside time to do it in the summer heat wasn't high on his list. The passing of Opal made him realize that he should stop putting it off and buckle down, so he woke up early and got to work on his list of repairs. Today's project involved gutting the old cabinets and installing new ones in the kitchen area. Once that was done, he would move on to the flooring issues.

"Wilbur? Wilbur, are you still in there?" Mavis called. Wilbur poked his head out of the front door and waved hello. "I'm in here," he called back, his voice echoing faintly against the aluminum siding. "But if you're here to put me to work, I was never born and you've never met me."

Mavis laughed as she climbed the three steps into the trailer. She was wearing her usual bright lipstick and a straw hat tilted at a dangerous angle, as if daring the sun to try her. In her hand was a tattered leather-bound notebook. "You're lucky," Mavis said, fanning herself with the bucket list journal. "I'm not here to make you work. I'm here to ask for your truck."

Wilbur stepped fully into view, brushing sawdust off his hands and onto his jeans. "That so? Should I be worried?"

"Only if you've grown attached to it," she laughed. "No! We're going on a quick little road trip."

Wilbur narrowed his eyes. "Define little, and who is we?"

"Just a hop, skip, and a jump to Nashville," Mavis replied.

Wilbur blinked. "That's almost five hours away."

"Only three and a half if you drive like Maude does" Mavis winked.

Wilbur leaned against the counter, arms crossed. "There's no way I'm letting Maude drive my truck. And I'm not so sure about you," he laughed. "Just you and Maude going on this quick little trip?"

"And maybe you," Mavis replied, tapping the notebook. "I've been making all kinds of notes about Opal's list. We've been combing through this thing for days. You wouldn't believe the stuff Opal wanted to do. Maude has been a wealth of information. Her memory is pretty solid still."

"Try me," Wilbur said.

"Well, I think we can manage zip-lining and go paintballing in Nashville," Mavis explained. "Something nice and easy to kick off the list."

"Paintballing and zip-lining with a woman in her mid-eighties is nice and easy?" Wilbur coughed.

Mavis shrugged. "It's going to be so much fun! Who doesn't love Nashville! I don't think it's necessarily the safest thing we could do, but it's not the most dangerous. Either way, it's on the list, and we're doing it. I know Emily doesn't have much time off right now, so I'll manage this leg of the race."

Wilbur looked around the trailer, his eyes resting on a crooked kitchen drawer he hadn't yet fixed. "You sure Maude is up for all this?"

Mavis sat down on one of the dinette benches and placed the notebook on the table like it was sacred. "I'm sure Opal wanted to live every last bit of her life. She may not have had time to do it all, but that doesn't mean we can't do it for her. You know how she used to say she'd haunt us if we didn't send her off in style. Maude has reminded me of that no less than ten times this week."

Wilbur stared at her for a long moment before letting out a breath through his nose. "I'll check the oil and air up the tires. When does this train depart?"

"Tomorrow, of course!" Mavis cheered. "You know you want to tag along!"

The following morning, the three of them,

Wilbur, Mavis, and Maude, met in front of Maude's house. Wilbur had already stopped for three coffees and a bag of biscuits. Mavis had packed enough luggage to imply they were going for a month rather than three days. Traveling with Mavis over the years had taught him that she packed for an army. When Wilbur hoisted Mavis' floral suitcase into the bed of the truck, he paused and asked, "Did you pack your entire wardrobe?"

"No," Mavis said dryly. "Just enough to change in case of spontaneous opera invitations or a wardrobe malfunction involving barbecue sauce."

"Fair enough," he grimaced.

The ride out of town was slow, winding past fields of corn and soybeans, through the parts of their county that hadn't changed in fifty years. Mavis played with the radio, cycling between Elvis, Dolly Parton, and gospel stations. Maude snoozed in the back seat; the erratic noise of her snores wasn't easy to drown out beneath the music. Wilbur drove with one hand on the wheel and the other out the window catching the wind. They talked about Opal most of the way. Mavis remembered one time when Opal snuck her pet chicken into the movie theater in her oversized purse. There was another time she ran the town's first unofficial matchmaking service from the beauty parlor, and yet another when she won the county fair pie contest with a homemade pie crust recipe that she took to the grave. By the time they rolled into Nashville, the sun was high in the sky and golden, lighting up the downtown buildings.

"We're staying at a place called The Melody

Inn," Mavis said, checking her phone. "Opal told me about it the last time we visited the Grand Old Opry here. Said she saw a ghost there in 1974."

"Perfect," Wilbur muttered. "Haunted and overpriced."

As it turned out, it was only one of those things. The Melody Inn had recently been updated, but there was still enough shag carpet and floral wallpaper to feel like Opal would've approved. Their first stop that night was karaoke. It wasn't on Opal's bucket list, but Wilbur knew that Mavis could never pass up the opportunity to grab a microphone and belt out a tune onstage. The bar was already full when they arrived, surrounded by cowboy hats, boots, and neon signs glowing like a mirage. Mavis signed them up for a group number without telling anyone. Maude nearly dropped her gin and tonic when the DJ called out, "Next up, we've got Maude, Mavis, and Wilbur singing a real classic!"

"I'm not singing," Wilbur said, standing his ground.

"Yes, you are," Mavis replied, linking her arm with his. "Opal would haunt you in your dreams if you sat this one out." Maude sighed loudly, but dutifully followed Mavis and Wilbur to the stage.

The performance was memorable. Wilbur croaked through the first verse, Mavis hammed it up like she was born for Broadway, and Maude shimmied like she had a secret past life as a backup dancer, thanks to the rum in her Coca-Cola. The crowd hooted and clapped, and by the end, Wilbur was grinning despite himself. "She would've loved that," he said as they exited into the warm night air.

"Loved it?" Mavis said. "She would've insisted we do five more."

They went to bed that evening feeling on top of the world. Wilbur hoped that feeling lasted, because the next day was when the real adventure began. Maude was already dressed when Mavis stumbled out of bed the next morning, her hair a frizzy halo and her pajama top on inside out. Wilbur, of course, was already downstairs, nursing a black coffee and scrolling through his phone like a man in search of a reason to back out.

"Guess what we're doing today?" Mavis said cheerfully after her shower, tossing Maude a granola bar.

"Eating like squirrels?" Maude mumbled.

"Zip-lining first," Mavis continued. "Opal always wanted to try it. I just hope we don't look too ridiculous up there." She flipped through her notebook and decided to call the zip-lining place one more time just to make sure that they were ready for them.

"I'm gonna need some real food before we do this," Maude said. While Mavis was on the phone, she and Wilbur decided to pick a place to eat. There were plenty of brunch style restaurants to choose from, so Wilbur let Maude scroll through the listings on his phone. It didn't take her long to settle on one.

"Thank God she already rode a bull!" Maude said as they left the steakhouse two hours later. "I could probably manage a mechanical one though."

"Maude, you'd break a hip," Mavis said.

"I'll break your face if you try to stop me," she replied with a smile. Wilbur and Mavis both laughed and continued to walk down the sidewalk. Mavis had insisted that the paintball and zip-line center wasn't too far from the restaurant, located in one Nashville's tourist traps.

"Are we lost?" Maude asked after a few minutes of walking past the same signs. "Didn't you call the place and they said it was nearby?"

"I'm sure this is it," Mavis said, peering at a faint outline of an old painted sign on the brick wall. "She said it was next to a place that sold wind chimes shaped like famous country singers."

"That's oddly specific," Wilbur said.

"Well, there's Dolly," Maude chuckled and pointed at a souvenir shop window. A single wind chime hung in the window shaped like Dolly Parton. They stood there for a moment, silent.

"I don't know what I expected," Mavis said quietly. "I guess I thought doing all this would make me feel, I don't know, closer to her."

"You don't feel closer to her?" Wilbur asked.

"I feel like she's everywhere. And also nowhere," Mavis whispered.

Maude slipped her hand into Mavis's. "That's grief, honey. She's stitched into everything, but we'll never get her back the way we want her."

Wilbur nodded. "But we carry her forward in stupid karaoke songs and wind chimes that look like Dolly Parton."

Mavis gave a teary laugh. "I hope she's watching," she whispered.

"She is," Maude said. "And she's mad you didn't try the tofu steak at lunch."

An hour later, they were standing on a wooded platform fifty feet off the ground, suited up in harnesses and helmets. Mavis was shaking. "This is a bad idea. This is a terrible idea," she said as the instructor clipped her harness to the cable.

Wilbur was already across the first line, cheering like he'd just won a prize fight. Maude, to no one's surprise, was next. "See you on the other side," she called, and with a joyful whoop, launched herself across the treetops. She had always been the one of the group of Ruby and Opal who had been less than pleased to go on such adventures, but she finally understood the brevity of life and had made a declaration to enjoy what time she had left. Plus, she was honoring her best friend.

Mavis followed, screaming the entire time, but somewhere between terror and exhilaration, something cracked open inside her. Wind in her face, eyes wide with disbelief, she let out a whoop that echoed through the trees. When her feet touched solid ground again, she was laughing so hard she couldn't breathe. "I almost peed myself," she said between gasps. "That was incredible."

Maude, brushing leaves out of her hair, nodded sagely. "Now we live like birds. Later, we go to war."

Wilbur turned, confused. "I'm sorry, what now? Oh Lord, paintball is next." They arrived at the paintball field that was in a giant field on the same complex. Spread out in front of them was an open terrain of wooden barriers, rusty cars, and inflatable bunkers. The three of them suited up again, now in full camouflage and protective gear.

"I feel like a GI Joe," Maude said, holding her marker like she'd just enlisted.

Wilbur rolled his eyes. "You're both going to break something."

"Only your ego," Mavis quipped, ducking behind a barrier.

The game began, and chaos broke loose. Mavis turned out to be oddly stealthy, popping up from behind a barrel to nail Wilbur square in the chest. "Traitor!" he yelled as the paint splattered across his shirt.

"You shouldn't have hesitated!" she shouted, already on the move again.

Maude was less stealthy but more enthusiastic. She charged directly into battle, cackling, firing wildly in every direction, and somehow managing to avoid getting hit. The teenage referee later admitted he was too scared to shoot her. By the end, they were exhausted, covered in paint, and hoarse from laughter. Mavis had welts on her arms and a triumphant grin that stretched ear to ear. "She would've loved that," she said, wiping her face with a wet wipe.

"We could start a league back in Rhinestone," Maude added.

"I'll never look at you two the same again," Wilbur chuckled.

"Good," Mavis said. "We're war heroes now. You should respect us."

That night, they wandered into a tattoo parlor

on a whim. The sign outside said it was open and it had the cozy, welcoming vibe of a place that wasn't trying too hard to be edgy. Inside, soft jazz played, and the walls were filled with framed art and quotes in fancy script. "It's so beautiful in here!" Mavis exclaimed. "I love the vibe. Look at these cute pictures!" She pointed to the wall that showcased available flash art.

Maude raised an eyebrow. "Are you suggesting we get matching tattoos?"

"You know what, why not?" Mavis said. "We survived zip-lining and survived paintball. This could be the souvenir we carry forever."

"I think I'm good," Wilbur shook his head. "Y'all two wild women carry on."

They browsed the flash sheets, then talked with the artist, a kind-eyed woman named Dani, about custom options. In the end, they settled on something simple and symbolic: a small magnolia blossom, outlined in fine black ink.

"Opal and Big Mama both loved magnolias," Mavis said softly as Dani prepped the stencil. "I remember one time when Opal said they were messy and unpredictable and beautiful, just like life."

She and Maude each got the flower inked. Mavis chose her wrist and Maude let the woman tattoo the small magnolia on her shin. When it was done, they stepped out into the night, their bodies tender, hearts full.

"Well," Maude said. "At least I'll remember getting this one. I guess I'm cool now."

"You were always cool," Mavis said.

That night back at the hotel, they ordered room service and poured three glasses of cheap champagne from a bottle Mavis had packed in secret. She raised her glass and cleared her throat. "To Opal, who never got to finish her bucket list, but made damn sure we'd be the ones to carry it through."

They clinked glasses. "To Opal," Wilbur and Maude echoed.

"And to us," Mavis added. "Because somehow, we're still standing. And still singing."

They drank and talked late into the night, telling stories that wandered and circled back again, until finally, silence wrapped around them like a blanket. The next morning, they packed the truck for the drive home. They had successfully crossed off three items from the list. Mavis glanced one more time at the journal, flipping through pages filled with checkmarks, dates, and little scribbled notes from the road. As they drove out of Nashville, Maude rolled down her window and let the wind rush in. Mavis pulled her hair into a messy bun and leaned her head on the seat. Wilbur turned up the radio, and Dolly's voice filled the cab again. Back home, the ShangriLa would be waiting, full of memories and projects to keep him busy for a while.

Chapter Nine

"I know we're all doing the bucket list adventures, but I want to find a way to honor Opal somehow," Mavis said over dinner one night. Emily nodded along like she had been thinking the same thing. "Maude has the highway named after her, and Big Mama has the children's home in Junction named after her, so it just seems right that Opal have something, too."

"What are you thinking?" Wilbur asked as he drank the last of his sweet tea.

"That's as far as I've gotten," Mavis sighed. "I can't think of anything that makes sense."

"Well, let's keep thinking on it. We'll know when it's right," Wilbur nodded. "This bucket list is keeping us all pretty busy as it is." He was already jittery at the idea of white water rafting in Yellowstone next week. This was set to be one of the biggest adventures he had ever been on: eight days in Colorado, Wyoming, and Montana to Yellowstone that could potentially cross off three of Opal's dreams. Emily, Mavis, Mona, Harry, and Harry's wife Tamara, had all planned to go with him and Maude. They were going to fly into Denver on Sunday and visit with Mavis' sister before boarding a train Monday that would take them through Rocky Mountain National Park to Glenwood Springs. From Glenwood Springs they would drive back to Denver and catch a plane to Bozeman, Montana, and drive to Yellowstone National Park. It was going to be an action packed eight days. Wilbur hoped that they were all up to it. He felt a little more at ease now that he had his dog, Bear, taken care of. He had never boarded him anywhere, but eight days was a lot to ask for one of their friends to watch him. Bear would be staying at the veterinarian's office as part of their pet boarding program. The ladies at the front desk were always so smitten with him. They had even agreed to board Mavis' trio of llamas while she was away.

"I'm all packed!" Mavis said as the conversation turned to their upcoming trip.

"Wilbur and I haven't even begun to pack. I don't even know where to start," Emily laughed.

"Eight days is a long time," Wilbur added. He had been quite nervous to be gone for so long, but Harlan had promised to keep an eye on things while he was away. It was nice to call the county sheriff your best friend.

"We're going to have the best time," Mavis said for what must have been the tenth time that evening. "You worry too much. This is going to be the trip of a lifetime."

"And you're going to Maude's tomorrow to help her pack, right?" Wilbur asked. Mavis nodded. "She swears she doesn't need any help, and she's probably right, but she's never been to that part of the country before. It's going to be quite the trek and I just want to make sure she is prepared."

"Well, remember, no touching the animals, no matter how cute they are. And we're not coming back with any new pets," Wilbur chuckled. He had read about tourists that would get out of their cars and attempt to pet the bison and other creatures that roamed the national park. He did not want any of them to become a statistic or a news headline.

"Opal was the one who brought back stowaways," Mavis smiled. She launched into the tale of how Opal had once brought back a kitten from Italy in the early 1960s. "I loved that cat. I can't believe he lived as long as he did."

"Opal hand fed him twice a day and he lived the true life of luxury," Wilbur added. "Leo was an icon in this town. Hated Maude though."

"I think the feeling was mutual," laughed Mavis.

"We've got so much to do before we leave," Wilbur reminded them.

"Of course," Emily nodded. "Oh, Mavis, let's get with Mona and Tamara tomorrow and see if they want to go shopping with us."

"Harry and I are going to have our hands full," Wilbur mumbled to himself.

"You knew that when you married me," Emily grinned. She leaned over and kissed him on the cheek and beamed back at Mavis. "I can't wait to meet your sister! Is she ready for all of our craziness?"

"She can't wait!" Mavis squealed. Wilbur cleared the dirty dishes off the table while the two women continued their conversation that centered around which animals they were most excited to see. Wilbur would have to keep an extra eye on them both.

When Monday rolled around, Wilbur loaded up his and Emily's luggage in the back of the truck, then drove to the Manor to pick up Mavis. She was waiting patiently on the front porch with her luggage ready to get the show on the road. They had one last stop before they made their way to Birmingham to catch their flight directly to Denver.

Wilbur was surprised to see that Maude's porch was empty when he, Emily, and Mavis pulled into her driveway. He figured she would be waiting for them, but she was nowhere in sight. "I'll go check on her," Mavis volunteered. Mavis walked up to the porch and knocked on the front door. A very grumpy looking Maude answered the door a few minutes later. "Is everything ok?" Mavis asked.

Maude grumbled something under her breath and ushered Mavis inside. "What was that?" Mavis asked.

"Don't worry about it," Maude sighed. Her luggage was piled up by the front door, but she herself did not look ready to go. "Are you dressed and ready?" Mavis asked hesitantly.

"I just need a few minutes," Maude replied.

"Can we load up your luggage while you finish up?" Mavis asked. Maude nodded and disappeared to her back bedroom. Mavis popped outside and requested that Wilbur help her with Maude's suitcases. He and Emily quickly walked inside to grab the luggage. "Everything ok?" Wilbur asked

Mavis. "I don't know, she seems to be in some sort of mood today," Mavis whispered. "We may have to stop for coffee or breakfast."

Wilbur checked his watch and grimaced. "I don't know that we have too much time to stretch," he replied. "Might have to make her a cup or two here and bring it with us."

"I'll take care of that," Mavis nodded. She headed to the kitchen and began preparing Maude's coffee. Wilbur and Emily made quick work of loading and organizing the luggage, and decided to sit back on the porch while they waited for Maude. When she didn't come out after fifteen minutes, Wilbur began to get even antsier.

"Maude? Everything ok in there?" Mavis called down the hallway. She had made enough coffee to fill two different insulated cups for Maude to enjoy on the way to the airport. She heard Maude's bedroom door open and heard her shuffle down the hallway. "I'm ready," Maude announced. She had her large purse in one hand and a small box in the other. "Alright, let's get a move on. I made you some coffee for the road. Have you had breakfast?" Mavis asked. She was surprised when Maude shook her head and said she didn't feel like eating this morning. "Are you ill?" Mavis gasped. "Do we need to stop and see a doctor?"

"Mavis, I'm fine. I'm just a little preoccupied this morning. Now are you ready or not?" Maude answered. Mavis nodded and walked outside to the porch while Maude locked the front door.

Mavis joined Emily in the backseat while Wilbur helped Maude into the front passenger seat of his truck. Maude handed her large bag to Mavis in the back seat, but kept the small box in her lap. Once they were on the open road, Mavis dared to ask another question. "So, Maude, what's in the box?"

"Less you know the better," Maude shrugged. Mavis and Emily exchanged nervous glances, but neither wanted to press the conversation any further. Wilbur caught Mavis' nervous stare in the rear view mirror and smiled to himself. He knew better than to ask Maude any questions when she was in a mood.

When they parked the car at the airport, Wilbur stacked the suitcases and bags onto a trolley and pushed it towards the double doors. Mavis texted with Mona to make sure they were still on time. "Oh goodness, Mona, Harry, and Tam are already at the gate waiting for us!" Mavis said in a panic.

"We don't board for another fifty minutes," Wilbur said as he checked his watch. He glanced toward Maude, who was still cradling the small box in her lap like it was made of crystal. He didn't have to guess what was inside, but he figured she wasn't ready to talk about it in front of everyone else. She'd speak her piece when she was good and ready. "Alright, ladies, let's get a move on," Wilbur said, grabbing the trolley's handle. "Denver isn't coming to us."

The automatic doors whooshed open, and the familiar scent of airport coffee and floor polish hit them all at once. Mavis took in the bustle with wide-eyed excitement, her suitcase wheels clicking rhythmically as she trotted to keep pace with Wilbur's long strides. Emily trailed just behind, already fishing around in her bag for her boarding pass. Maude didn't rush. She had her box tucked securely under one arm, her handbag on the other, and she walked as if she were crossing a small-town sidewalk on a Tuesday morning rather than a busy airport terminal.

"You know," Mavis whispered to Emily as they fell in step behind her, "if she slows down any more, we're going to have to put her on the trolley with the luggage." Emily stifled a laugh, but the sound still made Maude glance back.

"I heard that," Maude said without breaking stride. "And you wouldn't dare."

At the check-in counter, a young attendant in a crisp blue vest scanned their IDs and tagged their bags. Wilbur made quick work of it, but Mavis got tangled up in a conversation about seat upgrades and snack options. "Ma'am," the attendant said kindly, "you'll have complimentary drinks on the flight."

Wilbur groaned. "Mavis, you're holding up the line." Mavis rolled her eyes and finally surrendered her suitcase and joined the others as they moved toward security where Wilbur had to remove his shoes twice because he'd put them back on before he was told he was actually cleared. "Feels like we've been here an hour already," Wilbur muttered, collecting his belt and shoes from the gray bin.

Maude sailed through security with barely a pause, her box still clutched under her arm. "Experience," she said when Mavis asked how she did it. "I've been through enough airports to know how not to make a fool of myself."

They made it to the gate with fifteen minutes to spare, and sure enough, Mona, Harry, and Tamara were already there. Mona waved enthusiastically, her sparkly turquoise sweater practically glowing under the fluorescent lights. "There's the rest of our merry crew!" she said. "We've been watching them board folks for the flight to Miami. You should've seen the size of some of those beach bags."

Tamara leaned in to hug Emily and Mavis, while Harry gave Wilbur a wide smile. "Ready for eight days of chaos?"

"Not sure anyone can be ready for that," Wilbur replied.

When the boarding announcement finally came over the loudspeaker, they shuffled into line, presenting their passes one by one. Mavis was practically bouncing with excitement. "Denver, here we come!" she announced to no one in particular.

Onboard, Wilbur had lucked out with an aisle seat, Emily next to him, and Harry and Tamara across the way. Mavis was several rows in front of them with Mona, already chatting up the woman in the window seat next to them. Maude sat alone across the aisle, her box tucked into the carry-on space under the seat in front of her. As the engines roared to life, Mavis twisted around in her seat to look toward Maude. "You okay back there?"

"Just fine," Maude said, eyes fixed out the small oval window. The plane lifted off, tilting toward the sun, and the chatter in the cabin dimmed for a moment as everyone settled in. The layover in St. Louis was its own kind of circus. They only had an hour between flights, but Mavis still insisted on finding the best coffee in the terminal. She, Mona, Emily, and Tamara disappeared down a concourse while Wilbur, Harry, and Maude stayed behind with the carry-ons. When they returned, Mavis was clutching three cups and talking about a bakery she'd seen just past Gate C12 that apparently had life-changing cinnamon rolls.

"No," Wilbur said before she could even ask. "We're boarding in ten minutes."

The flight to Denver was longer, and somewhere over the Midwest, Maude finally leaned over to Wilbur. "You know where we're going after this, right?"

"Denver, Glen something, and then Yellowstone," he said. "Then back home."

Maude's voice was quiet, but steady. "There's a spot I need to see at some point. I'll know when I see it," she whispered. Wilbur just nodded. Maude would talk more about it when she was ready.

By the time they landed in Denver, the group was more than ready to stretch their legs. Mavis spotted her sister, Brandy, in the arrivals hall almost instantly and squealed loudly. "Mavis!" Brandy called out, weaving through the crowd to hug her. "Hello Wilbur! And you must be Maude!"

Introductions flew in every direction, and soon they were headed toward the rental cars, laughter echoing through the garage. Wilbur loaded the last suitcase into the trunk, then noticed Maude standing off to the side, looking out at the snow-dusted mountains in the distance. She held the box close, her thumb tracing slow circles on the lid. "You'll get your moment," he said softly.

She nodded, not looking away from the horizon.

Chapter Ten

Mavis rode in the front seat of her sister's vehicle while the rest of the group split into a rental SUV. Harry followed close behind Brandy's car so he wouldn't get lost. Wilbur rode up front with Harry, while Emily and Mona chattered away about how the air already smelled different in Colorado. Maude sat in the back eating from a bag of trail mix Mavis had insisted they buy in the airport gift shop.

They wound their way out of the airport, past flat stretches of prairie that suddenly gave way to nearby snowcapped peaks. Even the sky looked bigger out here than it did in Rhinestone. "Tomorrow we'll be weaving through the mountains," Emily said dreamily, her forehead pressed against the passenger window.

"Tomorrow," Wilbur reminded her, "which means tonight, we sleep. I'm already exhausted."

Brandy, Mavis' sister, lived in a beautiful house in a quiet Denver neighborhood. Her husband and children were away for a few days on a school trip. She greeted them all with the same energy she'd shown at the airport, ushering them inside, already talking about the dinner she planned to make. "I hope everyone likes pot roast," she said.

"It's not fancy, but after a day of travel, I figured something warm and filling was the way to go."

"You figured right," Harry said, already loosening his belt.

A few hours later, the dining room was set with matching plates and a pitcher of iced tea in the middle of the table. She reminded everyone that it was unsweetened tea, but she could add sugar to anyone's tea who needed it. Maude placed her box carefully on a nearby counter top before sitting down, almost like she wanted it to be in the room but out of the way. Over dinner, Brandy asked questions about the trip, wanting to know which bucket list items they were checking off first. "Well," Mavis said, counting on her fingers, "in the next few days we've got white water rafting and see a whole list of animals we want to check off our list. And no, Wilbur, I won't try to ride a bison or whatever you're afraid I'll do." The table laughed, but Wilbur noticed that even in the lightheartedness, Maude's eyes drifted toward the box every now and then.

After dessert, the group broke off into little clusters. Harry and Tamara went out for a short walk to stretch their legs, while Mavis, Emily, and Mona settled in the living room with Brandy to look through old family photo albums. Wilbur carried Maude's luggage upstairs to one the kid's rooms where Maude would be sleeping. "You good in here?" he asked, setting her suitcase by the bed.

"Thank you," Maude nodded.

Wilbur hesitated in the doorway. "You know,

you don't have to keep whatever it is to yourself. If you want help making arrangements, I can help you."

"I'll handle it," Maude said, not unkindly. "But I appreciate the offer."

The next morning came too soon, but Mavis was up before dawn with Brandy, making coffee and loudly organizing the day's schedule in the kitchen. "Train leaves at eight sharp," she announced to anyone within earshot. "Which means we need to be out the door by seven. And if you're not a morning person, well, too bad!"

With just a few minutes to spare, everyone was downstairs, bleary-eyed but ready, suitcases stacked neatly by the door. Maude's box was back in her arms, the same way she'd carried it yesterday. The drive to the station was quiet, the city just starting to wake up.

They boarded the train bound for Glenwood Springs, the cars warm and softly lit, with wide windows perfect for the views to come. Wilbur found them seats together, and soon they were gliding out of the station, the city fading behind them. The scenery shifted quickly from suburban neighborhoods to wide open plains, then slowly up into the foothills. Mavis pressed her phone against the glass, snapping picture after picture. "Every turn looks like a postcard," she said.

As the train began its climb, the mountains rose on either side with peaks dusted in powdered sugar type snow. They passed through tunnels that seemed to last forever, emerging into sudden bursts of sunlight and new landscapes. Maude sat quietly, watching it all, her hands resting in her lap over the box. At one point, Mavis leaned over. "Beautiful, isn't it?" she said in awe. Maude nodded slowly. "Opal would have loved this," she whispered. Something in her voice made Mavis squeeze her arm. She didn't press for more, but in her mind, she made a silent promise to keep a closer eye on the older woman.

In Glenwood Springs, they stepped off the train into crisp mountain air that smelled faintly of pine and woodsmoke. Their hotel was just a short walk away, and after checking in, the group scattered, some to explore the small downtown, others to rest before lunch. Wilbur, Emily, Tamara, and Harry ended up in a little cafe sipping hot chocolate. Across the street, Mona, Maude, and Mavis stood in front of a souvenir shop looking at postcards. From where he sat, Wilbur could see that Maude still carried the box.

The following morning, they would make their way back to Denver, then fly to Bozeman and drive into Yellowstone, but for now, the trip was unfolding in shared laughter and the kind of quiet moments that linger. The little town glowed as the group wandered toward somewhere to eat lunch. Mavis had read in a travel blog about a restaurant called The Pullman, and she wasn't about to let anyone talk her out of trying it. "It's farm-to-table," she explained for the fifth time that afternoon. "That means the menu changes every day based on what's fresh and available."

"Means you can't plan what you're ordering," Harry said. "Which sounds suspicious."

To his surprise, the food was well worth it. They all tried thick pork chops with rosemary potatoes, a trout dish fresh from the river, and for dessert, warm bread pudding with caramel sauce that made even Harry hum in approval. After lunch, a few of them strolled back through downtown, peeking in the windows of adorable shops. Maude walked a step behind the others, her small box in her handbag now, though she kept a hand hooked through the strap like it was anchoring her. Wilbur slowed his pace to match hers. "How're you holding up?"

Maude gave a small shrug. "Just thinking about tomorrow. And the next day."

"You don't have to rush anything," he reminded her.

"I know," she said, but her voice was far away. Wilbur wanted to know what was going on in her head and heart, but he knew that when Maude was ready to talk, she would. They spent the afternoon walking around the town, shopping, and trying whatever food options the little town had to offer. The next morning, Mona convinced almost everyone to try the hot springs before the return train to Denver. "It's basically soaking in history," she said, gesturing toward the steaming outdoor pools that had been drawing travelers since the 1800s. Emily slipped into the water first, sighing audibly. "Oh, this is worth the whole trip."

Wilbur eased in, wincing at the heat before relaxing. "Could stay here all day," he agreed.

Mavis floated over, her hair piled up in a messy bun. "Maude, you're missing out!" she called out, but Maude sat at the edge, her shoes still on, watching steam curl into the cool morning air. She didn't say why she wasn't joining. Wilbur guessed she didn't want to leave the box alone.

By mid-afternoon, they were back on the train to Denver, the mountains sliding past again, shadows growing longer as the day wore on. Mavis was already talking about the next leg of the trip. "Bozeman tomorrow," she said, almost bouncing in her seat. "Yellowstone by tomorrow evening!"

Brandy once again offered them a night's stay at her beautiful home and navigated them back to the Denver airport the next morning. The Denver airport felt busier than it had two days before. Their gate was packed with tourists in hiking boots, wide-brimmed hats, and brand-new backpacks that looked like they'd never seen dirt. During boarding, Maude made sure her box was tucked in her carry-on bag on her lap until they were in the air. The flight was short, less than two hours, but long enough for Mavis to make friends with the couple seated behind her, exchanging phone numbers in case they happened to bump into each other in the park. Mavis reminded Maude and Wilbur of Opal in those moments. Neither of them had ever met a stranger.

The large rental van Harry and Wilbur had rented smelled faintly of pine air freshener and sweaty feet as they loaded in. The road to the park took them through stretches of forest and open valleys, the mountains hemming them in on all sides. Every so often, someone would call out an animal sighting; first a cluster of mule deer, then an elk grazing in a meadow. "Reminder," Wilbur said, "no touching, no feeding, and no taking anything home, living or otherwise."

"Party pooper," Mavis teased.

They stopped at a small barbecue restaurant that resembled a log cabin for supper. While the food was good, they all agreed that it couldn't touch the smoked ribs and pulled pork from down south. By the time they reached their lodge inside the park, the sun was beginning to set in streaks of gold and pink over the mountains. The air had that wild, clean smell only found in places far from cities. They had rented three rooms in one of the lodges in the Park. Wilbur and Emily had one room, Tamara and Harry in another, which left Mona, Mavis, and Maude to share the third. Maude stood on the porch for a long time after everyone else went inside, looking at the horizon like she was searching for something.

The next morning's sun dawned bright and clear, which made it perfect for white water rafting. Their guide, a wiry young man named Tyler with sunburned cheeks, gave them the safety rundown while they stood shivering in their wet suits. "You'll get wet. You'll get cold. You'll probably scream," he said cheerfully. "That's all part of the fun. I love it."

Mavis was the loudest screamer in the boat, followed closely by Mona. Wilbur, wedged in the middle, kept shouting reminders to paddle in unison. Maude sat near the back, surprisingly strong with her strokes, her face lit with a rare, wide smile when they hit a rapid. Wilbur was just thankful that no one fell out or drowned. By the time they hauled the raft ashore, everyone was soaked, exhilarated, and starving. Back at the lodge Harry threw some hot dogs and hamburgers on the grill while everyone else showered and got into some comfortable clothes. They planned to make s'mores that evening and gear up for a day of sightseeing tomorrow. Mavis, Tamara, and Mona went over the list of all the animals they intended to see while at Yellowstone.

"Wilbur, Mavis?" Maude asked after everyone had eaten their fill of dinner. "I need y'all to walk down to the water over yonder with me this evening."

"Yes ma'am, we can do that," Wilbur nodded.

That evening while everyone else enjoyed s'mores around a campfire, Wilbur, Mavis, and Maude walked down to the rushing creek as the sun set. Steam rose in delicate curls from the geyser fields beyond. Maude cradled the wooden box close to her chest, her fingers curled around it like she was afraid the wind might take it. It wasn't heavy, but Maude carried it as though every ounce was sacred. Wilbur kept pace beside her, his hands shoved deep into the pockets of his jacket. The only sounds were the crunch of their boots on the packed trail and the distant hiss of a nearby hot spring. The others had stayed back at the lodge, giving them space. Mavis had squeezed Maude's arm before she left, her eyes shining in that way she got when she wanted to be strong but was two seconds from breaking. She walked a step or two behind Wilbur and Maude. Even though

Maude hadn't said what her plan was, Mavis knew that they were laying Opal to rest out here in the mountains where she could be with nature.

When Maude came to the stream, she stood there for a long moment, breathing in the sights, the sounds, and the smell of wild water. Wilbur glanced at her but didn't rush her. He knew better than to fill this space with words. "This was one of the last places she talked about," Maude said finally, her voice low and steady. "Said she wanted to see it before she went. I guess this is the closest I can give her." She sank to her knees at the edge of the water. The ripples licked at her boots, the cool water biting through the leather. Wilbur crouched beside her, his presence solid as the stones beneath them. Maude set the box on her lap and lifted the lid. Inside, the little drawstring pouch sat in the nest of soft fabric she'd packed for the trip. She reached in with both hands and held it for a moment, closing her eyes. When she opened them again, the water seemed brighter, like the sun had slipped out from behind a cloud.

Her hands trembled only a little as she loosened the pouch and tipped it toward the current. The ashes fell like pale silk, twisting in the air before the water claimed them. The water carried them away in a slow swirl, scattering them into glittering flecks before folding them out of sight. Wilbur put a hand on her shoulder. "She'd like this," he said, his voice rough. "Not just the water, but you doing this for her."

Maude let out a breath that was a half-laugh. "She always said I was stubborn enough to outlast her. Guess she was right. I put some of her in the creek behind the church and I'll put some in the forest behind Magnolia Manor. The rest I've got in that ugly old urn she chose."

They stayed there until the water looked like water again. Only then did Maude close the box and tucked it under her arm as they stood. The walk back felt lighter somehow, though nothing had really changed, except maybe the weight in Maude's chest. When they returned to the lodge, Emily held out a platter of s'mores for Wilbur, Mavis, and Maude to enjoy. "Now that you're back, how about I let you whip up on us in some cards, Maude?" Emily suggested.

Maude smiled delightfully.

Chapter Eleven

"This is it, this is how Mavis dies," Wilbur sighed. He had hoped that Harry would have at least been another voice of reason alongside him, but Harry was just as giddy at the sight of a herd of bison as Mavis was. Mavis, Emily, Tamara, Mona, and Harry had jumped out of the vehicle with gusto as Wilbur pulled over to the side of the road behind the caravan of spectators. Only Maude lingered close to the van snapping pictures with her camera. Wilbur leaned against the van close to her and shook his head. "I swear, if one of them gets gored, that's on them."

"You sound just like Ruby," Maude laughed. "She would have loved to see these mountains and all these critters, but she wouldn't get too close. You know Opal would have been out there howling at the moon with the wolves."

"Oh, Wilbur"! Mavis exclaimed. She was out of breath as she hurried back to the van. "You have to come see the little baby one in the middle of the herd. It's the cutest thing I've ever seen."

Wilbur chuckled at Mavis' excitement. Every animal they had seen throughout the trip had been the cutest animal she'd ever seen. They had already been able to cross off three of Opal's list items on the trip and they still had a full day left in the park before they flew home early the following morning. "I'd like to see a grizzly," Harry said as they all piled back in the van.

"I think I'm good," Wilbur replied. "These grizzlies are nothing like the little black bears we've got back home. And these mountain lions might put our panthers to shame."

"You're right about that," Harry agreed. "Might have to check their bags," he gestured to Mavis, Mona, Emily, and Tamara as he laughed. "I bet they'd snatch a cub before we even blinked an eye."

"Don't give them any ideas," Wilbur laughed.

The group spent the rest of the day winding through the twisting roads of Yellowstone, each curve in the road revealing another spectacle that sent the van erupting with gasps, squeals, or, in Wilbur's case, a long-suffering sigh. Every time Mavis gasped behind him, he was afraid he had run over something. The tall lodgepole pines stretched into the sky like endless green pillars, and the smell of pine sap and woodsmoke drifted through the cracked windows. Their first stop after the bison was Mammoth Hot Springs, where terraces of white and orange limestone tumbled down the mountainside like frozen waterfalls. Steam curled upward, blurring the edges of the cliffs in a dreamy haze. "Looks like a melted wedding cake," Mavis said, her camera clicking furiously as she leaned over the railing. Tamara giggled. "A wedding cake from the underworld. Can't you just imagine the devil popping out from behind one of those steam vents?"

"Don't give me nightmares," Mona replied, though her eyes were shining. "Still, it's beautiful. I've never seen anything quite like it."

"Smells like rotten eggs," Maude muttered.

"You're missing the point," Mavis teased, lowering her camera. "It's the earth breathing. That's what makes it magical."

Harry leaned in close to the rail, his grin mischievous. "Magical or not, I bet if you threw in a hot dog, you'd have it cooked in about five seconds flat." That set off a round of laughter from the women, and even Wilbur had to hide a smile behind his hand.

They lingered at the springs until Mavis dragged them onward, determined not to waste a minute. The next stop was Yellowstone Falls, where the river plunged in a thunderous sheet of white into the canyon below. The sound was so loud it shook through their bones. Mona gripped the railing with both hands, her face pale. "Oh my word, that's higher than it looked in the pictures."

"Don't lean so far!" Wilbur barked, moving closer behind her. His heart hammered as he watched the mist rise up in glittering clouds. "She's fine," Mavis said gently, laying a hand on his arm. "We're all fine. Look at it, Wilbur, it's unlike anything I've ever seen."

He did look, and despite himself, he had to admit it was breathtaking. The rock walls flared in shades of gold, orange, and russet, as though the canyon itself was on fire. A rainbow arched across the spray, and for a moment even Wilbur felt a sense of awe that silenced his complaints. "Opal would've loved this," Mavis said softly, breaking the quiet. Her voice trembled just a little, though she quickly tucked it back into brightness. "She would've been the first one leaning over that railing, daring the rest of us to do the same." They all nodded, each of them lost in their own memories of her wild, unafraid spirit. Mavis snapped another picture, but this time she didn't hide the tears that slid down her cheeks.

The afternoon sun slanted low, painting the meadows in streaks of light. Herds of elk grazed in the distance, their antlers catching the glow, and once they spotted a bald eagle gliding over the river. Mavis declared it was a sign that they were exactly where they were meant to be. When they finally reached Old Faithful, the parking lot was already packed with cars and buses. They squeezed onto the wooden benches surrounding the geyser with a crowd of tourists.

"How long do we have to wait?" Tamara whispered, fanning herself with a brochure.

"Anywhere from thirty minutes to two hours," Harry said confidently, as though he were a tour guide.

Mona groaned. "You're joking."

But just as she said it, a deep rumble shuddered beneath them. A plume of water shot skyward, followed by a great column of steam. The crowd gasped and applauded. The group jumped to their feet, laughing and cheering along with the rest. Mavis grabbed Mona's hand, and Emily clutched Wilbur's arm. Wilbur even let out a low whistle.

"Guess we got lucky," Harry said.

"Lucky," Maude repeated, smiling faintly as she snapped photo after photo. "Or maybe Opal pulled some strings."

By the time they piled back into the van, the sky was streaked in pink and gold. The air grew cooler, the kind of sharp mountain chill that nipped at their noses and made them pull sweaters tighter around their shoulders.

"Dinner?" Mavis asked, twisting in her seat to look at the group.

"Dinner," they chorused, though everyone looked too tired to think of where.

They ended up in a small diner in West Yellowstone where the neon sign flickered and the booths were patched with duct tape. The menu was simple, showcasing burgers, fries, and huckleberry milkshakes, but it tasted like the best meal they'd ever eaten. Mavis raised her milkshake glass with a grin. "To Opal! For keeping us on our toes and dragging us to the ends of the earth."

"To Opal," they all echoed, clinking glasses.

Wilbur took a long sip, then set his cup down firmly. "To Big Mama, too," he added. "She might not have wanted to get this close to the animals, but she would've loved seeing all of us together." There was a moment of silence, then Maude reached across the table and squeezed his hand. "You're right," she whispered.

The next morning came far too soon. The alarm clocks went off before dawn, dragging them from warm beds into the chilly gray light. The lobby was filled with the sound of zippers and luggage wheels, the group fumbling with coffee cups and boarding passes. Maude muttered something about never being a morning person, and Tamara nearly left her jacket behind until Harry swooped it up with a dramatic flourish. "Can't leave without this," he teased. "You'd freeze before we even reached the plane."

"It's not very cold out," Mavis said.

"Yes, but, Tam is always cold," Harry smiled at his wife who was pulling her jacket over hear arms.

Outside, Wilbur loaded the van one last time. It struck Mavis as bittersweet; this was the end of their Yellowstone adventure, and she wasn't ready to let go. As they drove north to Bozeman, the highway stretched quiet and endless ahead of them. Everyone dozed at some point, heads nodding against windows or shoulders. Maude snapped a photo of the rising sun casting golden light across the mountains, but then set her camera down in her lap. Emily broke the silence at last. "I don't want this to be over."

"It's not over," Mavis said quickly, squeezing her sister-in-law's hand. "It's just one trip on a longer road. We've got more of Opal's list to do. This is just the beginning."

That seemed to ease the heaviness in the van. They began tossing out ideas, laughing and dreaming of what was still to come. By the time they reached Bozeman, the group had already built half an itinerary for their next trip.

At the airport, they shuffled through security and found their gate. Wilbur sank into a chair with a groan, muttering about needing three days' sleep to recover. The women clustered around the big windows, watching planes taxi across the tarmac. When the call for boarding came, they moved as one, their steps light despite their tired bodies. The plane lifted off into the clouds, carrying them back toward Rhinestone, back toward the lives they'd temporarily set aside. They carried the laughter, the photographs, the memories of bison herds and boiling geysers, and most of all, the sense that Opal's spirit was still right there with them, pushing them onward, back with them.

The hum of the engines settled into a steady lullaby as the plane cut through the clouds. Most of the passengers closed their eyes or leaned into their neck pillows, but Mavis pressed her forehead to the tiny oval window, watching the world shrink and stretch below them. The mountain peaks had already faded from view, but she could still feel the smell of pine in her hair and the taste of huckleberries on her tongue. She knew, even as the plane climbed higher, that the trip would live in her bones for the rest of her life. Beside her, Tamara flipped idly through the in-flight magazine, scoffing at the glossy photographs of tropical beaches. "I don't know how anyone could look at this after what we just saw. White sand can't hold a candle to bison herds."

"Speak for yourself," Mona said, half-asleep, her voice muffled against her scarf. "I'd trade a herd of bison for a beach chair and a margarita right now."

Harry, sitting across the aisle, perked up. "Hey, that's not a bad idea. Zip-line through the rain forest in Costa Rica, then margaritas afterward."

Tamara sat up straighter. "Oh, I love that. Yes, that's perfect."

Maude groaned from two rows up, where she'd wedged herself into the window seat. "Don't even start planning another trip until I've had a month to recover. My knees aren't what they used to be."

"Your knees survived fine," Mavis teased gently. She reached over the seat in front of her and adjusted the small pillow behind Maude's head. "And admit it, you enjoyed yourself more than you thought you would."

The group settled into the flight's rhythm. Coffee came in tiny cups and peanuts and pretzels rustled in plastic bags. Harry told a long and embellished story about a near-run-in he'd once had with a moose on a camping trip, which had everyone howling with laughter until the flight attendant shushed them. Mona shared a pack of gum she'd brought along, and Tamara sketched the outline of a geyser in her notebook from memory. At one point, Mavis leaned her head back and closed her eyes, letting the hum of the engines wash over her. She thought about Opal, about how fiercely she'd lived, and how easily she'd laughed. She pictured her leaning out the van window, daring the wind to carry her voice to the mountains.

Hours later, the plane dipped through layers of cloud, and the familiar landscape of Montgomery came into view. Emily pressed her face to the glass, a childlike grin spreading across her face. "Home," she murmured. "I never thought I'd be so happy to see it and so sad all at once."

"I know what you mean," Mona said. "It feels different now. Like we're carrying Yellowstone back with us."

The wheels touched down with a jolt that made Wilbur grip the armrests, and the entire cabin exhaled in unison. Harry clapped him on the shoulder as they taxied to the gate. "See? Not so bad. No goring, no bear attacks, and the plane stayed in one piece."

As they said goodbye at the airport, Mona snapped a candid shot of Mavis hugging Emily, both of them rumpled and travel-worn, but radiant with joy. Tamara stretched her arms overhead and sighed dramatically. "I'm going to sleep for two straight days."

"Not before we unpack the car," Harry reminded her as they headed toward the exit.

Outside, the air was warmer and softer than the mountain chill they'd grown used to. The sun was just beginning to set, streaking the sky with lavender and gold. Their cars were waiting in long-term parking, familiar and ordinary in a way that felt almost jarring after the wildness of Yellowstone. For a moment, no one moved. They stood together in the fading light, their luggage at their feet, as if reluctant to scatter back to their separate lives. Finally, Mavis broke the silence. "Let's not let this be the last time. Promise me. We've got more of Opal's list to finish, and I don't want to wait too long."

They all nodded, one by one. "To Opal," Emily whispered.

"To Opal," the others echoed, their voices soft but certain.

Mavis, Emily, and Maude dozed on the drive back towards their charming town while Wilbur drove. Back home in Rhinestone looked the same as it always had. The quiet streets and the familiar storefronts all waited for them to resume their busy lives, but for the group of friends, nothing would ever feel quite the same again. They had stood together on the edge of canyons and watched the earth breathe fire. They had laughed until their sides ached and mourned the absence of the one who had brought them there.

Chapter Twelve

Mavis tugged at the hem of her cardigan as she stood outside the brick-fronted library in Junction, the next town over. It was a brisk evening, the kind that made the tips of her ears sting and her nose tingle, but the golden glow from the library's tall windows felt like a quiet invitation. She had been wanting to join the book club she'd heard about at the library for weeks, but she never worked up the courage to do so until that Tuesday morning. Come hell or high water, she was going to drive over to Junction and meet some new people who also liked books that evening. Helping Maude with the bucket list had given her purpose, and she had found joy again in small bursts, but she still missed the grounding habit of sitting with a book and losing herself in other people's stories. Reading had always been her favorite escape. Somewhere along the years of care-giving and chaos, though, her books had gathered dust.

She pushed the library door open, warmth wrapping around her like a welcome hug. In the back room where the flyer said the club met, she saw a cluster of chairs set up in a loose circle, with half a dozen people already chatting with cups of coffee and tea in their hands.

"Hello there!" an older woman with short silver hair waved her in. "You must be new. Come join us," she smiled.

Mavis smiled nervously and crossed the room. She introduced herself, and one by one, the members gave their names. There was Eleanor, the retired teacher who had apparently run the club since it began twenty years ago. Lee, who worked at the post office. Jenny, a younger woman with a toddler at home who said she barely had time to shower, let alone read, but insisted the club was her sanity. A few others smiled warmly at her, and Mavis felt her shoulders start to loosen. Mavis looked around at the last person in the circle who smiled. "Mackenzie Potter," he said with a half-smile, lifting his hand in an easy wave. "But everyone calls me Mac." He looked to be in his early forties, dressed in a neatly pressed button-down shirt, sleeves rolled just enough to suggest he was more relaxed than formal. His eyes were a clear hazel that crinkled a little at the corners when he smiled.

The group settled in, and Eleanor launched into discussion about the book of the month: a contemporary novel about family secrets and forgiveness. Mavis had devoured it in just two nights, and as the conversation unfolded, she felt a spark light up inside her. She loved the way people read the same sentences yet took away such different meanings. She found herself leaning forward, gesturing with her hands, laughing at Lee's jokes and agreeing with Jenny's thoughtful comments. By the time the meeting wound down, her cheeks ached from smiling. As people rose to gather their coats, Mavis reached for her tote bag and nearly bumped into Mac, who had stood to stretch. "Good thoughts tonight," he said, nodding toward her.

"Thank you. I wasn't sure if I'd remember how to talk about books with other people," Mavis smiled.

Mac chuckled. "It didn't seem like you'd forgotten. You came out swinging."

She laughed, feeling a little blush rise in her cheeks. "I just really liked the story. It's been a while since I let myself read."

"Then I'd say you came back at the right time," Mac nodded. There was a pause, the kind that could drift into awkward silence, but instead, Mac tilted his head. "Forgive me for asking, but you're friends with Harry and Mona, aren't you?"

Mavis blinked in surprise. "Yes, I am."

"We've worked together a few times. I'm an accountant, small businesses mostly, and Harry and I go fishing sometimes. He's a good guy," Mac explained.

Mavis's surprise softened into delight. "Small world. We just got back from the vacation of a lifetime with them both!"

"I heard all about it," Mac nodded. He gave her another smile, this one a little warmer. They both reached for their coats then, and as Mac shrugged his on, he said casually, "You planning to come back next week?"

"Oh, definitely. I think I needed this more than I realized," Mavis nodded.

"Good. Then I'll see you here," Mac grinned. The simple exchange lingered with Mavis as she walked back to her car, the cool night air brushing against her flushed cheeks.

The next morning, Mavis woke with the faintest smile tugging at her lips. She rolled over and glanced at the book they'd discussed still sitting on her nightstand. For so long, her nights had ended with half-watched television or scrolling through her phone, but last night she'd fallen asleep with the quiet hum of a story still in her chest. She hadn't realized how much she missed that feeling. By mid-afternoon, she couldn't resist a trip back to the library. She scanned the shelves, pulling titles she'd meant to read years ago, as well as the next selection Eleanor had announced: an adventurous historical novel set during World War II. She checked them all out, the stack so tall she had to balance it against her hip, and left feeling like she'd gathered old friends.

That evening, as she curled into her favorite armchair with a blanket and tea, she let herself get lost in the pages. Every so often, though, her mind wandered a little to Mac Potter's easy smile. Harry knew him and seemed to enjoy spending time with him. Harry kept a pretty tight circle, so Mac had to be something special if he had broken through Harry's tough exterior. If he'd worked with Mac, that meant Mac was trustworthy and capable. And from the way he'd carried himself in the library, Mac seemed attentive but not overbearing, quick to laugh but not desperate for attention. She was drawn to him, even though she told herself it didn't matter. She had joined the book club for the books, not for whatever it was her stomach did when she thought of Mac.

The following Friday, Mavis had errands in Junction, and she found herself lingering near the bakery on Main Street. She had just picked up a loaf of sourdough and was fumbling with her wallet when she heard a voice behind her. "Well, there's the book club celebrity," a familiar voice laughed.

She turned, startled, to find Mac standing a few feet away, holding a paper bag of his own. His hazel eyes caught the afternoon light, and that same easy grin spread across his face. Mavis laughed, shaking her head. "Celebrity? I think that's stretching it."

"You should've seen Eleanor's face when you countered that the ending wasn't about forgiveness but about acceptance. I swear she was impressed," Mac replied.

Her cheeks warmed. "I didn't realize anyone was paying that close attention."

"Interested readers always pay attention," he said simply.

For a moment, neither of them moved. Then Mac gestured toward the small café next door. "Got time for coffee? My treat. It's the least I can do for the woman who out-debated Eleanor Thompson."

Mavis hesitated, then nodded. "All right, but only because I was craving caffeine anyway," she smirked playfully.

The café was cozy, its windows steamed from

the warmth inside. They found a small table by the window, and Mavis set down her bakery bag as Mac ordered for them. He returned with two steaming cups and a couple of biscotti balanced on napkins.

"So," Mac said, settling in. "Tell me, how long have you been friends with Harry?"

"Feels like forever," Mavis said, smiling at the thought. "We grew up in the same town, ran in some of the same circles growing up. Mona and I are best friends. It was so nice to go to Yellowstone together."

"I saw some of the pictures! It looked incredible. Though I'm a little surprised at how Harry has become such a traveler. He's changed so much over the last few years. It's nice to see him happy," Mac said. "He's a straight shooter. I respect that."

"You must be good at what you do if Harry didn't scare you off in business," Mavis laughed.

"Numbers don't scare me. They're honest. People, well, people are usually more complicated," Mac shrugged.

Mavis tilted her head, intrigued. "You like working with businesses then? Helping them make sense of the messy parts?"

He nodded. "It's satisfying seeing someone's livelihood stabilize because you balanced their books or planned for taxes so they could breathe a little easier. I like being the guy in the background making sure things run." He smiled at her and asked, "So, what do you do for work?"

Mavis studied him for a moment. He wasn't

flashy. He didn't talk like he was selling himself, the way some men did. There was a solid sense of grounding about him, a reliability that intrigued her. "I used to be a full time travel agent," she offered. "Before everything shifted in my life. I liked planning trips for people and helping them find an adventure that suited them."

"Sounds like we're in the same business, then," Mac said. "Different tools, but the same goal of getting people where they need to be with as little stress as possible."

The comparison made her laugh, and the sound felt freer than it had in months. They lingered longer than either of them probably intended, talking about books they'd loved as teenagers, television shows they watched in the evenings, and the quirks of small-town life. When Mavis finally glanced at the clock on the café wall, she gasped. "Oh no! I'm late for picking up a few things before supper." She gathered her bag quickly and stood up. Mac stood, too, and walked her to the door. "It was nice running into you, Mavis. I hope it happens again soon."

She smiled up at him, surprised at how natural it felt. "Me, too," she admitted. As she drove home, she found herself humming along to the radio.

By the time the next book club rolled around, Mavis felt more confident walking into the library. The hesitation that had tugged at her cardigan hem that first night was gone, replaced by a sense of anticipation. She carried the thick World War II novel tucked under her arm, its corners softened from the nights she had spent turning page after page. Inside, the group was already gathering. Lee greeted her with the same cheerful warmth, and Eleanor insisted Mavis sit beside her. Jenny gave a tired wave, her hair pulled back in a messy bun, but her eyes sparkled as she admitted she'd stayed up late actually finishing the book for once. Mac sidled in and sat across the circle, already flipping through his copy. When his gaze lifted and found hers, his face broke into a smile that felt like a private hello. Mavis felt a little flutter low in her chest, and she told herself to focus on the novel instead. Discussion began with Eleanor posing her usual opening question: "What did this story make you feel?"

Mavis had scribbled notes in her notebook, but as the conversation wove through themes of sacrifice, loyalty, and hidden courage, she let herself speak from the heart. She talked about how the protagonist's bravery reminded her of her grandmother who had always carried herself with quiet dignity. Others nodded and chimed in. Mac spoke, too; his comments were thoughtful and precise, like he had weighed them carefully before letting them out. When the session ended, chairs scraped back, and Eleanor announced that they would be taking the next two week offs, but to be ready for next month's pick, a mystery this time. Mavis was already intrigued.

As she gathered her bag, Mac came around the circle to her side. "So," he said lightly, "coffee again?"

She laughed. "You're going to make this a habit, aren't you?"

"Depends," he said. "Do you mind?"

The truth was, she didn't mind at all. They sat with their steaming mugs comparing notes on the book, then sliding easily into other conversations. Mavis was eager to learn more about him. At forty, Mac carried himself with the quiet steadiness of a man who had built his life carefully. He loved his work as an accountant, a profession that suited his sharp mind and love of order. He told her that he had moved to Junction ten years ago from Daytona, but his Florida roots ran deep. His father, a well-respected professor, and his mother, a judge with a keen sense of justice, had raised Mac and his siblings with high expectations and plenty of love. His younger brother still lived near Daytona, and his older sister lived in Vermont. They were both married and had families of their own. Mac adored his siblings and his beloved two nieces and three nephews. Mac had never married, never had children of his own, though it wasn't for lack of wanting companionship. He'd simply been cautious, preferring to wait for the right person rather than rush into the wrong thing. In town, Mac had settled comfortably. Folks knew him as reliable and polite, with a dry sense of humor that surfaced at the most unexpected times. He volunteered occasionally, kept his house tidy, and enjoyed a quiet beer at the Junction tavern on Fridays with friends from work. "And Harry is one of them?" she asked one evening.

"One of the memorable ones," Mac said with a grin. "He's got a way of making you feel like you're stepping into a tornado, but then somehow, you're standing steady in the middle of it."

"That's Harry," Mavis agreed with a chuckle.

For a moment, the air between them shifted into something deeper than book talk or friendly banter. Mavis felt it, and judging by the way Mac's expression softened, he did, too. They exchanged phone numbers and to Mavis' surprise, Mac began texting her in the evenings after work. He sent her a picture of a snapping turtle he and Harry had caught early one Saturday morning before easing it back into the river. Mavis chuckled and set her phone down to put away the groceries she had just bought. When her phone rang an hour later, she thought it might be Mac continuing the conversation, but as she glanced at the caller ID, she smiled. "Harry! Speak of the devil."

His gruff voice came through, amused. "Why am I always the devil in these sayings?"

"Because angel doesn't suit you," she teased.

"Fair enough. Hey, listen, Tam and I went fishing with Mac today," Harry continued.

Mavis froze for half a second, then forced her voice to stay casual. "How fun!"

"He mentioned you've been coming to book club. Said you're keeping someone named Eleanor on her toes," Harry said.

Mavis laughed. "I don't know about that."

"I told him he ought to be careful. You'll run circles around him if he's not paying attention," Harry laughed.

Mavis rolled her eyes, though her heart was beating faster. "Did you call just to tell me you gossiped about me?"

"Pretty much." She could hear the grin in his voice. "Also, he's good people, Mavis. I trust him."

Her chest warmed at the unspoken meaning. Harry didn't vouch for many. "Thanks, Harry," she said softly.

"Don't thank me. Just keep reading your books and giving Eleanor headaches. Anyway, don't forget Wilbur and I are fixing up Ruby's trailer this tomorrow. Bring coffee, or I'll never forgive you," Harry laughed.

"Deal," Mavis grinned. They hung up, but Mavis lingered in the kitchen, her hand still resting on the counter. Harry trusted Mac. Somehow, that made her feel like she could trust herself a little more, too. Mac must be pretty interested if he was talking to Harry and Tamara about her.

Chapter Thirteen

The more that Mavis saw Mac at book club and on their scheduled coffee meetup after club, the more she wanted to get to know him. He seemed genuinely interested in her and her hobbies, family, and the bucket list adventures she had already been on and were in the planning stages of. Maude had decided that the next adventure would be racing a car over one hundred and fifty miles per hour at a speed park near Atlanta. Emily was going with her and Mavis didn't know who was more excited, Maude or Emily! Going too fast in a car wasn't quite Mavis' speed, nor did Wilbur pitch a fit a go. This was right up Emily's alley, so when a free Saturday opened up, she whisked Maude away on the drive to Atlanta for the thrill of a lifetime.

Emily had learned a long time ago that if Maude got a certain glint in her eyes, the best thing to do was hold on for dear life and say a prayer. That glint was back this morning, sharp and eager, as they stood in the parking lot of the Atlanta Speed Park. The roar of engines echoed across the wide stretch of asphalt, vibrating through the ground and into Emily's shoes. She could practically feel her heart thumping in rhythm with the revving motors.

"Are you sure about this?" Emily asked, tugging her cardigan tighter against the cool Georgia breeze. The weather was pleasant enough for late summer, warm with just a hint of coolness underneath, but that wasn't why she was bracing herself. She was a woman who loved a good thrill, but Maude was in her mid-eighties and Emily would be lying if she said she wasn't at least a little concerned.

Maude's grin widened, deepening the laugh lines on her sun-browned face. "Emily, I was born sure about fast cars. If they put me behind the wheel of a tricycle with an engine, I'd find a way to make it fly."

"That's what I'm afraid of," Emily muttered, though her lips smirked despite herself.

"Finally something I was born to do. Lord knows Opal would've hated this. I'm not even sure why it's on her list. She always said I was the fastest driver this side of the Mississippi," Maude laughed.

The building at the center of the park was sleek and modern, with big glass windows overlooking the track. Inside, the hum of conversation mingled with the faint smell of rubber and gasoline. A young man in a black polo shirt with the speed park's logo greeted them at the counter. "Morning, ladies," he said brightly. "Are you here for a ride-along or a driving experience?"

Emily immediately lifted a hand. "Ride-along. Definitely ride-along. We are not driving these machines."

Maude leaned against the counter, grinning like she had a secret. "Well, I wouldn't say no to driving," she shrugged.

"Maude," Emily's tone was loving, yet firm.

The young man chuckled. "We get both kinds in here. Don't worry, ma'am. If you choose the driving option, you'll have an instructor in the car with you at all times. But the ride-along's a thrill, too. We've got professional drivers who'll push the cars past one hundred and fifty easy."

"Ride-along," Emily repeated, eyeing Maude like she was daring her to argue.

Maude held up her hands in mock surrender. "Alright, alright. Ride-along it is."

They filled out waivers and were led into a small briefing room where a short safety video played. Emily sat stiffly, her hands clasped in her lap, while Maude leaned back with her arms folded, looking as relaxed as if they were at the movies. When the video finished, the instructor reminded them, "These cars can hit speeds of one hundred and seventy miles per hour. Trust your driver, follow their instructions, and most importantly have fun." In the prep area, racks of racing suits and helmets lined the wall. The staff helped them gear up, zipping Maude into a fireproof jumpsuit that felt far too snug for her liking. "Do we really need all this?" she asked as the helmet was placed in her arms.

Emily laughed. "You want to go flying down that track in your Sunday clothes? This makes us look official. I feel like Danica Patrick already."

"You look like you're about to rob a bank,"

Maude said, unable to stop herself from chuckling at the sight of Emily in the oversized helmet.

"Oh hush. At least I'm pulling it off. You, on the other hand," Emily tilted her head, studying Maude. "Well, bless your heart. Nobody's ever accused you of being intimidating, have they?"

Maude gave her a playful swat. They both dissolved into laughter, the nervous tension melting just a little. For a fleeting second, Emily felt the kind of joy Opal would have wanted them to feel doing something wild and memorable in her honor. They could see the cars lined up on the pit road as they gleamed under the sunlight, their paint jobs a rainbow of sponsors and bold designs. The engines growled with life, sending shivers up Emily's spine. "Lord have mercy," she whispered. "They sound like beasts."

"They are beasts," Maude said, practically vibrating with excitement. "Beautiful, glorious beasts."

A driver in a red and black suit approached, removing his helmet to reveal a young face with sandy hair and an easy smile. "One of you ladies ready for the ride of your life?" he asked.

"That'd be me," Maude said before Emily could get a word in.

The driver introduced himself as Kyle, explained how to climb into the passenger side, and reminded her to keep her hands and feet clear. Maude listened with half an ear, her grin stretching from ear to ear. Emily shook her head. "You're enjoying this far too much," Emily snickered.

"You better believe it," Maude said.

Emily stepped back with the staff as Maude climbed awkwardly through the window into the passenger seat with a team of help guiding her in. The moment the car roared to life, Maude gave a thumbs-up out the window like she was already in love. Emily clasped her hands together. "Dear Lord, please keep her safe!"

The car lurched forward, rolled down the pit road, and then, like a shot from a cannon, it blasted onto the track. Emily gasped out loud as the engine screamed, the car blurring into color as it hugged the curve of the asphalt. "Oh my word," she breathed. She could see Maude's helmeted head bobbing slightly, and she could almost imagine the wild grin underneath. The car streaked past the stands at a speed Emily couldn't even comprehend. The staff member beside her glanced at the digital readout. "One-fifty-five. One-sixty."

Emily's heart leapt into her throat. "She's really going that fast?"

"Yes ma'am. And loving every second of it, I bet!" he cheered.

Emily pressed her hands together, torn between horror and admiration. She knew that Maude had always been bold, sometimes recklessly so, but watching her fly around that track, Emily saw more than just thrill-seeking. When the car finally slowed and pulled back into the pit, Maude was practically glowing as they helped her climb out. She yanked off her helmet and whooped. "Did you see me, Emily? Lord, that was better than chocolate cake!" Maude yelled happily.

"I don't know if I've ever seen you so happy," Emily grinned.

"I hit a hundred and sixty! Maybe more!" Maude's eyes were shining. "Opal would've been hollerin' right there with me. I swear I felt her."

Emily's chest tightened. "I know she was with you," she nodded.

Maude reached out, grabbing Emily's hand. "Now it's your turn," she yelled. The track was extremely loud and Emily was hopeful that Maude's hearing would return to normal soon.

The staff member smiled encouragingly. "It's safe, ma'am. And trust me, once you're out there, you'll love it," he smiled. "Are you ready?"

Emily looked at Maude, at the way her joy radiated so brightly, and then she thought of Opal; brave, fearless, big-hearted Opal who'd written this list not just for herself, but for all of them in a way. Emily squared her shoulders. "Alright. But if I die, I'm haunting you," she chuckled.

Maude grinned. "Fair deal."

Emily climbed in through the window and braced herself. The world narrowed to a blur. The instant the car shot forward, Emily's breath caught in her throat. The wind roared against the helmet, the engine thundered like a beast beneath her, and the track whipped by in dizzying streaks of gray. She clutched the harness across her chest, too stunned to scream, too exhilarated to think. And then something happened. Somewhere between terror and thrill, Emily felt a rush of release and a burst of laughter escaped her. When the car finally slowed, she was breathless, yet she felt more alive than ever before.

As she climbed out, Maude caught her in a fierce hug. "You did it!" Maude cried. "You crazy, wonderful woman, you did it! God, you remind me of her so much!"

They sat on a bench afterward, sipping cold water, their helmets resting on the ground. The track buzzed with activity, but for a moment it felt like the world had narrowed to just the two of them. Maude leaned back, sighing in contentment. "That was one for the books. Another checkmark for Opal."

"I think she'd be proud of us," Emily nodded. "I'm glad we didn't push Wil too hard to come along. He would have hated that."

Maude chuckled at the thought of Wilbur hanging on for dear life. "Opal would definitely be proud of us," she nodded. "I think maybe in a way she was right here with us. I swear I felt her hollerin' in my ear."

"I think she wanted us to feel this, not just the thrill, but the reminder that life is meant to be lived full speed sometimes," Emily smiled softly.

"Full speed," Maude repeated, her grin returning. "That oughta be our motto." They clinked their water bottles together like champagne flutes, toasting their friend, their courage, and the road ahead. When the water bottles were nearly empty, Emily and Maude had finally caught their breath. "Lord, my face hurts," Maude groaned, rubbing her cheeks. "I haven't laughed this hard since the time Nadine got her girdle stuck in the gymnasium bathroom stall and we had to call the janitor."

Emily bent forward, shaking with mirth. "Oh my!"

The afternoon sun had shifted, casting long shadows across the track. A breeze picked up, carrying with it the faint, hot-metal tang of engines cooling. Emily tipped her head back and closed her eyes. "Do you feel younger?" Maude asked suddenly.

Emily opened one eye. "Younger?"

"Yeah. Like we shaved twenty years off, just by hittin' one-sixty out there," Maude beamed.

Emily chuckled. "If that's the case, then I'd better book another ride before supper."

"That's the spirit," Maude nodded. She leaned back against the bench and squinted at the sun overhead. "I guess we better get on back home. Unless there's more adventure to be had."

Neither of them wanted to rush home just yet. The adrenaline made their stomachs growl, and the little concession stand at the speed park hadn't been enough. So Maude suggested a diner she knew off the highway, the kind of place where the pies were stacked in glass cases by the register. Emily didn't argue. She figured she deserved a slice of something decadent. They slid into a red vinyl booth, as the waitress, a round woman with hair the color of sweet tea, raised an eyebrow at their windblown looks. "Y'all look like you've been through a tornado."

"Close enough," Emily said. "Two coffees and two slices of your best pie, please."

"Coming right up," Fran, their waitress, smiled.

Emily rested her chin on her hands. "Do you realize how ridiculous we must look? Two grown women grinning like schoolgirls, hair a mess, and smelling faintly of gasoline."

Maude shrugged. "Ridiculous is underrated. You should've seen the looks I got when the state trooper pulled me over on the highway that time. Said I was goin' ninety in a fifty. I told him my foot slipped."

Emily gasped. "Ninety? Maude!"

"What? The car wanted to go. I was just obliging," Maude shrugged.

Emily shook her head but smiled. "I've heard that you've always been a daredevil. I think everyone secretly loves that about you."

"I don't know about that," Maude said softly. "One time Ruby rode with me to Savannah and we made it in record time? She got out of the car and kissed the ground, but then she winked and said it was the most fun she'd had in years."

"I wish I could've met her," Emily smiled softly.

The waitress returned with steaming mugs of coffee and two slices of pecan and chocolate pie. The women dug in, their conversation flowing as easily as the coffee. By the time they paid the bill and slid back into Emily's sedan, the sun had dipped lower, painting the sky with streaks of peach and lavender.

"Now don't you get any ideas," Maude warned playfully.

Emily smirked. "What ideas? Don't worry, I'll

keep it right on the speed limit."

"You're no fun," Maude sighed.

The hum of the tires and the rhythm of the highway made Emily drowsy, but her thoughts kept circling back to the track. "You think we're doing this right?" Emily asked quietly.

Maude glanced over. "What do you mean?"

"The bucket list. These adventures. Sometimes I wonder if we're really honoring her, or just distracting ourselves," Emily asked.

Maude tapped the glove box in front of her. "Maybe it's both. But I think Opal knew what she was doin' when she wrote that list. I think she wanted to feel alive. So we can keep that going, too, even without her."

Emily nodded slowly. "She always did know what was best for us all, didn't she?"

"Bossy as a preacher on Sunday," Maude said fondly. "But usually right."

They rode in companionable silence after that, the highway stretching out ahead of them like a ribbon leading back to Rhinestone. As she pulled into Maude's driveway, Maude yawned and stretched her arms over her head. "I think I'll sleep good tonight," Maude said. "Thanks for a fun day." Emily watched as Maude ambled up her porch steps and disappeared into her house.

The ride to her home with Wilbur didn't take long. The beautiful log cabin style home glowed softly in the dusk as she pulled into the gravel drive. Lights flickered in the windows, and the faint smell of firewood drifted through the air. Emily's heart swelled at the sight; no matter where she went, this place was home. Wilbur was on the porch, rocking slowly in his chair, a glass of sweet tea sweating on the table beside him. He raised an eyebrow as Emily climbed out of the car. "Well," he drawled, "you look like you've been up to mischief."

Emily puffed out her chest. "Mischief of the best kind." Emily hurried up the steps and leaned down to kiss her husband's cheek. "You won't believe how much fun we had today."

"Try me," Wilbur chuckled.

"We went over a hundred and sixty miles an hour!" Emily squealed as Wilbur opened the front door for her. Wilbur's brows shot up. "You're pullin' my leg."

"I swear on my good dishes," Emily said, grinning. "Fastest I've ever gone, and that's saying something." Emily clasped Wilbur's hand. "It was terrifying at first. But then, oh, Wilbur, it was incredible. It was just like flying. I laughed until I cried."

Wilbur looked at his darling wife with a mix of amazement and amusement. "Well, I'll be. My Emily, the speed demon."

"I wouldn't go that far," Emily said with a blush. "Another checkmark on Opal's list. Maude said she would be proud."

Wilbur grew thoughtful. "She'd be proud of y'all no matter what, but I reckon she's smiling extra wide tonight."

The two of them sat together on the couch inside as the crickets began their nightly chorus. Emily rested her head on Wilbur's shoulder, her heart full.

Chapter Fourteen

As July came to a close, the dog days of summer stretched on. Wilbur and Emily had gone over to Magnolia Manor to have dinner with Mavis one Friday evening. Talk had soon turned to the old bucket list and what all was left on it. Mavis wanted to knock off quite a few items in Europe for the next adventure, but Wilbur was skeptical.

"Mavis, I don't know that Maude is able to go traipsing around Europe," Wilbur said over dinner a few nights later. He looked at Emily for confirmation, but she was strangely quiet as she picked at her green beans. "I'm not saying it's a bad idea, I just think it's a lot for anyone, let alone someone almost ninety." Wilbur didn't mean to sound like the bad guy. He knew Maude was unlike anyone else, but it worried him to take her across the world for a strenuous two week adventure. There was no way Emily could take off that much time for work, not after going out west for ten days two months ago, so it fell to him and Mavis to accompany Maude. Fourteen days across the pond was indeed a long time to be gone from their homes and daily life, but Mavis insisted that it needed to be done sooner than later.

"September in Europe is great weather wise,"

Mavis countered. "And they have better healthcare than we do here, so it's not like that's going to be an issue. Come on, Wilbur, if we don't do it now, then when? None of us are getting any younger. We don't know how much time any of us have left. I want to do this for Opal and for Maude. Heck, for me, too." Her eyes had filled with tears and Wilbur began to soften.

"I guess it could be fun," he sighed.

"Oh, Wilbur, is that a yes?" Mavis squealed. Emily chuckled and reached over and hugged her husband. "Fine, but I wish you could come with us," Wilbur said to Emily.

"That just means we'll have to go one day. By then you'll know all the best spots to take me to," Emily grinned.

Mavis jumped up and grabbed her notebook and began making copious notes. "Wilbur, do you have your passport? I bet not. Oh Lordy, we're going to have to get on that tomorrow. I think we can leave by September first, but not if you don't have a passport. Ok, let me make some calls and see if I can expedite that."

"Do you ever take a breath?" Wilbur asked.

"No time for that," Mavis shook her head. "I need to call Maude. Oh heavens, I bet her passport expired fifty years ago. Maybe September isn't going to work after all." She jumped back up and rushed to the living room to call Maude.

"What have I gotten myself into?" Wilbur asked a giggling Emily.

Mavis returned to the dining room a few minutes later, her expression a mixture of shock and delight. She plopped her phone down on the table and leaned forward, almost breathless. "You are not going to believe this," she announced.

Wilbur raised an eyebrow. "That Maude's passport expired in 1974?"

"Wrong!" Mavis jabbed a finger toward him. "She has a passport. A current passport. I nearly dropped the phone when she said it. Apparently she's kept it up to date all these years just in case."

Emily laughed. "That sounds exactly like Maude. You know she's more prepared than all of us put together. Remember how she had an entire sewing kit in her purse at the church picnic last month? She doesn't even know how to sew!"

Wilbur groaned. "So I'm the only one who isn't ready to jet off to Europe at the drop of a hat? Figures."

"Don't you worry," Mavis said, already scribbling in her notebook again. "I know a lady at the county office who owes me a favor. And if she can't get it done, then her cousin works for the passport agency in Atlanta. Between the two of them, we'll have you holding a shiny new passport in no time."

"Why do I feel like you're running some kind of underground operation?" Wilbur muttered.

"Because she is," Emily teased. "You should've seen how fast she got those tickets for our Yellowstone trip back in May. It was like watching a magician at work."

Mavis waved a dismissive hand. "Oh, that was nothing. This is more important. Europe, Wilbur! We're talking castles, cathedrals, history, and croissants. Opal always wanted to see the Eiffel Tower sparkle at night. We can't waste time."

Wilbur looked at her, then at Emily, then back to Mavis again. He realized he was surrounded, outnumbered, and overruled. "Fine," he said. "But if I end up in some foreign jail because of forged documents, I'm blaming you."

"Please," Mavis said, rolling her eyes. "My connections are all above board. Mostly." She grinned and snapped her notebook shut. "Tomorrow morning we're going to get your photo taken. Wear a collared shirt. No hats, no glasses, and try to smile without looking like you're smiling. It's all in the eyes. They're very particular about how the photo can look."

Emily nearly spit out her tea laughing. Wilbur sighed, resigned. "This is going to be a disaster."

The next morning came with the usual Southern humidity thick as syrup, but Mavis was at Wilbur and Emily's doorstep by seven o'clock sharp. She was armed with a large tote bag, her ever-present notebook, and an alarming amount of energy for someone who had clearly already had three cups of coffee. "Rise and shine!" she sang out as she marched into their kitchen like she owned the place. "Time to get this passport situation handled."

Wilbur shuffled into the kitchen, hair sticking up in every direction, clutching his coffee mug like a lifeline. "You're enjoying this far too much."

"Someone has to," Mavis said cheerfully. "Now drink up, and then we're headed to the Walgreens for your photo. I've already made an appointment at the post office after that. We're going to knock this out in one morning."

Emily leaned against the counter, amused. "She's scary when she gets like this."

"I heard that," Mavis said. "And thank you. Scary gets things done."

"Y'all have fun!" Emily smiled. She kissed Wilbur goodbye and headed to work. Mavis waited quite impatiently for Wilbur to get dressed and ready for their day. As soon as he emerged from his bedroom, Mavis clicked her tongue in disapproval. "Oh no, that shirt won't do. Here, I'll just pick one for you." Before Wilbur could argue, Mavis had disappeared into his room and returned a few minutes later with a long-sleeved pale blue shirt that she said would match his eyes better than the red one he had picked out. Rather than argue, Wilbur changed shirts and finished his coffee quickly. Mavis was already behind the wheel of her car waiting for him as he locked his front door.

The photo, predictably, was an ordeal.

"Stand up straight, Wilbur. No, straighter. Lord, you look like you're about to fall over," Mavis fretted behind the photographer.

"I am about to fall over," Wilbur grumbled. "This is humiliating."

"Stop frowning. You can't frown in a passport photo. Try to act more neutral," Mavis instructed.

"This is my neutral face, or whatever that means," Wilbur said solemnly.

"Neutral does not mean angry-at-the-world face. For heaven's sake, just look approachable. It's all in the eyes, Wilbur," Mavis explained.

"Approachable? For what? The customs agent? You think they're going to invite me to dinner?" Wilbur laughed.

"No laughing!" Mavis frowned. The Walgreens clerk cleared his throat politely, clearly trying not to laugh. "Sir, just look at the camera like you normally would." He snapped a few pictures and as soon as they printed, Mavis inspected the printed proof like she was a casting director auditioning head-shots. "Hmm. Not bad. You don't look like a criminal. More like a tired farmer. It'll do."

Wilbur muttered something under his breath that sounded suspiciously like, "I am a tired farmer."

By mid-afternoon, Mavis's miracle connections had worked. The paperwork was in motion and Wilbur was assured he'd have his passport within two weeks. Mavis was practically glowing with satisfaction. "See?" she said, sliding into the booth at the diner where she and Wilbur had collapsed after the errands. "Easy peasy. We're going to Europe, folks."

Mavis smiled, but Wilbur just shook his head. "You know, I thought this season of life was supposed to be about slowing down. Sitting on porches. Fishing. Napping. Instead, I've got a travel agent-turned-taskmaster dragging me across the world."

"And aren't you lucky?" Mavis beamed.

"Lucky," Wilbur repeated dryly. But when he caught her amused glance, he couldn't help but chuckle. Maybe he was lucky, in a strange, exhausting sort of way. "So, what's for dinner tonight?" Wilbur asked. He assumed Mavis had planned the rest of the afternoon and evening for them, so he might as well ask.

"Oh, I have plans," Mavis blushed.

"Plans?" Wilbur repeated. "And what is this gentleman's name?"

"How do you know?" Mavis gasped.

"I was merely guessing," Wilbur chuckled. "Your face is redder than a sunburn from a hot July sun. What's going on?"

"Oh, Wilbur, I've been meaning to tell you, but I just wanted to see how things went first," Mavis began. She told Wilbur all about how she had met Mac at book club two months ago and had been to a few coffee meetups. They talked on the phone and texted most days, but when Mac asked her for an official date a few days ago, Mavis began to get nervous. She was more than excited, but there was something special about Mac that made her want to take things slowly.

After lunch, Mavis dropped Wilbur off at his house where he gave her a big hug. "Thanks for always pushing me to live a little more. I'm excited about this big trek we're going to take. Be careful tonight and have fun. We're meeting at Opal's in the morning, but call me if the plans change," he smiled.

Mavis had been nervous all day. Not the kind of nervous that left her hands trembling or her voice quaking; she'd been through far too many storms to let jitters undo her. This was a lighter sort of nervous, one that fluttered in her stomach and sent her to the mirror one too many times to adjust her earrings and smooth her blouse. She had told herself not to make too much of the evening. After all, she and Mac had already shared several cups of coffee after book club. They'd talked about novels, about work, about little quirks of life in Junction and Rhinestone, but tonight was different. Tonight, it was a real official date. Mac Potter, an accountant by trade, book lover by nature, and self-professed numbers nerd, had asked her out with the most charming mixture of confidence and awkwardness. "I thought maybe," he'd said, scratching the back of his neck at the last book club meeting, "we could do something outside of coffee sometime. Something official. There's a painting class at The Art Nook downtown, and I thought you might like it. And, well, dinner after?"

Mavis had surprised herself by answering immediately. "I'd love to!"

Now it was Friday evening, and she was standing at her dresser, debating between the green cardigan or the navy blazer. The cardigan felt too casual, but the blazer felt too stiff. She settled on a flowing teal blouse and a pair of dark jeans. By the time she arrived at The Art Nook, her nerves had transformed into excitement. The little studio glowed with warm light, its windows lined with cheerful painted canvases of sunflowers, seaside sunsets, and rolling hills beneath lavender skies. Inside, the scent of acrylic paint mingled with coffee brewing in a corner. A handful of easels stood ready, each with a pre-sketched beach landscape waiting for color.

Mac was already there. He was dressed in a crisp button-down shirt that was a light shade of green and dark slacks. His brown hair had just enough curl to look perpetually unruly, and his glasses slid down his nose in that way that made him look both serious and endearingly boyish. When he saw her, his face lit up. "Mavis!" He waved her over with the enthusiasm of a man genuinely happy she'd come. "I saved us a spot by the window. The light's better, or at least that's what the artist at the front told me. Not that I know the first thing about painting."

"Neither do I, so we can learn together," Mavis smiled.

The instructor, a woman with streaks of cobalt paint on her apron, cheerfully announced that tonight's theme was "Sunset Over the Waves."

"Perfect," Mac whispered. "I love the beach. I'm might hang this in my office."

The class began with broad strokes of sky and outlines of sand dunes. Mac, meticulous with numbers, approached painting with the same care. He measured each brushstroke as though precision would win him an invisible prize. Mavis, meanwhile, let herself go. She dabbed, blended, smudged. Where Mac's sky turned out pale and even, hers was streaked with fiery oranges and pinks. At one point, Mac leaned closer, peering at her canvas. "Yours looks like an actual sunset," he said, sounding both impressed and a little defeated. "Mine looks like someone ironed the sky flat."

"That's not bad," Mavis teased. "A flat sky

means perfect weather for accountants. No surprises."

He chuckled, the sound warm and easy. "Touché. Still, I think your painting will win the gallery prize tonight."

"Is there a prize?" she asked, arching a brow.

He grinned sheepishly. "Not officially, but if there was, I'd vote for you."

They fell into an easy rhythm after that, alternating between concentration and conversation. Mac told her more about his childhood of little league games and the way his mother used to make pecan pie every Sunday. He had moved to Junction years ago for work and stayed because the small town felt like the right size for him, but he missed those weekly pecan pies.

By the time the class ended, their canvases were dry enough to carry. Mavis' sky blazed with bold colors, her beach waves shaded with deep greens and blues. Mac's painting, though more restrained, had a calm and peaceful look. They posed for a quick photo together, holding up their masterpieces, and laughed at the contrast. Outside, the August evening was cool as the sky deepened into twilight. Mac opened the passenger door of his car for her, a small gesture, but one that made Mavis' heart skip. He'd made reservations at Casa Azul, the new Mexican restaurant in town.

The restaurant was bustling, its walls painted with murals of desert landscapes and flag shaped banners were strung overhead. A mariachi trio played near the bar, and the scent of sizzling fajitas and fresh cilantro filled the air. Mac had clearly planned ahead; they were seated at a quiet corner table, away from most of the noise. The waiter brought chips and salsa, and Mavis tried not to devour them too quickly.

"So," Mac said, leaning forward on his elbows. "What do you recommend? I feel like I should trust someone with better taste than me."

"You don't give yourself enough credit," she said, scanning the menu. "But the enchiladas look tempting. So do the carnitas."

Mac ordered carnitas and Mavis chose the enchiladas verdes. Over dinner, their conversation meandered from lighthearted stories to deeper reflections. Mac admitted he had never married, though he'd come close once. Mavis shared bits of her past too, which surprised her because she was normally quite private about her life. As she told him about her adventures with her ex, Earl, from Louisiana, Mac listened intently and didn't pass any judgment. At one point, he told her about a disastrous attempt to impress a girl in college by joining an improv troupe. "I froze on stage and ended up quoting numbers from my statistics textbook," he said, grimacing. "The audience didn't know whether to laugh or feel sorry for me."

Mavis laughed until tears sprang to her eyes. "At least you were authentic. No one could accuse you of faking it."

As the meal wound down, Mac grew a little quieter, more thoughtful. "Mavis, I just want you to know that I've really enjoyed these past weeks. The coffee chats, book club, and tonight. You make things feel lighter, like I don't have to try so hard."

Her chest tightened. "I feel the same," she said softly. "I didn't expect to, but I do."

The waiter brought churros for dessert, and they shared them, dipping the sweet dough into chocolate sauce. By the time Mac drove her back to her car that was still parked outside of the paint studio, the stars were bright against the night sky. He walked her to the car door, her painting tucked carefully under her arm. They lingered, neither rushing to say goodnight. Finally, Mac cleared his throat. "I'd like to see you again soon. Maybe without a pre-sketched canvas this time."

Mavis smiled, her heart warm. "I'd like that too." Then, before she had a chance to react, Mac leaned closer to her and kissed her on the cheek.

"Goodnight, Mavis," he said.

"Goodnight, Mac," she stuttered softly. She opened her car door and slipped inside the driver's side. She set the painting on her passenger seat and watched as Mac got back in his car. Mavis realized she was still smiling when she pulled into the driveway of Magnolia Manor thirty minutes later.

Chapter Fifteen

The morning sun had just begun to burn off the last of the dew when Mavis pulled into Opal's driveway the next morning. The air smelled faintly of honeysuckle, and the steady hum of bees carried across the yard. She spotted Wilbur already at work, his broad shoulders bent over a hive, gloved hands steady as he adjusted straps. Emily stood nearby with a clipboard, as though she were overseeing a major operation, and Maude perched on the porch steps in her wide straw hat, her arms crossed in mock impatience.

"'Bout time you showed up," Maude called, though her lips twitched into the barest smile. "We thought maybe that fancy accountant of yours had kidnapped you."

Mavis blushed, her cheeks still carrying the warmth of the evening before. "I am not late. Y'all are just early."

Wilbur looked up with a half-smile. "You look awful chipper for this time of morning. Must've been some coffee you had with Mac."

"It wasn't coffee," Mavis said, setting her purse down. "It was dinner and painting."

"Painting?" Emily asked, bright-eyed.

"Yes!" Mavis squealed. "He took me to a

painting class. They had these little canvases all sketched out already. Mine turned out all right, I think. And then," Mavis went on, "he took me to that new Mexican place in town. Ordered queso for the table, even though there were only two of us. We sat there for hours talking. He's funny, and kind, and easy to talk to."

Maude tilted her head, her eyes soft despite her teasing tone. "Well, I'll be. Sounds like the book club finally paid off. Guess Opal knew what she was doing with that helpful nudge."

Mavis tried to wave it off, but the truth was she felt lighter than she had in years. The moment lingered, warm and easy, until the hum of bees reminded them of the task at hand. Wilbur clapped his gloves together. "Alright. Y'all can swoon over Mavis' love life later. We got bees to move."

Moving bees was not a task to be rushed. Wilbur had spent most of the morning preparing, sealing the hives with mesh screens so the bees could breathe but wouldn't come spilling out when lifted. A smoker sat nearby. "Opal would've told us the best way to do this," Wilbur said as he crouched, inspecting the first hive. "She had her own way of enchanting everything. I bet she could speak to the bees."

"She really could. She'd be standing right behind you, giving step-by-step instructions," Emily agreed, jotting something on her clipboard as if to imitate her late friend.

They all smiled at the memory. The bees had been one of Opal's great joys. The honey jars had lined her kitchen window sill, the sunlight glowing through them like amber. It was only right they be moved carefully, with reverence. Wilbur squatted down and heaved the first hive onto a dolly. "Alright, someone keep these wheels steady."

"I'll do it," Emily said, hopping into place.

Maude stood with her hands on her hips. "And what am I supposed to do, look pretty and swat at bees?"

Mavis bit back a laugh. Bees weren't exactly her specialty. She hovered close but not too close, her heart jumping each time one of the little striped workers buzzed past her ear. She watched as they maneuvered the hive slowly, Wilbur guiding the weight while Emily steadied the dolly. Mavis held her breath as the box tilted over a bump in the path, but it settled safely again.

"There," Wilbur said with satisfaction as they reached the truck. He and Emily lifted together, sliding the hive carefully into place in the truck bed.

"That's one," Emily said, checking her clipboard.

"Six more to go," Wilbur answered.

Maude groaned. "Six? Lord help us. We'll be here all day."

"Unless you plan on lifting something heavier than your coffee mug, you don't get to complain," Wilbur laughed.

They fell into a rhythm as the morning wore on. Wilbur handled the heavy lifting, Emily fussed with her notes, Maude alternated between helping and heckling, and Mavis did her best to pitch in where she could. She fetched water, held doors open, steadied the dolly when asked. The bees, surprisingly, remained calm. During a break beneath the pecan tree, Emily passed out cold bottles of lemonade she'd brought in a cooler. The four of them sat in mismatched lawn chairs Opal had collected over the years.

Mavis sipped her drink, still thinking about Mac. "You know," she said softly, "I didn't realize how much I'd missed just laughing with someone. Not about anything big, just silly things. He told me this story about his cat that I'm still laughing about."

"Hold it," Maude interrupted, pointing with her bottle. "The man has a cat? That's either a good sign or a red flag. Yes, I know what red flags are. I watch the television."

"A good sign," Mavis insisted with a smile. "He adopted her from the shelter. She's missing part of her tail and apparently has a habit of knocking over his paperwork at the worst possible times."

They all chuckled at the thought, but then Maude's gaze drifted toward the house, and the laughter faded. The white paint was peeling around the eaves, the flowerbeds grown wild without Opal's careful tending. The screen door sagged slightly on its hinges. It still looked like Opal's place, but it also looked like a place waiting for its next chapter. "I've decided," Maude said quietly, almost to herself. "Once we finish with the bees and get through the last of her things, I'll call the realtor. It's time." No one spoke for a moment. The thought of letting go of Opal's house was heavier than any hive. Mavis reached over and squeezed Maude's hand. Maude nodded, her jaw set tight. "Just feels strange."

Emily leaned forward, her voice gentle. "We'll go through the house together. Make sure everything that matters finds a home with us."

Wilbur took a long sip of lemonade and looked toward the truck, where the hives sat ready. "Alright then," he said. "Let's finish what we started."

By late morning, the truck bed was lined with hives strapped neatly in place, their soft buzzing a low chorus that rose and fell with the breeze. Wilbur wiped his brow with the back of his arm, his shirt damp with sweat. "Well," he said, stretching his shoulders. "That's the bees handled. Now for the hard part."

Maude, who had been half leaning against the porch rail, raised an eyebrow. "You mean harder than hauling fifty-pound boxes of buzzing stingers across the yard?"

"Yep," Wilbur said simply, nodding toward the house.

The four of them stood there for a beat, looking at the familiar front door. Opal's house had always been more than just walls and a roof. It had been the backdrop for countless Sunday dinners, late-night phone calls, emergency cups of coffee, and the steady presence of a woman who had made everyone feel at home. Emily finally broke the silence. "I'll make lists," she said, lifting her clipboard again like a soldier raising a sword. "One pile for what we're keeping, one for what goes to charity, one for throwing away."

Maude groaned, "Lord help us, she's making piles."

"You'll thank me later," Emily said primly, marching up the steps.

The back screen door squeaked when she pulled it open, just as it always had. They followed her inside, the familiar creak of the floorboards greeting them. The air smelled faintly of lavender and lemon polish, though it had grown stale without Opal's constant bustling. The living room looked frozen in time, like Opal might walk in any minute with a tray of cookies. Afghans were neatly folded on the back of the sofa, and the bookshelf bulged with novels and gardening guides, and gemstones and crystals adorned the room in various places.

"Alright," Emily said, setting her clipboard on the coffee table. "Let's start here. Books, knickknacks, photo albums."

Maude wandered over to the mantle, picking up a porcelain figurine shaped like a rooster. She turned it in her hand, lips twitching. "I told her this thing was ugly as sin. She said it gave the place character."

Wilbur snorted, "That's one word for it."

Mavis, meanwhile, had drifted to the bookshelf. She ran her fingers along the spines until she pulled out a photo album wedged between gardening books. She sat down and opened it, the first page revealing snapshots of backyard picnics, birthday cakes, and one particularly lopsided Christmas tree. "Oh," she breathed, her chest tightening. "Look at this."

They gathered around as she flipped through the pages. There was Opal in her fifties, hair windswept, looking unimpressed at some long-forgotten family barbecue. Wilbur appeared in a photo wearing shorts, holding a fishing pole proudly beside a very small fish. Emily laughed so hard she nearly dropped her clipboard. "Wilbur, that fish wouldn't feed a kitten!"

"It was a good catch," he grumbled, but even he was smiling at the memory.

They lingered there, flipping through pages, laughing and wiping at their eyes, until Maude closed the book gently and set it aside. "We'll keep the albums, of course."

Emily dutifully scribbled on her list. After working their way through the small living room, the kitchen was next. The counters were cluttered with jars of honey, each labeled in Opal's tidy handwriting. Mavis picked one up, holding it to the light. It glowed like amber. "She'd always slip me a jar when I came by," Mavis said softly. "Said it was good for my tea, good for my soul, good for whatever ailed me."

"And she was usually right," Maude nodded.

Wilbur began boxing up empty jars he found in the cabinet, his movements slow and careful. "These'll go with me. I'll keep bottling honey when the time comes. Figure it's the least I can do."

They worked slowly, each drawer and cupboard tugging out another memory. Emily kept her piles neat, fussing only when Maude tried to toss a mug without writing it down. "Don't you dare mess up my system," Emily teased.

"It's a cracked mug, not a government file," Maude retorted, but she sighed and let Emily note it down.

By early afternoon, the four of them had filled half a dozen boxes and made surprisingly little progress. The emotional weight of each item slowed them more than the physical lifting. In the hallway, they found Opal's sewing basket, stuffed with spools of thread and unfinished projects. Mavis picked up a half-finished quilt block, the fabric soft beneath her fingers. "She was always making something for someone. Baby blankets, wedding gifts, and sometimes just because. She was so thoughtful."

Maude touched the quilt square, her tough exterior cracking just a little. "Guess she didn't get around to this one."

"We could finish it," Emily suggested quietly. Mavis nodded, tears pricking her eyes. "Yes. Let's do that," she whispered. She and Emily gathered up the sewing basket and Wilbur lifted the sewing machine and table to carry to Mavis' car. The antique sewing machine would look perfect in Mavis' craft room under the bay window.

Wilbur cleared his throat, clearly uncomfortable with the emotion rising in the room. "Alright then. Who's hungry? We've been at this for hours."

"Lunch sounds good," Maude admitted. Emily opened the refrigerator and pulled out a platter of sandwiches she had brought over for the occasion. Mavis opened a grocery bag that had chips and a box of cookies. They carried their sandwiches, sides, and lemonades to the porch, grateful for the breeze. The truck with its hives sat quiet at the edge of the drive, and the house behind them seemed to exhale with the day's work.

After lunch, the group lingered a little too long on the porch, reluctant to head back inside. The shade of the pecan tree was forgiving, the cicadas droning their late summer song, and the hum of the hives in the truck gave a steady reassurance that part of Opal's legacy was already secured. Emily, ever the taskmaster, clapped her hands. "Alright. Break's over. Bedroom is next."

Maude groaned. "Heaven help us. That's where she kept everything she didn't want people poking at."

"That's the point," Emily replied crisply, heading toward the front door again. "If we don't do it now, it'll never get done."

Mavis brought up the rear, bracing herself. She had been in Opal's bedroom many times, but today it felt different. Today it was no longer just Opal's room; it was a space that needed sorting, a space that would soon belong to someone else. The bedroom smelled faintly of lavender sachets and cedar. The quilt on the bed was one Opal had finished years ago, a patchwork of blues and greens, frayed in places from years of use. Mavis smoothed her hand over it, the fabric cool beneath her palm. "She always said this was her ocean quilt" Mavis murmured. "Said it made her dream of the beach."

"We'll keep it," Emily said at once, scribbling it

on her clipboard. "No question."

The dresser drawers revealed neat stacks of folded sweaters, soft and worn from years of wear. In one drawer, Maude discovered a bundle of letters tied up with a faded ribbon. She held them up, eyebrows arched. "Uh oh. Look what I found," she murmured.

"Maude," Mavis said quickly, "don't you dare read those out loud. They're private."

But Maude was already tugging one free. She skimmed a few lines before gasping and cackling. "Would you believe it? Love letters. And not from anyone we know!"

"Maybe we should put those back," Wilbur cautioned.

"Oh, don't be such a prude," Maude teased. "Listen to this! "My dearest Opal, you looked like summer sunshine last evening. I couldn't stop thinking of you after you left the dance hall.""

"Maude!" Mavis yelped. "Those aren't yours to share."

"I'm just saying," Maude grinned, tucking the letters back into their ribbon. "Our Opal had more secrets than she let on."

Wilbur muttered into his collar. "Good thing she took most of them with her. Y'all make your piles and I'll start on the closet."

The closet was stuffed with dresses from decades past, coats in every shade, and stacks of shoes in their original boxes. Wilbur immediately began making piles. "Keep, donate, toss. Some of these vintage pieces might even be worth something."

Maude pulled out a sequined dress the color of champagne. She held it against herself and did a little shimmy. "Lord, I forgot she had this. I remember when she wore it to the New Year's dance and nearly slipped on the floor because she insisted on those ridiculous heels!"

Even Wilbur chuckled, though he quickly busied himself with boxing up shoes. "Y'all are gonna waste time playing dress-up if you're not careful."

As the afternoon wore on, the work grew heavier. They found Opal's jewelry box, filled not only with gemstones but with quirky brooches, clip-on earrings, and strands of faux pearls she had loved to wear. Each piece carried a story. "Wilbur, look! It's the opal you gave her!" Mavis cried.

When Wilbur was a teenager, he found a few opals in the woods behind Magnolia Manor. He had surprised Ruby, Opal, and Maude with them one afternoon. All three Stone Sisters adored the gift almost as much as the young boy who gave them such a priceless gift. Ruby had turned her opal into a necklace that she was buried with. Maude kept her gem as a whole stone in her jewelry box. Opal had her stone turned into a ring. "Well, Wilbur, I reckon it should go back to you," Maude smiled. She handed the opal ring to Wilbur who immediately caught his breath. "I remember where I found this," he whispered. "Feels like yesterday."

"Mavis, I'll make sure you get mine in the will, so now you both will have original pieces from the Stone Sisters. It'll be full circle or whatever they say," Maude nodded. Mavis hugged the older woman and motioned for Wilbur to join in.

"Don't forget about me!" Emily smiled. She, too, joined in on the hug before Maude broke it apart. "Ok, enough of that. We've got things to do."

At last, they came to the nightstand. Inside was a small notebook with a worn leather cover. Mavis opened it and discovered pages filled with Opal's looping handwriting. Lists of honey yields, recipes for herbal remedies, half-finished poems, and a few prayers. By the time they finished with the bedroom, the sun was slanting low through the windows, painting the room in gold. Boxes lined the hallway now, labeled neatly in Emily's perfect handwriting. The house looked both emptier and more alive, as though the memories stirred by their work had filled the air.

On the porch again, they sank into the lawn chairs with exhaustion. The lemonade was long gone, but Emily produced a thermos of sweet tea she'd tucked in her bag, pouring it into paper cups. They drank in silence for a while, the cicadas now joined by the soft croak of evening frogs. Maude looked at the familiar porch rail, at the flowerbeds gone wild, at the rooms now boxed and labeled behind her. "I'll put it up for sale. It's time. I thought I'd never be able to do it, but we've kept the pieces that matter. The rest, well, it's just walls and wood. Opal lives on in us, not in this place," she nodded.

Mavis reached over, her hand covering Maude's. "She'd be proud of you."

Emily nodded, tears glimmering in her eyes. "And whoever moves in here will feel her warmth. I swear it."

Wilbur said nothing at first, staring out at the hives in his truck, but then he gave a short nod. "I'll keep the bees. That's my part. Rest of it, you're right. Time to let it go."

The decision settled over them like the evening air. Maude leaned back, her hat shading her face, and let out a long breath. "Well then. This week, we'll call the realtor."

They sat together as the sun dipped behind the trees, bees humming softly in the distance, the porch creaking beneath their weight. The work of the day had been hard, but it had been good. They had moved bees, sorted memories, unearthed laughter and tears. They had tended to Opal's legacy with care. As fireflies began to flicker across the yard, Mavis thought of her painting class, of Mac's easy smile, of the way life kept finding ways to surprise her. The night stretched gently before them, and for the first time in a long while, it felt like they were all ready for whatever came next.

Chapter Sixteen

Wilbur had never been on a flight that lasted more than five hours. He'd flown to Denver most recently, and even that had been enough to make his palms sweat and his stomach twist in ways he didn't care to remember. So when Mavis cheerily reminded him for the fiftieth time that their flight from Atlanta to London would take nearly nine hours, he considered backing out.

"Emily's got everything under control at home," Mavis said for the tenth time as she wrestled her suitcase into the back of Wilbur's aging pickup. "She promised to water your plants, feed your chickens, and double-check that all your tools are locked up in the shed. And the bees, yes, she knows how to take care of the honeybees."

Wilbur rubbed the back of his neck. "It's not the house I'm worried about. It's the idea of being in the air that long. Nine hours, Mavis."

Maude, climbing into the cab, snorted. "You'll be fine. They feed you, give you free drinks, and you can watch movies. Just pretend you're at home in your recliner with a television strapped to the seat in front of you. That's what I do."

Mavis chuckled while buckling her seatbelt with a click. "Oh, it'll be wonderful! Think of it, England! The Globe Theatre! We'll see Buckingham Palace, double-decker buses, the works. We'll do everything Opal always dreamed about."

"Fine," Wilbur said at last, starting the truck. "But if that plane falls out of the sky, don't say I didn't warn you."

At the airport, Wilbur clung to his carry-on bag like it was a life preserver. Mavis breezed through check-in, chatting with the ticket agent about how excited she was. Maude grumbled about overpriced airport sandwiches. By the time they boarded, Wilbur's nerves had spread to his hands, which shook slightly as he fumbled with his seatbelt. "This thing doesn't look strong enough to hold me in if we hit turbulence."

"That's because it's not," Maude said, already fluffing the airline pillow behind her head. "If we go down, we go down. Nothing you can do about it."

"Maude!" Mavis gasped. "Don't say things like that!"

"I'm just saying," Maude shrugged.

As the plane lifted, Wilbur gripped both armrests so tightly his knuckles went white. Mavis patted his arm. "Just think of London," she whispered. "Fish and chips, the Globe, all the history."

"I'm thinking of the ground getting farther away," Wilbur muttered.

"How about you go to sleep? It's almost midnight our time, so by the time we land and get all of our things, it'll be lunch time there."

Hours passed uneventfully. Mavis watched movies and made cheerful conversation with a British woman sitting across the aisle. Maude napped and complained about the food being a level above microwaved slop. Wilbur barely moved, too afraid of jinxing the plane's balance. When they finally landed at Heathrow, Wilbur staggered off the plane with relief. "Thank the Lord for solid ground," he breathed.

They gathered their luggage without much fanfare. Their first stop after checking into a modest hotel was grabbing something to eat from the pub across the street. The three of them shuffled across the cobblestone street, weary from the long flight but grateful to be on solid ground. The pub's wooden sign creaked above the door as they pushed inside, welcomed by the warm hum of conversation and the savory aroma of roasted meats and ale. The low ceiling beams and mismatched tables gave the place a lived-in charm, and Wilbur immediately spotted an open booth tucked against the wall. He gestured them in, and the three slid gratefully onto the worn leather seats.

A cheerful waitress with a lilting accent greeted them and handed over menus, though Wilbur waved his off almost immediately. "Fish and chips," he declared. "When in England, I reckon you've got to do it right." Mavis laughed, agreeing that something hearty sounded perfect, while Maude, ever non-adventurous, squinted at the chalkboard specials until she settled on fish and chips. They decided to order pints for the hell of it. Wilbur chose a bitter, Maude a stout, and Mavis something lighter that promised citrus notes she couldn't quite pronounce.

When the food arrived, it was everything they had hoped for: the golden-crisp batter on Wilbur's and Maude's fish broke at the touch of his fork, and Mavis's shepherd's pie carried the comforting scent of rosemary. They ate slowly, savoring each bite, their earlier exhaustion softened by the comfort of good food. The pub's laughter and clinking glasses wrapped around them like a blanket, and for the first time that day, the three friends leaned back and felt the excitement of their adventure settle in.

As they lingered over the last sips of their drinks, Mavis dabbed her mouth with a napkin and leaned forward. "You realize tomorrow morning we're getting the full works, right? None of this toast-and-coffee business. I've read all about the proper English breakfast. If I'm going to do this trip, I want the authentic experience."

Wilbur chuckled, wiping crumbs of fried fish from his face. "You'll regret that by lunchtime. That's enough food to put a man down for the day."

"Maybe you," Maude teased. "But I'm built for adventure."

Mavis, still savoring her shepherd's pie, smiled into her glass. "I'm just glad we're all here together. Tomorrow feels like the start of something special. Breakfast, sightseeing, and then the Globe Theatre. Can you believe it? Shakespeare performed in London. Opal would have loved it."

Her voice softened at the end, and both Maude and Wilbur nodded.

Wilbur reached across the table and gave Mavis' hand a squeeze. "Then we'll love it twice as much. For us, and for her."

That settled, they spent the rest of the meal tossing around ideas for the day like riding the double-decker bus to Buckingham Palace, maybe strolling along the Thames before the play. By the time they stepped back out into the cool London afternoon, noise from the city surrounded them. They were exhausted form such a long flight and the time change, so after walking around to see the shops on their street, they headed to the hotel to get some rest. Tomorrow promised history, laughter, and a touch of Shakespearean magic. Wilbur was looking forward to getting a good night's sleep.

The next morning, sunlight slipped through the heavy curtains of the hotel room, though it felt far too early for anyone who'd crossed the Atlantic the day before. Wilbur was the first to stir, grumbling at the brightness. His body clock was still stubbornly back in Rhinestone, and he would have much preferred a few more hours of sleep, but he could already hear Mavis in the next room, humming as she got ready, and he knew there was no chance of sneaking in another nap.

By the time they all met in the lobby, Mavis had her guidebook tucked under her arm, looking eager despite the faint shadows under her eyes. "They serve breakfast just down the street," she announced. "A proper English one. Maude, you'll be pleased."

Maude gave a triumphant grin. "I told you. Bacon is for everyone."

They followed the smell before they saw the café, its windows fogged from the steam of frying pans. Inside, the place was cozy, with mismatched tea cups stacked on the counter and an old radio playing faint jazz. They were seated at a small table by the window, and before long, steaming plates began arriving one by one. "Good heavens," Maude muttered as the waitress slid a plate in front of her. Eggs, sausages, rashers of bacon, a fried tomato, mushrooms, toast, a heap of baked beans, and a plump, round object fried to golden brown.

"What is this?" Maude asked, pointing at the mysterious item with her fork.

"Black pudding," the waitress said cheerfully, already moving on to Maude.

Maude blinked. "Pudding? That's not pudding."

Mavis snatched up her fork. "Only one way to find out." She took a bite and chewed thoughtfully. "Mm. Spicy. Kind of like sausage."

"Do not tell me what's in it," Wilbur said quickly, pushing his to the far side of his plate. "Some things are better left a mystery."

Mavis, ever the peacemaker, picked at hers and smiled. "It's not so bad. Different, but good. I like the tomatoes."

"What's this?" Maude demanded, pointing at the English bacon with her fork.

"That would be bacon, madam," the waiter said politely.

Maude narrowed her eyes. "This is not bacon. Bacon is crispy. Bacon crunches. This is ham that gave up."

Wilbur nearly spit out his tea laughing. "Told you not to expect biscuits and gravy."

"And what are beans doing on my breakfast plate?" Maude went on, horrified. "That's not breakfast food, that's a cookout gone wrong."

Mavis, meanwhile, happily spooned beans onto her toast. "I think it's delicious."

Maude pushed her plate away. "England might be nice, but their food is a crime."

Mavis, to nobody's surprise, cleaned hers with gusto. Wilbur waved the white flag halfway through, dabbing his forehead with a napkin. "If I eat another bite, they'll have to roll me out of here."

"That's the point," Mavis said smugly. "Now we're fortified for the day."

After breakfast, they set out into the bustle of London. The morning air was crisp, carrying the mingled scents of fresh bread from corner bakeries and exhaust from the double-decker buses rumbling past. Mavis insisted they buy day passes for the Underground and the buses, and before long they were climbing the narrow staircase to the top deck of a bright red double-decker.

Wilbur eased himself into a seat by the window and looked out over the city. "Well, I'll be. You can see everything from up here."

The bus rumbled past rows of stately Georgian townhouses, corner pubs with flower boxes spilling geraniums, and shops with names that sounded exotic to their small-town ears. Maude leaned across Mavis to point. "Look! Buckingham Palace!"

They hopped off at the stop, joining the crowd gathered at the gates. The guards in their tall black bearskin hats stood ramrod straight, unflinching even as tourists posed and tried to make them laugh.

Maude studied them with narrowed eyes. "I bet I could crack one of them."

"Don't you dare," Mavis said quickly, clutching her arm. "You'll get yourself arrested on the first full day of our trip."

Wilbur chuckled. "Wouldn't surprise me. You know Opal could! She would probably have them and the horses eating out of the palm of her hands."

"She could speak to horses," Maude nodded.

They stayed long enough to watch the Changing of the Guard, the spectacle both impressive and a little surreal. The pomp and precision, the gleaming instruments of the marching band, the rhythmic stomp of boots was unlike anything they had ever seen back home. From there, they strolled along the Mall, shaded by rows of trees, and found themselves at Trafalgar Square. The fountains sparkled in the sunlight, pigeons flapped noisily across the stones, and Nelson's Column rose high above them. Maude climbed halfway up one of the lion statues for a photo before Mavis scolded her down. "How does she do that?" Wilbur asked.

By afternoon, their feet ached, and they ducked into a small riverside café for tea. Wilbur stirred sugar into his cup, skeptical. "I still say coffee is better."

"You're in England," Mavis reminded him gently. "You have to try it their way."

He sipped, then gave a reluctant nod. "Not bad. Needs pie, though."

"Everything needs pie," Maude said dryly, but she smiled into her cup.

As evening crept in, they made their way toward the Globe Theatre. The building stood out against the city's modern glass and steel as a round, timbered replica of Shakespeare's original, its white walls crisscrossed with dark beams. A crowd gathered outside, buzzing with anticipation, programs in hand. Wilbur looked up at the thatched roof. "Doesn't look like much from the outside. Kind of like a big barn."

"History never looks fancy until you step inside," Mavis replied, her voice reverent. She had dreamed of this moment ever since they decided on England for the bucket list.

They found their seats on simple wooden benches, not built for comfort but for tradition. The air buzzed with excitement as the stage came alive with music. Actors in Elizabethan dress strode out, their voices rich and booming, every word of Shakespeare made fresh and immediate.

Maude leaned over halfway through and whispered, "I can't understand half of what they're saying."

"Shh," Mavis hissed, though she was grinning. Her eyes were alight, drinking in every moment.

Maude shifted on the hard bench and

whispered back, "I'd enjoy it more if they sold popcorn." But when an actor delivered a soliloquy so moving that the audience fell into hushed stillness, even she was struck silent, her rough hands folded in her lap. As the play drew to a close and the actors bowed, the three friends clapped until their palms stung. Mavis felt tears prick her eyes, not of sadness, but of wonder, of gratitude that they had made it here together. Walking back through the lamplit streets, Mavis looped her arm through Maude's. "What a day. Buckingham Palace, double-decker buses, and Shakespeare himself, well, close enough. Opal's smiling down on us, I know it."

Wilbur trudged beside them, weary but content. "I'll admit, it wasn't half bad. Long as tomorrow doesn't involve any more mystery puddings." They laughed together, their voices carrying down the quiet street, London unfolding around them in the glow of the evening.

The alarm went off the next morning far earlier than any of them liked, the sharp trill echoing in the quiet hotel room. Wilbur groaned and rolled over, fumbling to silence it. "Whose bright idea was it to leave at the crack of dawn?"

"Hers," Maude said from the other bed, already sitting up with her hair sticking out in every direction. "Mavis is the one who said we ought to beat the crowds."

Mavis was already bustling about, checking her bag for tickets and guidebook. She had a knack for travel organization that neither of the others shared, and without her, it was unlikely they'd have gotten farther than Heathrow. "Up, both of you. We've got a train to catch at Waterloo."

By the time they shuffled downstairs, the lobby was quiet except for the clatter of dishes from the breakfast room. A sleepy taxi ride brought them to the station, where the vast arched roof of Waterloo stretched above like a cathedral of steel and glass. Trains rumbled in and out, carrying commuters and tourists alike toward destinations written on the great board overhead. "Feels like we're about to march into battle," Wilbur muttered, eyeing the swarm of passengers darting through the concourse.

"Battle of finding the right platform," Maude said cheerfully. "Lucky we've got General Mavis leading the charge."

Mavis ignored them, striding ahead with determined purpose. "Platform nine, Wilbur. Try to keep up."

Once aboard, they found seats near the window. The train pulled out of London, gliding past row houses and warehouses until gradually the scenery shifted to rolling fields and hedgerows. Morning mist clung low to the ground, making the countryside look almost dreamlike.

Wilbur leaned back with a sigh. "Now this I can appreciate. Beats driving through cornfields back home," he grinned.

Mavis pressed her forehead to the glass. "It looks like something out of a painting. Sheep in the distance, little cottages with thatched roofs. I half expect a knight on horseback to come galloping by."

"Wrong century," Wilbur said, but even he looked out the window with quiet admiration.

The rhythm of the train and the soft countryside made Maude's eyelids droop. She jerked awake when the ticket collector arrived, flustered as she dug for their passes. Mavis tried to cover a laugh behind her hand. "You were about two minutes from snoring," she giggled.

"I was resting my eyes," Maude insisted.

"Uh-huh. Just like Wilbur rests his eyes during the Sunday sermon," Mavis giggled.

At Salisbury station, they switched to a coach bus bound for Stonehenge. The vehicle rumbled along narrow country lanes, hedges brushing close against the windows. Villages dotted the way, with cozy pubs and crooked church spires peeking above the trees. As they neared the site, Mavis grew restless in her seat, bouncing her knee with excitement. "Can you believe we're actually going to see it? The real thing. One of the wonders of the world, right here in front of us."

Wilbur shifted his cap. "Bunch of rocks in a field," he shrugged.

Mavis gave him a look. "You hush. This is history."

When the bus finally pulled into the visitor center, the three of them joined the line of travelers making their way toward the shuttle that carried guests closer to the stones. But the moment the great circle came into view across the grassy plain, even Wilbur fell silent. The stones loomed against the horizon, massive and weathered, their arrangement both deliberate and mysterious.

Sheep grazed in distant fields, the wind sweeping steadily across the open land. There was a hush among the visitors, a reverence that seemed to come naturally.

"Well," Wilbur said softly, "I'll be. That's something."

Maude, hands shoved in her jacket pockets, studied the towering stones with a frown of concentration. "Makes you wonder, though. How'd they get 'em up there without cranes and bulldozers? Folks say aliens, but I don't buy that."

"Aliens?" Mavis scoffed. "It was people! Brilliant, determined people. They found a way. That's the beauty of it, isn't it? We don't know for certain how they did it. It's the mystery that keeps us coming."

They lingered until the chill wind drove them toward the café at the visitor center. Over cups of hot tea and scones, they reflected on the morning. "Worth the trip," Wilbur admitted between bites. "Even without aliens."

Maude clinked her cup against his. "Here's to Opal's bucket list. One more checked off."

Mavis raised her cup as well, her eyes shining. "And still many more to come."

The bus ride back toward Salisbury was quieter. Maude dozed against the window, Mavis flipped through her photos, and Wilbur stared out at the fields, thoughtful. When the bus jolted to a stop, he turned back to them. "You know," he said, "I used to think these trips were just indulgences. Fool's errands. But standing out there today, it's like being reminded the world is bigger than us.

Older, too."

Mavis reached over and patted his hand. "That's exactly why Opal wrote it all down. To remind us to keep reaching."

Wilbur nodded slowly, the corners of his mouth twitching. "Well, I guess the old girl knew what she was doing."

Chapter Seventeen

Mavis woke Wilbur and Maude up early the next morning. She was so excited to experience the canals and the narrow-boats. Mavis loved the cozy interiors and colorful paint. "Can you imagine living like this? Traveling the waterways all summer?" she mused.

Wilbur shook his head. "I'd sink it in a week."

Maude looked at the picture of the narrow-boat on Mavis' phone and scowled. "Too cramped. Can't even turn around without hitting something," he grumbled.

They climbed back aboard a bright red double-decker bus that waited outside. Wilbur looked uneasy as the driver navigated London's crowded streets. "They're on the wrong side of the road," he kept muttering.

"That's the right side for them," Mavis corrected. She took dozens of photos, leaning over the railing to capture shots of Big Ben and every statue in sight.

"You pay taxes for both sides of the road," Maude shrugged. "Might as well drive on whatever side you want."

The bus rattled to a stop near Paddington, and the three friends filed off with the morning crowd.

The air smelled faintly of roasted coffee and damp stone, and just beyond the bustle of the station, the city seemed to exhale. Streets narrowed, trees leaned over quiet lanes, and then suddenly they were staring at the beautiful canal. The canal stretched ahead, calm as glass, reflecting the rows of willows and pastel townhouses. Narrow-boats lined the water, their hulls painted in jewel-bright colors, each with its own personality. Some had flower boxes bursting with geraniums, others displayed whimsical names in bold script: The Jolly Otter, Daisy May, Endless Summer. A couple of ducks paddled lazily past as if to say, welcome to our neighborhood. Mavis clasped her hands together, beaming. "Isn't it wonderful? Look at the curtains in that one! And oh, that one has a tiny rooftop garden." She snapped photo after photo, her excitement bubbling over.

Wilbur squinted at the boats, adjusting his cap. "They're almost like floating tin cans. I don't know, Mavis. You couldn't put ninety percent of your stuff in one of these. You'd need four or five just to house your basics."

"Wilbur!" Mavis said, scandalized. "They're charming."

"They're cramped," Maude corrected, pointing at a boat with windows barely wider than her forearm. "You'd have to go outside just to stretch your elbows."

Still, even Maude couldn't hide her interest when they approached the dock where a narrow-boat was open for tours. A cheerful man in a striped jumper greeted them, explaining how his family had lived on the boat for years, traveling the waterways each summer. He waved them aboard.

The boat rocked gently as they stepped onto the deck, and Wilbur grabbed the rail with both hands. "Steadier than I expected," he admitted.

Inside, the narrow-boat was a marvel of clever design. A compact kitchen with gleaming copper pans led to a snug sitting area lined with bookshelves. Beyond, a cozy bed was tucked into an alcove with quilts folded neatly at the foot. Everything smelled faintly of woodsmoke and chamomile tea. "It's like a dollhouse you can live in. I could spend all summer like this," Mavis sighed happily.

"Till the plumbing broke. Or a joist," Wilbur muttered playfully, though he lowered himself into one of the little chairs, testing it out. "It's not bad though. Better than I figured."

Maude ducked her head into the sleeping nook and immediately bumped her forehead on the low beam. "Ow! See? Cramped."

The owner chuckled. "You get used to ducking. And you learn not to bring too much with you. The waterway life is all about simplicity," he explained.

That struck something in Mavis. She stood at the window, watching another boat glide slowly past, its captain whistling as he steered. "Simplicity," she echoed. "That doesn't sound bad at all."

"Mavis, you're a glorified hoarder," Wilbur chuckled.

"She gets it honest," Maude nodded.

After the tour, they took a boat ride along the

Regent's Canal. The narrow-boat chugged steadily forward, carrying them past bridges arched with ivy, quiet stretches of leafy shade, and bursts of street art splashed on old brick walls. Families waved from the towpaths, cyclists zipped by, and the occasional heron lifted gracefully from the water's edge. Mavis sat up front, leaning over the railing as though she could drink the whole scene in at once. "This is my favorite day so far. Look at how peaceful it is," she mused.

Wilbur lounged on the bench behind her, arms crossed but eyes half-closed. "I'll give you that. Beats the noise of the city."

Maude, however, couldn't help critiquing. "It's lovely for a ride, but living here? No privacy. Every tourist with a camera would be snapping shots through your window," she smirked.

"You'd just pull the curtains," Mavis laughed.

"You know I'd shout at them instead," Maude replied, and Wilbur nearly choked on his chuckle.

The boat glided through the famous Maida Hill Tunnel, lights twinkling off the damp brick walls as the sound of water echoed around them. Mavis held her breath at the sight, enchanted, while Wilbur muttered, "Feels like being swallowed whole by a whale." When they finally emerged into sunlight again, the relief was audible.

They disembarked near Camden Market, where the air filled with the mingling aromas of sizzling street food. Stalls offered everything from steaming curries to fresh crêpes to quirky souvenirs. Maude made a beeline for a leather goods booth, testing the zippers on bags with a critical eye. Wilbur, meanwhile, was drawn toward a stall selling meat pies. "Now this is what I call sightseeing," he said, handing over a few pounds for a piping hot steak pie. He took a bite and closed his eyes in bliss. "Better than the fish and chips."

Mavis wandered slowly from stall to stall, charmed by handmade jewelry and colorful scarves. She bought a small painted trinket box shaped like a boat, tucking it carefully into her purse. "A little reminder," she explained when Wilbur raised an eyebrow.

By late afternoon, the three of them sat on a bench by the canal, the water rippling gold in the lowering sun. Mavis cradled a cup of tea, Wilbur gnawed the last of his pie crust, and Maude inspected the new bag she had haggled for with satisfaction. "You know," Wilbur said, "this one wasn't half bad. Peaceful ride, good food, no one tried to arrest Maude for climbing on statues. I'll count it a win."

"Day's not over yet," Maude insisted.

Mavis chuckled softly, her gaze drifting back to the slow-moving boats. "Opal would have adored this. She always said she wanted to live simply, without clutter. I think she would've felt at home here." They fell quiet for a moment, each imagining their friend perched on one of the narrow-boats, her laughter carried on the canal breeze. The thought settled warm in their hearts. As evening approached, they caught the bus back toward their hotel, the city alive with twilight energy. Wilbur dozed, and Maude leaned her head against the window, a rare smile tugging at her lips. Tomorrow would bring another adventure, but for tonight, the memory of sunlight on water and brightly painted boats was more than enough.

Mavis was up before dawn again, bouncing quietly on her heels as she nudged Wilbur and Maude. "Come on! Today we're taking the train to Paris. Eiffel Tower, Versailles, and everything the city of love has to offer!"

Wilbur groaned from beneath the covers. "We just got the hang of British time, and now you're dragging us back into early mornings."

"You'll survive," Mavis said with a smirk, already packing her bag. "Besides, it's Paris. You can sleep on the train if you have to."

Breakfast at the hotel was quick, a few pastries and strong coffee, and soon they were walking toward St. Pancras International, the sleek Eurostar terminal gleaming in the morning light. The station hummed with travelers speaking a dozen different languages, rolling suitcases clattering across the floors. Once aboard the Eurostar, Wilbur sank into his seat with a long sigh. "At least this one doesn't wobble like those canal boats."

Mavis laughed and leaned toward the window. "Just wait. You're going to love watching the countryside blur past as we shoot under the English Channel. It's like magic." She unfolded her map of Paris, tracing their route. "We hit the Eiffel Tower first, then Versailles. It's going to be a long day, but worth every step," she shrieked.

The train roared forward, whisking them

through green fields and sleepy villages, past river bends and wind-whipped hills. When they reached Folkestone, the sudden jolt signaled the start of the undersea tunnel. The cabin lights dimmed slightly as the train slipped beneath the Channel, and even Wilbur found himself staring in awe. "Under the sea," he muttered, shaking his head. "Crazy."

"Not as crazy as people calling that pudding atrocity breakfast," Maude said, earning a chuckle from Mavis.

By mid-morning, they emerged into France. Fields of golden wheat and poppy-dotted meadows flashed by before Paris itself came into view: rooftops, the Seine snaking through the city, and the unmistakable silhouette of the Eiffel Tower rising above the skyline. They arrived at Gare du Nord and followed the signs to the Metro, the language barrier a minor challenge but easily navigated with smiles, gestures, and Mavis's trusty phrasebook. Stepping out near the Champ de Mars, the tower loomed above them, majestic and impossibly intricate against the clear afternoon sky. Wilbur tilted his head back. "Bigger than I imagined. You can't really understand it until you're right here," he mused.

Maude squinted upward, shading her eyes. "My neck hurts just looking at it. How many pieces of metal is that thing made of? I bet I could climb it back in my day."

"You're afraid of heights," Wilbur laughed.

Mavis ignored them, already snapping photo after photo, circling the tower to capture it from every angle. "Imagine coming here at night, all lit up. It's like stepping into a dream."

They queued for the elevator, the excitement palpable. From the upper deck, Paris sprawled beneath them: the Seine glinting in the sunlight, the rooftops a patchwork of red and gray, streets lined with trees, and monuments rising at every turn. Wilbur was silent, taking in the view with a rare expression of wonder. "Alright," he admitted, "I'll give it to you. That's impressive."

After descending, they strolled along the Champ de Mars, watching street performers, artists sketching portraits, and children feeding pigeons. Mavis insisted on a quick picnic with baguettes, cheese, and pastries from a nearby boulangerie. Sitting on the grass beneath the tower, they shared bites and laughter. "You know," Mavis said between bites of brie, "I can't believe we're really here. Eiffel Tower, Paris, together. It's like living inside one of those travel magazines we used to dog-ear."

Wilbur munched thoughtfully. "Better than a magazine. At least you don't have to smell the page glue."

Mavis nudged him. "You're impossible, you know that?"

"Compliments come in time," Wilbur said with a wink.

By mid-afternoon, they boarded a train to Versailles. The palace and gardens awaited, and the closer they got, the more stately the approach became. Carriage paths lined with trimmed hedges, fountains shimmering in the sunlight, and the palace itself, vast and imposing, drew gasps from the three of them.

Inside, they wandered through hall after hall of opulent rooms: gilded mirrors reflecting crystal chandeliers, painted ceilings, and tapestries telling stories in rich colors. Maude muttered under her breath, "You'd need a week just to see all of this!"

Mavis ran her fingers over a delicate banister. "It's incredible. Imagine the history here, the kings, the queens, the banquets."

Wilbur tilted his head. "All that gold. I'd be too nervous to touch anything," he whispered.

They stepped into the gardens next, sprawling expanses of geometrically precise lawns, flowerbeds bursting with color, and fountains that played in choreographed sprays. Mavis walked ahead, marveling at the fountains and sculptures.

"Can you imagine living here?" she asked, turning to her friends. "Waking up to this every day?"

Wilbur shrugged. "I prefer no king or queen yelling at me."

Mavis laughed. "We could do a palace version of that, Wilbur. You scrubbing the floors, Maude rearranging the fountains, and me taking endless photos."

They walked along the Grand Canal, taking in the symmetry, the distant fountains, and the occasional tourist boat gliding past. Time seemed to slow in the golden afternoon light. Evening found them back in central Paris, hungry and tired but radiant. They found a small bistro near the Seine and sat outside, sipping wine and enjoying the street music drifting past. Mavis leaned back, sighing. "I don't think this day can get any better. Eiffel Tower, Versailles, a little wine, the Seine! I think we're living someone else's dream."

Wilbur shook his head, smiling faintly. "I'd say the same, except with Emily here with us. And I don't even like wine," he shrugged.

Maude clinked her glass against his. "To Paris, then. And to Opal, who got us started on all of this."

They laughed and ate, the lights of the city shimmering on the water, and the Eiffel Tower glowing faintly in the distance. Tomorrow would bring more adventure, but tonight, Paris belonged to them. The train ride back to London was nearly silent as Wilbur and Maude both snored as they leaned against the window. Mavis was too excited to miss a single second of the trip. They decided to spend the next day resting and walking around the street their hotel was on. It was their last full day in London, as they were headed to Ireland early the next morning per Mavis' itinerary. "I think I want one more fish and chips," Wilbur said. "Yea, that sounds good."

Lunch that day brought Wilbur immense happiness. He posed for a picture with his plate of fish and chips, crispy and golden, with malt vinegar on the side. "It's perfect," he declared as Mavis snapped the photo.

Maude poked hers with a fork. "This one is a little bland. Needs pepper. Needs something. How's your whatever that is, Mavis?"

"Well, it's not terrible," Mavis frowned. She

had ordered haggis after misunderstanding the menu. One bite, and her face twisted. "This is an abomination. Who thought it was a good idea to stuff a sheep's stomach with oats?"

After their late lunch, they headed back to the hotel to pack and make sure everything was ready for their departure in the morning. While Wilbur showered, Mavis and Maude walked downstairs to the lobby to take a few more pictures of the evening sun.

While Mavis chatted with the woman at the front desk, Maude looked around and struck up conversation with a Scottish man in the lobby who greeted her warmly. His accent was thick as porridge. "Aye, lass, ye heading oot tae the Highlands the morn?" he asked.

"Come again?" Maude asked.

He repeated himself, slower. "I still didn't catch a single word," Maude frowned. The man rolled his eyes and stomped off.

"What was that all about?" Wilbur asked. "Why did he throw his hand sin the air as he ran away? You didn't snap, did you? You always joked about it."

"Maybe she did," Mavis said wide-eyed. "Big Mama always said it was coming."

"No!" Maude rolled her eyes. "That man said some kind of curse or something."

Mavis, trying not to laugh, leaned in. "He asked if you're headed to the Highlands tomorrow," she giggled.

Maude threw up her hands. "Well, how on earth am I supposed to know that? He's ain't speaking English. I swear they speak a different language over here. Like that guy this morning!"

"What happened this morning?" Mavis asked.

"He told me to get in the queue," Maude said, confused. "I thought he meant some kind of trap. Turns out it just means a line."

"He probably thinks you have an accent, not him," Mavis smirked.

"And don't even get me started on them calling the elevator a lift. I nearly asked a stranger where the elevator was, and she looked at me like I'd asked for a rocket ship," Maude grumbled.

Chapter Eighteen

Mavis came out of the bathroom in a puff of steam and lilac perfume, cheeks rosy with energy. She had braided her hair and tucked it into a jaunty bun that made her look ten years younger. "Today's the day!" she sang, clapping once. "Oktoberfest begins today, September sixteenth, right on schedule. Opal would be so tickled that we're hitting it on opening day."

Wilbur smiled at the thought and sat down on the small couch near the door. "Okay," Mavis said, bright again. "Bags zipped? Passports? Phone chargers? I brought motion-sickness pills just in case, Wilbur."

"Just in case the pilot forgets how to drive, you mean," he moaned.

Mavis rolled her eyes and shouldered her purse. "We better get a move on. Maude said she would meet us down in the lobby with her luggage." Together she and Wilbur grabbed their suitcases and bags and shuffled downstairs. The lobby smelled of coffee and furniture wax. A bell tinkled every time someone passed through the revolving door. Maude was standing at the front desk and demanded a fresh look at their bill.

"What's this charge?" she asked, tapping the

printed out receipt.

The clerk, a pale young man with a tie too tight at the throat, smiled over-pleasantly. "That would be the tea you ordered in the lounge yesterday and the day before, madam."

"I couldn't even drink it," Maude frowned. "Who serves unsweetened tea!"

Wilbur eased their suitcases toward the door like a man escorting misbehaving children from Sunday school. "She's gonna get us banned from the whole country."

Mavis stepped in with a sunny, diplomatic grin. "We're square. Thank you for a lovely stay. The breakfast tomatoes were delightful. Hate that we won't make breakfast today, but we really must be off."

Maude muttered, "Delightful if you like tomatoes at breakfast," but she let herself be shepherded to the curb.

They piled into a black cab that smelled faintly of patchouli. Outside, London wore its rain like a thin veil. The driver navigated roundabouts and red buses with cheerful curses under his breath.

"You'd think after all this time they'd fix which side of the road they're on," Wilbur said, watching cars slip by on the opposite side.

Mavis squeezed his arm. "They think the same about us."

"At least in Rhinestone you can tell where the sky is going to come from," he said. "Here it's gray in every direction."

"Stop narrating the weather," Maude said, digging in her purse. "Find me a mint and your cheerful attitude."

The airport unfurled as a long, glassy riddle of lines that fed into other lines, trays for shoes, belts for bags, questions about liquids in small bottles that made Wilbur feel like he was smuggling contraband even when he wasn't. He held tight to his passport as if the wind from a passing trolley could snatch it. "This is why people never leave home," he muttered as they padded sock-footed through security.

"You say that every time," Mavis said, then craned up to catch the departure board. "Munich: Gate B37. We're good! We're early! Oh, listen to this," she continued. She cracked open the guidebook and read in a conspiratorial whisper. "The mayor taps the first keg and shouts 'O'zapft is!' That means 'It's tapped!' And then the drinking begins."

"That's a lot of pomp just to say the beer's ready," Maude said.

Boarding went smoothly, smoothing Wilbur's lungs along with it. The plane was smaller than the transatlantic bus-with-wings they'd ridden before. He gripped the armrests for takeoff, held his breath through the bump and lift, and then blinked in surprise when they were already skating along above the quilt of cloud and countryside.

"Short hop," Mavis said, and pressed a ginger candy into his hand. "Chew this. It helps."

Out the window, England slipped away in squares of green and brown, and then the Channel, and then patches of land that might as well have been Alabama if you couldn't see the neat, red-roofed villages peeking from clusters of trees. Mavis read more bits about dirndls and lederhosen, and pretzels you had to carry with two hands. Maude dozed with her arms folded, lips pursed as if challenging the plane to try something.

"Cabin crew, prepare for landing," the overhead voice said before Wilbur felt ready for it. He unclenched his jaw and pretended he'd been calm the whole time.

Munich's airport was bright and brisk, all light wood and clean tile. Signs in German and English pointed them toward baggage claim and the S-Bahn into the city. People were dressed for the festival in every direction they turned. Men in crisp shirts with leather suspenders, socks bunched around their calves smiled as they walked by. Women in dirndls the colors of bright candies hummed as they followed suit. Wilbur and Mavis were awestruck at the hats with feathers and buttons pinned to vests and the happy hum of a city that had decided to make room for celebration.

"Oh," Mavis breathed, clutching the guidebook to her chest. "It's like walking into a storybook."

"Looks like walking into a boot catalog," Wilbur said, eyeing the sturdy footwear. "Those folks are ready to stand."

"They're ready to dance," Maude corrected. "And so am I, if the food's as good as they say."

They rode the S-Bahn into the city, a smooth thread gliding through suburbs into denser blocks full of bakeries with braided loaves in the windows, signs for pharmacies with green crosses, bicycles everywhere. When they stepped back onto the street near their hotel, the air held a cool, yeasty smell of beer and bread just out of ovens, and the faintest whisper of roasted meat riding the breeze.

Their hotel was small and square and smiled at them with flower boxes. The innkeeper, a rosy-cheeked man with iron-gray hair, greeted them in German first and then in an easy English that set Wilbur at ease. "Welcome, welcome! You have just arrived in time. Today the first keg is tapped. Your room is on the third floor. Lift is just there. Breakfast is finished, but we have coffee."

"Coffee is fine, thank you," Mavis said, and then, unable to help herself added, "We're here for Oktoberfest. It's on our friend's bucket list." She tapped her purse where the notebook rested.

The innkeeper's eyes softened. "Then you must make a toast for your friend. Ein Prosit! This is the song you will hear again and again. It means we wish you good cheer."

"We'll wish her the biggest cheer you've got," Maude said, surprising them with gentleness.

The lift was slimmer than it looked. Wilbur held his suitcase to his chest like a toddler while Maude pressed the button. Their room had lace curtains and feather duvets plumped like small clouds. The window looked over a courtyard where bikes leaned against rails and a cat performed the solemn duty of washing its paws in the sun. They had chosen two connecting rooms since they would only be in Germany for two nights, but already it was feeling cramped.

"This'll do," Maude said, already fluffing a

pillow in her small room. "Now change shoes. I aim to put a dent in German cuisine."

After Mavis and Wilbur were ready, she led them back outside towards the festival. It wasn't difficult to find. They followed the crowd. The river of people shimmered with color, dirndls like banners, and lederhosen like parade uniforms, with laughter stitching everything together. Vendors had set up along the walkways with gingerbread hearts strung on ribbons, each iced with messages in curly white script. Mavis cooed over one that read "Ich liebe dich" and bought it to hang from her purse.

"What's it say?" Wilbur asked.

"It says 'I love you.' I'll pretend Opal wrote it for all of us," she smiled.

Maude sniffed suspiciously at another stand. "What's in those wheels of cheese?" she asked in her sternest voice, as if she'd catch Germany trying to sneak unseasoned potatoes past her.

"Paprika, onion, a little beer," the vendor said, beaming. "It is obatzda, a soft cheese for your pretzel."

"Say no more," Maude replied, and bought a tub without tasting. "I respect a cheese with ambition."

Theresienwiese spread ahead like wide avenues of trampled grass, rides spinning bright as hummingbirds, and beer tents that were all uniquely painted and towering, each with its own identity and music rising from within. "This isn't a festival," Wilbur said, craning. "This is a city that built another city just to have something to do."

"And we are precisely on time," Mavis said, bouncing. "Opening day! Oh, listen, do you hear it? They're singing already."

A hostess in a dirndl shepherded them inside a tent where the ceiling was painted like a Bavarian sky, blue and white, with clouds drifting and wreaths hanging like little green halos. Long wooden tables ran in tidy lines, jammed with people who had already made friends with everyone within stein-clinking distance. They squeezed onto a bench between a family from Stuttgart and a cluster of college students from who-knows-where. The table smelled of varnish and spilled beer and roasted chicken. A waitress appeared who could have carried a pickup truck on each arm; she balanced six steins as if they were empty.

"Drei Maß?" she asked, and Mavis nodded hopefully. The waitress set three glass columns of beer in front of them, each crowned with a snowy head.

Wilbur inspected his. "This mug is a weapon," he mused.

Maude lifted hers with both hands, took a heroic sip, and wiped a foam mustache with dignity. "Bless the Germans," she said. "They understand volume. It's smooth, like bread and sunshine had a baby."

The band broke into a song that sounded like a polka glad to be alive. People stood on benches and swayed. The family from Stuttgart clinked their steins gently against theirs, smiling. "Prost!" they chorused.

"Prost!" Mavis answered brightly.

Food arrived in the lane of the table like floats in a parade: half chickens with skin blistered and crisp, platters of sausages snaking around mounds of sauerkraut, pretzels big enough to moonlight as life preservers, bowls of potato dumplings glossy with brown gravy. Maude went very still with happiness.

"Nobody talk to me for the next few minutes," she said. "I must commune with my plate."

"You said that in Paris at the pastry counter," Wilbur reminded her.

"And I was right then, too," she replied, cutting into a dumpling with reverence.

Mavis put a little of everything on her plate and then a little more. "This is exactly what she wanted," she said softly, glancing at her purse. "To be here, in it, not just reading about it."

Wilbur cleared his throat and lifted his stein. "To Opal," he said. "Who dragged us across oceans without so much as lifting a finger."

"To Opal," they echoed, and drank.

It happened during the second Ein Prosit. That was how Mavis would tell it later, two toasts in, one polka over the line, the band roaring, the whole tent rising to clink and sing while the words tunneled through her heart with happy insistence. She saw the stall just outside the tent flap: leather shorts and suspenders, shirts embroidered with flowers, feathered hats. "I'll be right back," Mavis told them, which was the most dangerous sentence she knew how to say.

"What are you doing?" Maude asked, still

engaged in a meaningful relationship with a sausage.

"Errand," Mavis said, and slipped into the stream of festivalgoers.

The stall smelled like new leather and cedar. A woman with bright eyes and a braid the size of a thick rope greeted her in quick German and then in English. "You would like a dirndl?" she asked, hands already sifting through fabrics.

"Actually," Mavis said, her mouth forming the sentence before prudence could catch up, "I would like lederhosen."

The woman blinked and then brightened. "For you? But of course! We have ladies' cut." She swept aside a curtain and revealed a row of soft brown shorts with green embroidery curling like vines. "This, with a blouse, very nice. Very strong."

Fifteen minutes and some delighted squeaks later, Mavis stepped from the makeshift fitting room wearing brown leather shorts that hugged her hips, a white blouse with gathered sleeves, and braces stitched with edelweiss. She turned in front of the mirror, surprised by the way she looked both ridiculous and entirely herself. "It suits you," the vendor declared, fastening a brass buckle. "You have the joy for it."

Mavis bought the set, including a little hat that sat at a jaunty angle on her bun. She marched back into the tent like a one-woman parade. Wilbur, mid-sip, sputtered beer out his nose. "Good night, Mavis!"

Maude slammed both palms on the table and howled in laughter. Mavis planted her fists on her hips and grinned. "Opal would have dared me. Consider it done!" she grinned.

"Next thing you know she'll be buying me a pair," Wilbur said. "And I got knees nobody needs to see."

"Correct," Maude said. "Cover those, but let the girl live."

A passerby raised a thumb and called, "Schön!" Mavis, flustered and pleased, tipped her tiny hat.

Between songs, the young people down the bench tried to teach Wilbur a phrase or two. He learned "bitte" and "danke" and then tried to string them together until he accidentally told a waiter, "Please thank you more beer" and received exactly what he asked for, which was both not at all and exactly what he meant. Maude gleaned what she truly needed to learn to say was Schweinshaxe with the proper throaty authority so that a pork knuckle the size of a small football appeared. She cracked the crisp skin with her knife and closed her eyes. "Seasoned," she whispered. "Bless the spice rack of Bavaria."

Mavis discovered that if she stood and clapped when the band played Ein Prosit, she was immediately part of a hundred-person friendship. She learned the hand motions, the little sway that meant you were ready to toast anything from the weather to the hat you'd just bought, or to the memory you were trying to hold still long enough to show someone you loved. At some point, Wilbur excused himself to find the restroom and returned twenty minutes later wearing the expression of a man who had fought a mild war.

"You get lost?" Maude asked.

"I went in a door that wasn't a door," he said. "I thought it was the men's, but it was a closet with a mop that looked like it had seen things. Then a fella in an apron rescued me and pointed me the right way, but everything was labeled like a riddle. Herren is men, in case either of you ever need to know. Damen is ladies. I almost asked a woman to explain it to me, but I thought better of it because she had a stein that could've knocked me into next week."

"You survived," Mavis said, touching his elbow.

"I did. And I washed my hands like someone was grading me," he said gravely.

Course followed course as if the kitchen were determined to test the limits of physics and appetite: white sausages tender as clouds, served with sweet mustard; sauerkraut tangy enough to reset a person's temperament; potato pancakes that crackled at the edges and went soft as you bit in. Mavis, who had come to the table hungry and curious, found herself laughing between bites at the impossible bounty. "How is anyone grumpy in a place like this?" she asked, wiping a dot of mustard from her lip.

"Because their shoes are foolish," Maude replied, cutting another slice from her pork knuckle. "Stand like this for six hours and see what it does to your spine. That's why Germans invented benches."

"Pretty sure benches were already invented," Wilbur said, but he stretched his legs in grateful agreement. His initial caution had softened into a good-natured looseness; the music braided through him. He looked down the table to where the Stuttgart father was showing his little boy how to clink a tiny root beer mug without spilling. The boy looked up at Wilbur with the solemn intensity of children and held out his mug. Wilbur clinked it gently and the boy beamed, then immediately drank with exaggerated gusto.

"Careful," Wilbur said. "You'll have a foam mustache."

The boy swiped his lip and giggled. His mother said something in German that was surely "Say thank you," and the boy chirped, "Danke!" as if he'd invented manners.

"Bitte," Wilbur replied, proud of having the right word ready.

Mavis watched it all with her heart folded open. She thought: This is what Opal would have loved best. Seeing her people tangled together with strangers growing familiar over something simple and good. She slipped her hand into her purse and brushed the notebook with her fingertips, as if the touch alone could transmit the sound and heat and joy to its pages.

Chapter Nineteen

Wilbur woke the next morning with a start to the sound of Maude's suitcase zipper rattling like a machine gun in the adjoining room. Each snap and clack echoed through the hotel room, assaulting his still-sleeping brain. He groaned, burying his face in the pillow, silently willing the sound to vanish. "Why must y'all start so early?" he muttered, his voice muffled by the pillow.

"Good morning, Wilbur!" Mavis called cheerfully, perched on the edge of the bed like a bird ready to take flight. "Today's the day! Bran Castle!"

Wilbur peeked out just enough to see her enthusiastic smile. "Ah, yes, Dracula's castle. I almost forgot!" he chuckled sarcastically.

"Yes! Vlad the Impaler! Bram Stoker! Legends! History! All of it!" Mavis practically bounced with excitement. "Opal would have been beside herself if she could see us now. Of course it's not really Dracula's castle, but for all intents and purposes, it's a fine choice. Don't get me started on Vlad the Impaler."

Maude rolled her eyes, tugging her sweater closer around her shoulders. "I know I'd like breakfast that isn't just stale bread or a pastry before we risk broken bones on stairs."

"You'll get food," Mavis promised. "We're stopping at the village below the castle. It's quaint and charming. You'll love it."

Wilbur groaned. "Satisfying or not, my heart rate is already double just thinking about climbing stairs and encountering," he waved vaguely at the ceiling, "potential ghosts."

The room descended into the familiar chaos of packing. Maude methodically arranged snacks and hand sanitizer, muttering about castle germs as she did so. Mavis triple-checked the tickets, fanning them out like prized playing cards. Wilbur hovered nervously by the door, unsure whether to help or hide entirely. By the time they were done, the hotel room looked like a tornado had struck with piles of clothes, stray snack wrappers, and a lone, bewildered travel pillow left in the corner. By the time they reached the Munich train station, the platform buzzed with activity. Travelers dragged oversized suitcases, musicians strummed guitars, and street vendors hawked pretzels and coffee. Wilbur eyed the sleek, gleaming train waiting to whisk them to Romania. "It's too shiny. Too smooth. Trains don't move like that," he fretted.

Once aboard, Mavis immediately pressed her face to the window, squealing at every passing field, village, and mountainside. "Look at those vineyards! And the houses! Isn't this lovely?"

Maude, meanwhile, was already halfway through a bag of pastries she had purchased at the station. Crumbs rained down onto her lap like confetti. Hours passed as the train glided through rolling hills, dense forests, and sleepy villages.

Mavis narrated with unrestrained enthusiasm about Romanian history, Vlad the Impaler, and Bran Castle. Wilbur tried to nap but woke every few minutes, convinced that the train was teetering on the edge of a cliff. Maude alternated between eating, napping, and quietly judging him.

At one point, Wilbur dozed off so deeply that his head toppled onto a neighboring passenger's shoulder. The man startled awake. Wilbur bolted upright, crimson-faced. "I, uh, sorry, vampire dreams," he muttered. Mavis stifled a giggle, then gasped.

"What in the world?" Wilbur asked.

"Oh my heavens! This guidebook says that Vlad never even lived in Bran Castle. It's all a marketing ploy! I know Bram Stoker never even visited Romania, he just saw pictures, but oh my goodness!" Mavis read.

"So, we aren't going to the castle?" Wilbur asked.

"No, we are going!" Mavis answered. "It's commonly called Dracula's castle, but he's not there."

"Well, he's a literary character," Wilbur reminded her.

"Wilbur, shh," Mavis sighed. She dove back into her book and continued reading.

Eventually, the train slowed into Brașov. The town's colorful rooftops and cobbled streets were picturesque, framed by the Carpathian Mountains rising dramatically behind. The crisp mountain air carried hints of pine and wood smoke from distant stoves. Mavis immediately began snapping photos, dragging Wilbur along by the elbow. "We need to get to the castle before the crowds," she said eagerly.

A shuttle bus awaited at the base of the hill, winding up narrow, twisting roads toward Bran Castle. Wilbur gripped the seat in front of him, muttering about failing brakes, crumbling guardrails, and the likelihood of wolf attacks. Mavis leaned out the window, snapping photos and laughing at his panic. She squealed every time the bus crested a ridge, pointing to the looming silhouette of the castle through the fog. The castle loomed larger with every turn of the winding road, its jagged silhouette cutting into the pale morning sky. Mavis practically bounced in her seat, hands pressed against the window. "Can you believe this? Opal would have insisted on at least twenty photos already!"

Wilbur swallowed nervously. "I am not looking forward to this walking part. I'm fairly certain every step up that hill is an invitation for disaster," he whispered to Mavis. "Maude is almost ninety!"

Maude rolled her eyes but smirked. "Worry about your own self. You're about to become a legend yourself, Wilbur. People will tell tales of the man who nearly fainted halfway up the hill to Dracula's castle."

The bus hissed to a stop at the base of the castle path, and they disembarked among a throng of tourists. The smell of roasting chestnuts and wood smoke mingled with the crisp mountain air. Maude immediately spotted a vendor selling carved wooden bats. "Oh, for heaven's sake," she muttered, picking one up. "I suppose I should get you one for your nerves, Wilbur."

Mavis skipped ahead, chattering about the castle's history. "This is Bran Castle! Vlad the Impaler may not have ruled here, but it's still so impressive! The architecture, ah! Look at those battlements! The Gothic windows! Opal would have been enchanted by the sheer history!"

Wilbur followed, hesitating at every step, his hand brushing against the rough stone walls. "History is fine, as long as it doesn't involve me falling down a spiral staircase. Or ghosts. Or," he paused, shivering, "vampires."

A Scottish tourist passed by and said something that Wilbur swore sounded like, "Yer blood will be mine, laddie!" Wilbur jumped back, almost tripping over his own feet. Maude laughed so hard she nearly lost her balance, catching herself on the vendor's table. "Relax, Wilbur! That was just someone speaking in a thick accent. Isn't that what you and Mavis told me the other day?"

The path to the castle was steep, flanked by vendors selling everything from Dracula key chains to fangs to T-shirts with "I Survived Bran Castle" printed on them. Maude stopped at every stand, examining each item with exaggerated seriousness. She picked up a wooden stake, waving it at Wilbur. "Here, just in case. You can defend yourself."

"I think I'll survive by staying away from the windows," Wilbur muttered.

Mavis was already several steps ahead, snapping photos of every turn, every arch, every curious detail. "These walls! The towers! The fog! The view!" she howled gleefully.

Maude tugged Wilbur forward. "Come on, Wilbur. You're going to look back one day and laugh about this. Maybe. If you survive," she shrugged.

Finally, they reached the castle's massive arched entrance. A guide greeted the tourists, leading them through corridors that smelled faintly of stone dust and history. Wilbur's eyes widened at every creaking floorboard. Maude whispered, "I'd be happier in a soft chair with a plate of food."

The first room they entered was a narrow hall lined with suits of armor. Wilbur instinctively backed up against a wall, muttering, "Do they move? Do they bite?" Maude leaned over to him. "They're not real, you dramatic man. You're probably giving the other tourists a show. Does Emily know how scared of all this you are?"

Mavis darted from room to room, reading plaques aloud. "This is the armory! Oh, look at these windows! The view is spectacular!"

Wilbur shuffled along, careful to avoid stepping on any loose stones. He muttered complaints under his breath about drafty hallways, low ceilings, and mysterious shadows. They entered a dimly lit room dedicated to Vlad the Impaler. A portrait stared menacingly in a corner, eyes glaring from beneath a furrowed brow. Maude jumped back. "Good grief! Warn a person next time!"

Wilbur, pale, poked the frame. "Looks too alive for me," he whispered.

Mavis shushed them, her eyes wide with delight. "Honestly, you two are worse than children."

The corridors twisted and turned, leading them to spiral staircases and hidden chambers. Wilbur's legs began to wobble. Maude leaned over to steady him. "Just take it slow. Look at the walls, not the drop."

Eventually, they emerged into a courtyard where the castle's towers rose like jagged teeth into the sky. Mavis gasped, clicking photos at every angle. "The view! Opal would have wanted us to climb every tower!"

"She's not wrong," Maude nodded. "Opal would have done left us behind to explore like she did at Graceland."

Outside, vendors beckoned with souvenirs. Maude haggled over a carved wooden sword, lowering the price by an outrageous amount before finally relenting. Mavis purchased a delicate hand-painted egg. Wilbur refused to buy anything, claiming stair climbing was payment enough. They stopped for a quick lunch at a café in the village below the castle. Wilbur stuck to sausage and potatoes, Mavis sampled mici, and Maude ordered a hearty stew. The food was satisfying but unfamiliar. Wilbur poked suspiciously at the spices. "They're serious about this, aren't they?"

Mavis laughed. "Yes, Wilbur. Just eat it. You're alive, aren't you?"

Afterward, they wandered through the village streets. Maude bought a tiny wooden bat and a Dracula figurine, joking, "For your protection,

Wilbur."

Wilbur muttered, "I'll be the first to meet the real Dracula if he shows up."

Mavis continued snapping photos of every shop, every fountain, and every cobblestone. She leaned over Wilbur's shoulder. "Look at this! Opal would have loved this. The architecture, the culture, the people!"

Wilbur sighed, half-awake and half-panicked. "I'll admire it from a safe distance. Possibly from the bus. Or the train."

By late afternoon, they returned to the shuttle bus for the journey back to Brașov. Wilbur clutched the rail nervously, while Maude teased him endlessly about his theatrics. Mavis continued to click photos, insisting that every ridge, every tree, every cloud needed to be documented. The return train to Munich was quieter. Wilbur dozed intermittently, muttering about imaginary bats. Maude read and nibbled snacks, and Mavis gazed at the passing scenery, still thrilled by the day's adventures. Wilbur occasionally woke, whispering warnings to anyone within earshot: "Vampires. Bats. Spooky corridors. Dangerous staircases." Maude rolled her eyes, handing him chocolate.

The German countryside stretched out in shades of amber and green as the sun set. Mavis leaned back, content. "I'm so glad we came. Opal would have loved this. I know I keep saying this, but she really would have. She loved everything. I swear she lived more life than anyone I know."

Maude patted her hand. "Yes, sugar. We feel it."

"Opal would have laughed at us today. Probably for hours," Wilbur nodded.

By the time Munich appeared in the distance, the three were exhausted but satisfied. Mavis was already planning tomorrow's adventure. "Where to next?" Wilbur asked warily.

Mavis' eyes twinkled. "Tomorrow we fly to the Netherlands. I can't believe our trip is over halfway over," she smiled.

As they exited the train to walk back to their hotel, Wilbur muttered, "I swear I felt something in that armory. It was like a cold breath of doom and gloom."

Maude raised an eyebrow. "I think you're imagining things. You're probably just hungry. Or tired. Or both. Or slightly hysterical," she shrugged.

"I was perfectly sane until I saw that portrait!" Wilbur protested. "It glared at me. I know it did!"

Mavis, perched upright with her camera still dangling around her neck, laughed. "You're imagining it, Wilbur. And even if it did glare, you were safe. Opal would have laughed at how dramatic you are!"

Wilbur nodded and grinned, "You're right. Opal would have laughed at me while she rolled her eyes and gave me a history lesson."

"Well, at least we're making memories," Maude agreed. She tore a piece of chocolate from her bag and handed it to him. "Eat. You'll feel better. Or at least sugar will help your courage."

Wilbur accepted it reluctantly, popping the piece into his mouth while walking in the middle of the two women. He suddenly ducked down and shook his head. "That bat flew right at me!" he shrieked. Mavis and Maude exchanged glances and burst out laughing. "We're going to have to get you a vampire repellent, Wilbur," Mavis said. "A little garlic, some silver, you know, standard precaution."

The smell of pretzels, roasted chestnuts, and evening pastries filled the air from the ongoing Oktoberfest festival. Maude pointed to a bakery. "Shall we indulge before bed? You can rest afterward, Wilbur, if you survive the pastries' sugar rush."

Wilbur groaned but followed, muttering, "If a vampire jumps out of the bakery, we're doomed."

Mavis laughed, linking her arm with his. "No vampires, Wilbur. Just pastry and memories. And perhaps a little chocolate."

They sat at a small outdoor table, savoring their pastries, and watched the city transition into night. Lights reflected in puddles from a recent rain, and the hum of Munich in the evening surrounded them. Wilbur finally leaned back, exhaling a long breath. "I think we survived."

Maude smiled. "Barely. But yes, we survived. And it was memorable, wasn't it?"

Mavis nodded vigorously. "Absolutely! Opal's list is getting smaller, and our adventures are getting bigger. Just think of everything we've seen today. The castle, the village, the mountains. And tomorrow, who knows?"

Wilbur peered at her cautiously. "Please tell me tomorrow does not involve more castles, more stairs, or more imaginary vampires."

"Tomorrow is another adventure. But perhaps one with slightly fewer heart attacks," Mavis giggled. "I can't wait to see the gardens in Netherlands. Keukenhof gardens is so richly beautiful."

"I'll admit, those gardens from the pictures you showed me online looked beautiful. No wonder Opal wanted to see them. I have never seen such big tulips. But I ain't gonna wear any wooden shoes that I also saw on the internets. Don't even try," Maude warned.

"No promises," Mavis replied.

As the night grew deeper, the three of them walked slowly back to their hotel. The streets were still rowdy, full of people drinking and dancing in the streetlights. Maude hummed a soft tune and Mavis talked excitedly about all the photos she had taken. By the time they reached their room, exhaustion had set in. Wilbur collapsed onto the bed and took several deep breaths. Maude dropped into a chair, brushing crumbs from her lap as she ate another chocolate croissant from her bag. Mavis, still glowing from the day's adventures, began organizing her outfit for the next day.

"Sleep well," Maude said, smiling after a few minutes. She stood up and walked the few steps to her room. "Tomorrow is another day, but tonight, we rest."

Wilbur muttered something incomprehensible about garlic and daylight as he walked to the bathroom to take a shower. Mavis laughed, tucking herself into her corner of the room.

"Goodnight, everyone. Y'all sure are some jumpy people." She made a mental note to tell Emily that Wilbur would not be accompanying them on their Halloween haunted house tour next month. Her big brother got more skittish and jumpier the older he got.

Chapter Twenty

The flight from Munich to Amsterdam was less than two hours. They touched down right at lunch time. Maude kept checking her watch and sighing audibly. The coffee and pastries she had for breakfast hadn't carried over very long, and she was starving. She wasn't sure what kind of food people in the Netherlands ate, but she was willing to immerse herself into the culture if they had food she recognized. Surely every country ate fried chicken!

Wilbur let out a low whistle as the plane touched down in Amsterdam, the smooth glide to the runway earning a small round of applause from a few of the passengers. He glanced across the aisle at Maude and Mavis, who were both craning their necks to see out the small oval window.

"Well," Maude said, her tone as dry as ever, "the ground looks about like any other ground to me."

Mavis gave her a playful swat. "Oh, hush. We're in the Netherlands! Can't you feel the history, the charm, the culture already?"

"The culture smells faintly like jet fuel," Maude muttered, but her lips twitched in a half-smile.

By the time they collected their luggage and navigated the airport, Wilbur was already looking forward to a sit-down and a plate of something hearty. Their hotel was a short drive away, a modern building with glass walls that reflected the cloudy Dutch sky. The lobby was sleek, all pale wood and tulip arrangements on every surface. At the reception desk, Mavis did most of the talking, her voice bright and full of energy despite the hours of travel. "Three rooms, please. We're here for a few days to explore the gardens." She beamed at the receptionist as though she had just announced their arrival to the queen. She couldn't bear another night sharing with Wilbur or Maude; they all needed some space to relax and get a full night's sleep.

They dropped their bags upstairs and soon found themselves wandering a nearby street lined with cafés. The air was cool but pleasant, tinged with the faint scent of fresh bread and roasted coffee drifting from open doorways. Mavis, her eyes darting from menu boards to flower boxes, finally pointed toward a corner café with wicker chairs spilling out onto the sidewalk. "This one," she declared. "It's charming, and look at that pea soup!"

Wilbur grunted his approval. Their server, a cheerful young woman with hair pulled into a bun, rattled off specials in English that carried a lilting accent. Mavis ordered traditional pea soup with rye bread, Wilbur pointed to an open-faced sandwich layered with cheese and ham, and Maude requested coffee strong enough to "stand up in the cup." When the food arrived, steam curling into the air, they fell into a companionable silence. The soup was thick and hearty, filled with bits of smoked sausage; the bread crackled at the crust.

Maude leaned back in her chair, savoring her first sip. "All right," she admitted, "this isn't bad. I could get used to this." Mavis clasped her hands. "Good, because this afternoon we're going to see the tulip gardens! I've waited my whole life to walk through them. Just imagine the colors, the rows and rows of blooms, the scent in the air. It's like stepping into a painting."

Wilbur buttered a piece of bread and gave her a fond glance. "You'd better hope the rain holds off, or your painting might turn into a mud puddle." But Mavis only laughed, undeterred. She had already pulled out her guidebook and was pointing to the glossy photograph of a rainbow field of tulips stretching to the horizon.

"We'll have plenty of time," she said firmly. "Lunch, then tulips. That's the plan."

And as they finished their meal, the energy of a new adventure hummed between them, tugging them toward the gardens that waited just outside the city. After lunch, they walked to the shuttle stop, where a line of tourists had already gathered. The bus carried them out of the city and into the countryside, the landscape flattening into endless green pastures dotted with sheep. Canals stitched the land into neat squares, and in the distance, windmills turned lazily against the pale sky.

Wilbur pressed his nose nearly to the glass. "Well, would you look at that! Real windmills. I love that."

Maude snorted. "We have windmills back in the States."

He shrugged. "Something different about them here."

Mavis leaned forward, practically vibrating with excitement. "You two hush. This is even better than I imagined. Just wait until you see the tulips."

When they finally arrived, the entrance gates of Keukenhof welcomed them with bright banners and music floating faintly through the air. It was as if the earth itself had exploded into color. Rows upon rows of tulips unfurled in sweeping curves, ribbons of scarlet, gold, purple, and ivory stretching as far as the eye could see. The air was soft with perfume, the breeze carrying the sweetness of blooms.

Mavis clapped both hands over her mouth. "Oh. My. Stars."

Even Maude faltered, her eyes widening. "Well, I'll be. That's something else."

Wilbur gave a low whistle. "I'll admit, I wasn't expecting this."

They walked slowly, as though afraid to disturb the beauty. Each bend revealed a new arrangement: fiery oranges paired with soft pinks, delicate fringed tulips beside sturdy double blooms that looked like peonies in disguise.

"Oh my word! Look at this one! What a beautiful flower," Mavis said, snapping a photo. The blossoms were nearly black, velvety petals catching the light. Maude pointed to a ruffled variety in pale yellow. "That one looks like it overslept and showed up in its pajamas."

They laughed, their voices mingling with the chatter of tourists and the shrieks of children chasing bubbles. As they strolled, Wilbur's steps slowed. He stopped at a bed of bright red tulips and leaned on the railing. "You know," he said quietly, "Opal would've loved this. She always had a thing for flowers. I bet she could grow these in Rhinestone. Even if no one else could, she could. She could do it all."

Mavis touched his arm, her eyes soft. "That's why we're here. To see it for her. To bring her with us." For a beat, silence settled. Then Maude, ever the realist, cleared her throat. "If she were here, she'd probably tell us to quit standing like statues and keep walking, after she pocketed a few of these flowers and stuffed them in my bag."

At one pavilion, orchids cascaded from hanging baskets, filling the air with sweetness. In another, tulips stood in tall glass vases arranged by color gradient, fading from ivory to crimson like a painter's brushstroke. Mavis insisted on taking photos at every turn. She snapped Wilbur in front of a bed of purple tulips and then begged Maude to smile beside a field of orange ones. "Smile," Mavis coaxed. "Pretend you're having the time of your life."

"I'll pretend I'm tolerating you," Maude muttered, but her lips twitched into a grin just as Mavis clicked the picture.

They stopped for coffee inside one of the pavilions, sipping from delicate cups while surrounded by blooms. Mavis struck up a conversation with a couple from Canada, swapping travel stories and recommending the best pie in Rhinestone. Wilbur wandered off and had to be retrieved before he joined the wrong tour group. By the time they reached the gift shop, their feet ached pleasantly. Mavis cooed over tulip-patterned scarves, Maude bought a tin of stroopwafels for emergencies, and Wilbur picked out a tiny wooden windmill key chain for Emily.

The ride back to the hotel was quieter. The bus hummed along, the fields receding into memory. Mavis leaned against the window, eyes dreamy. "This is exactly how I pictured it," she sighed. "More, even."

Maude patted her arm. "Don't get used to perfect. Tomorrow, we'll probably get rained on."

Wilbur smiled faintly, watching the fading colors of the sky. "Rain or not, it's worth the trip. You were right, Mavis. This was something to see."

"Dream of fields of tulips tonight," Mavis smiled as she closed to the door to her hotel room. Maude and Wilbur walked down the hall to their rooms and both fell into their own bed and fell right to sleep.

The morning light slipped through the tall hotel windows in pale stripes early the next morning, soft as watercolor. Mavis had been awake since dawn, her heart thumping with the kind of excitement she hadn't felt since she was a girl waiting for Christmas morning. She threw on a cardigan, tied her scarf with flair, and marched down the hall in her slippers to knock on Maude's door. "Rise and shine! The canals are waiting!"

From inside came Maude's muffled groan. "Tell the canals I'll meet them after lunch." Mavis knocked again, firmer. "We didn't come all the way to Amsterdam for you to sleep the day away." By the time she reached Wilbur's door, he was already up and dressed, tugging on his shoes. His freshly washed hair stuck out at odd angles, but there was a spark of amusement in his tired eyes.

"I figured you'd come knocking," he said. "You never could resist dragging people out of bed."

"Because adventure doesn't wait," Mavis declared.

"Neither does my stomach," Wilbur said, and together they went downstairs to breakfast.

The dining room was bright and cheerful, tables set with white cloths and little vases of tulips. The buffet was unlike anything they'd seen back home: baskets of crusty bread, platters of cheese and cold cuts, little pancakes dusted with powdered sugar, yogurt with fruit and granola, and pitchers of fresh juice. Mavis made herself a plate with a little bit of everything, humming happily as she went. Wilbur piled on scrambled eggs and bacon. "I'm sticking with what I know." Maude dragged herself in last, hair only half brushed, and poured herself the darkest coffee she could find.

"These pancakes are called poffertjes," Mavis said brightly, sliding a few onto Maude's plate as she shuffled to the table. "Try them."

Maude squinted at the tiny golden discs. "They look like pancakes that didn't grow up right."

"Just eat one," Mavis urged. Maude stabbed one with her fork and took a bite. Her eyebrows rose despite herself. "Well, I'll be. Not bad. Sweet."

"See?" Mavis beamed. "You're already enjoying yourself." Maude muttered something about not going that far, but she didn't put the fork down.

After breakfast, they set out into the crisp air, the city already humming with life. Bicycles whizzed past on every street, their bells ringing like a language of their own. Narrow houses leaned shoulder to shoulder along the canals, their gables cut into fanciful shapes. The water glinted between them, dotted with houseboats. "Oh, look at them!" Mavis clasped her hands as she peered over a bridge. "These houses are like a storybook come to life. Can you imagine waking up every morning with this view?"

"Imagine trying to park a car here," Wilbur muttered, eyeing a particularly narrow street. "I'd rather mow a field than back into one of those spots."

"They don't park cars," Mavis said, exasperated. "They ride bikes."

"Which is why I nearly got run over twice already," he grumbled. They wandered through the Jordaan, a maze of cobbled streets where cafés spilled onto sidewalks and shop windows displayed everything from antiques to handmade jewelry. At a flower stall, Mavis bought a bouquet of tulips so bright they looked painted. "For the room," she explained.

"You know we can't take those home," Maude said.

"They're for now," Mavis replied. "Beauty is worth having, even if it doesn't last."

They paused at a café for coffee. Wilbur ordered a slice of Dutch apple pie, thick with cinnamon and topped with a cloud of whipped cream. One bite and his eyes closed in satisfaction. "Now this," he said, "is worth the plane ticket."

Mavis snapped his picture with the pie, ignoring his protests. "Proof you're enjoying yourself."

Afterward, they joined a line for a canal cruise. The glass-roofed boat slid smoothly along the water, the guide narrating in English and Dutch. Mavis pressed her face to the glass like a child, pointing at every bridge, every houseboat, every flower-boxed balcony. "Look, look, there's one with a little garden on top!" she exclaimed. Maude leaned back in her seat, unimpressed. "Looks like weeds to me. I've got those all over my yard back home." But even she couldn't hide her smile when a family of ducks swam alongside the boat, the ducklings paddling furiously to keep up.

The tour guide explained how the city was built on wooden piles driven into marshy ground, how the canals served as both transportation and defense centuries ago. Maude listened with interest, nodding slowly. "So the whole place is basically floating," she mused. "Explains why all the houses lean like they've had too much to drink."

"They're charmingly crooked, not drunk," Mavis gasped.

After the cruise, they walked to the Anne Frank House. The line wound around the block, and though the wait was long, Mavis insisted they go. Inside, the narrow staircases creaked beneath their feet, the hidden rooms preserved in solemn stillness. The weight of history pressed close, and for once, even Maude had no smart remark. When they emerged back into the daylight, Wilbur exhaled slowly. "Puts a lot of things in perspective," he said.

Mavis squeezed his hand. "Yes. It makes me grateful for every little thing."

They moved on quietly, the bustle of the city slowly lifting their mood again. At a street market, Mavis bought stroopwafels still warm from the griddle, handing one to each of them. The thin waffle cookies, sandwiched with caramel syrup, melted sweetly in their mouths. Maude's eyes widened. "All right, I'll admit it. This is divine."

Wilbur licked a bit of syrup off his finger. "Better than pecan pie, maybe," he chuckled.

"Don't let the folks back home hear you say that," Maude warned.

Later, while Mavis wandered into a shop selling Delft blue pottery, Wilbur strayed down a side street and promptly got himself turned around. When he reappeared twenty minutes later, Maude arched an eyebrow. "Where'd you vanish to?"

"I, uh," Wilbur scratched the back of his neck. "Let's just say I ended up in a part of town where the windows were full of things I don't think they'd sell at Macy's." Maude burst out laughing. "Wilbur! You wandered into the Red Light District, didn't you?" His ears went scarlet. "I didn't know! I was just trying to find the cheese shop you two kept talking about." Mavis nearly dropped her tulip bag from laughing. "Oh, Wilbur, only you could accidentally stroll through the Red Light District in broad daylight."

He grumbled something about needing better signs and stomped off toward the nearest canal, which only made them laugh harder. By late afternoon, they found themselves in Vondelpark, Amsterdam's sprawling green heart. Families picnicked on the grass, cyclists zipped along shaded paths, and children climbed on jungle gyms. They sat on a bench beneath tall trees, tulips resting in Mavis's lap, stroopwafel crumbs still on Maude's jacket.

"This city," Mavis sighed, looking around with shining eyes, "is alive. I could spend a month here and never run out of things to see."

Maude stretched her legs. "A month? I'd need stronger shoes." Wilbur leaned back, watching a dog chase a frisbee across the lawn. "I'll admit, it grows on you. Crooked houses, bike traffic, funny little pancakes; it all kind of fits together."

Chapter Twenty-One

Mavis, Maude, and Wilbur had such a wonderful time in Amsterdam that they almost didn't want to leave. After another restful night and a good cup of coffee with poffertjes the next morning, the trio headed to the airport for their last stop of this epic European vacation. The flight from Amsterdam landed in Dublin under a soft drizzle, the kind of misty rain that made the city look like a watercolor painting. Mavis pressed her forehead to the airplane window, watching the patchwork of green fields stretch toward the horizon. "I heard it's always raining here. It smells different," she said, inhaling deeply as they disembarked. "It smells fresh, damp, and very green."

Maude adjusted her scarf, already mentally cataloging the streets Mavis was about to drag them down. "Adventure smells like rain, apparently. And Guinness," she added with a wink.

Wilbur, lugging the heaviest of their suitcases, grinned. "Well, let's see if Dublin lives up to the hype. If we're lucky, we might even spot a leprechaun or two before lunch."

Mavis' eyes sparkled. "It is on Opal's bucket list, don't you dare forget."

"I would never forget," Wilbur laughed.

"Leprechauns aren't real," Maude sighed while rolling her eyes. "I told her time and again that she would never see one of those jokers. Probably just a kid in a suit with jingles on his feet!"

"We'll see," Wilbur shrugged. "You never know. I'll be sure to keep two eyes out."

The taxi ride into the city gave them their first glimpse of Dublin's charm: red-bricked Georgian houses, narrow streets with bright shop signs, and the occasional pub spilling warm light onto slick cobblestones. Buskers strummed fiddles and sang old Irish ballads as the trio passed, and Mavis couldn't stop grinning. "It's like the city's alive, literally breathing music and stories."

Their hotel was small but cozy, tucked between two older brick buildings. The receptionist greeted them warmly, pointing out a little café around the corner for breakfast. The only problem that arose was that there was only one room available. Somehow the booking had gotten misplaced and Wilbur, Maude, and Mavis would have to share a room. Thankfully, the room had two large beds, but it still wasn't ideal. By the time they dropped off their bags in their room, the rain had lightened to a gentle mist, perfect for wandering.

Mavis grabbed her travel journal. "Okay, first stop: Trinity College. I want to see the Book of Kells. Then, well, everything else," she said, giving Wilbur a conspiratorial look. "You're too organized for your own good," Maude teased, slipping on her raincoat. "Let's just start wandering. The city will tell us where to go."

They walked along the cobblestone streets,

popping into little shops and stopping to peer into bakeries. The smell of fresh soda bread and pastries made their stomachs rumble. "Lunch first," Maude declared, and they ducked into a café painted in cheerful yellow hues. Wilbur chose the potato and leek soup, while Maude decided on the hearty seafood chowder. Mavis couldn't make up her mind, so the waiter brought her a cup of colcannon, a potato and kale soup, along with a cup of Irish vegetable soup. Mavis insisted on trying two slices of soda bread with butter and jam, which she pronounced heavenly.

After lunch, Trinity College loomed ahead, its stone facade regal against the gray sky. They joined the line of tourists, Mavis practically bouncing in place. Inside, the Long Room's towering shelves seemed to stretch forever, and Mavis pressed her hands to her chest in awe. "This is like stepping into a dream," she whispered. Wilbur and Maude shared a quiet smile, enjoying her delight. After soaking in the centuries-old manuscripts, the trio wandered out into the courtyard, where students hurried between buildings. A street musician nearby played a haunting tune on the violin, and Mavis dropped a coin into the open case, her heart swelling. "Opal would have loved this," she murmured.

As the afternoon rolled on, they strolled along Grafton Street, watching performers juggle, dance, and play music for tips. Mavis purchased a bright scarf from a market stall, Wilbur snapped dozens of photos, and Maude insisted they try the famous Dublin chocolate from a tiny shop tucked into an alley. By the time evening settled in, the rain had stopped, leaving the streets glistening. The city lights reflected off the wet cobblestones, turning every puddle into a tiny mirror. Mavis stopped mid-step. "Can we maybe try an Irish pub one night? Just one? I want to soak it all in."

"You've been waiting for that since we booked the trip," Wilbur laughed.

"Then it's settled. One pint, a bit of music, and maybe, just maybe a leprechaun sighting," she teased.

"Let's do that tomorrow," Maude yawned. "I am getting old after all." She grinned at Wilbur who went slightly pink in the ears.

The next morning, Mavis bounded out of bed before anyone else. "Come on! We can't waste a single second. Dublin won't wait for us!" she exclaimed, shaking Maude awake. Wilbur groaned from under the covers. "Can't Dublin wait for an hour?"

Breakfast was a lively affair at a café near their hotel. Mavis insisted on ordering the full Irish breakfast, complete with sausages, rashers, eggs, and a mound of black and white pudding. Maude opted for scrambled eggs on sourdough with a side of rashers, while Wilbur went modest, choosing just eggs and toast. He didn't want to have too much on his stomach while walking for hours on end on the uneven streets.

Fueled and ready, they set off on foot, determined to explore as much as possible. Their first stop was St. Patrick's Cathedral. The stone walls and stained-glass windows left them all momentarily speechless. Mavis traced her fingers along the intricate carvings and whispered, "Opal would've told us every story behind these stones. I bet she could even speak Irish Gaelic."

From there, they wandered to Dublin Castle. The sunlight broke through the clouds in golden patches, casting playful shadows across the courtyard. A group of tourists asked to take a photo with Wilbur, thinking he looked distinguished in his raincoat. He posed reluctantly, muttering about how he'd never been famous for his raincoat before. By midday, hunger struck again. Mavis pulled out her guidebook. "We have to try fish and chips at The Woollen Mills!" she insisted, practically dragging the others across the city. The shop was cozy and bustling, the smell of fried batter mingling with fresh bread. Maude sighed with satisfaction as she took her first bite. "I could eat this every day," she declared, wiping grease from her fingers.

Wilbur bit his tongue and didn't mention the fact that her beloved catfish, Clive, would probably taste just as good as this fish had Mavis allowed him to be battered and fried. Clive was Mavis' pet catfish who had quickly outgrown his aquarium at Magnolia Manor. It had taken Wilbur and his friend half a day to load the fish into the bed of a truck and haul him down to the giant pond on the property. Mavis still wandered down there frequently to feed him his favorite diet of deli meat sandwiches that she lovingly made for him.

After lunch, they wandered through the

Temple Bar area, stopping to admire the colorful doors, street art, and performers juggling everything from flaming torches to hula hoops. Mavis paused in front of a street musician playing the fiddle. She dropped a coin into the case and clapped along to the lively tune, making the musician grin. Wilbur, ever the practical one, pulled out his map. "Okay, we've still got the Guinness Storehouse and Phoenix Park on the list. We should pace ourselves," he announced.

Mavis, undeterred, pointed to a tiny shop tucked in a corner. "Look! A shop selling fairy doors and tiny charms. We have to go in!" Inside, a woman with twinkling eyes greeted them. Mavis and Maude immediately fell in love with a shelf full of miniature houses. "Do you think a leprechaun lives here?" Mavis asked, her eyes wide. The shopkeeper leaned in and whispered, "If you listen closely at night, you just might hear the pitter-patter of little shoes."

Maude rolled her eyes, but even she smiled. "We're officially in the land of magic," she admitted.

As the afternoon stretched on, they visited Kilmainham Gaol, where they walked the historic halls and felt the weight of Ireland's past. Mavis took careful notes in her journal, while Maude and Wilbur listened quietly, moved by the stories of resilience and hope. Evening fell, and it was finally time for the pub. A dimly lit place, tucked down an alley, beckoned with the warm glow of lanterns. Music spilled into the street, fiddle and bodhrán setting a merry rhythm.

They settled into a corner table, clinking pints of Guinness. The first sip made them all sigh with contentment. "This is heaven," Maude said, her voice muffled by the frothy beer mustache she promptly licked away. Mavis leaned in and whispered, "I'm watching for leprechauns."

"Sure, and I'm watching for fairies. Maybe we'll spot a banshee next," Maude snorted.

Just as the laughter settled, a small man in a green vest and cap shuffled toward their table. He was no taller than Mavis's shoulder, his wiry red beard twinkling in the firelight. "Would ye like a riddle or a song, perhaps?" he asked, his accent thick and musical.

Maude's eyes went wide as she spit out her beer. "Mavis! He's real!"

The man winked, tapping his nose, then slid a shiny coin across the table. "Keep this safe. Might bring ye luck," he said, before disappearing as suddenly as he'd appeared.

Mavis picked up the coin and held it close, her eyes misty. "Opal's bucket list, check!"

Maude laughed until tears came. "I don't care if it's magic or Guinness-induced hallucination, I'm believing it." Wilbur chuckled, shaking his head, but the smile on his face betrayed him. "Well, I'll be. A proper leprechaun sighting."

They stayed in the pub for hours listening to stories, tapping along with the music, and sharing moments of quiet reflection about Opal and the adventures they'd had. Laughter and music filled the space, the warmth of friendship and the little pinch of magic settling around them like a soft cloak.

The next morning, Mavis woke to a soft drizzle tapping against the hotel window. She peeked outside, hoping for a last burst of Dublin magic. The streets glistened in the early light, quiet except for a few early risers and the occasional bicycle bell. "Rise and shine," she called, shaking Maude gently. "One last day to soak it all in!"

Breakfast was a cheerful affair over a shared plate of scones, fresh fruit, and steaming cups of tea. Mavis insisted on taking one last walk to the little café they'd discovered the day before, just to savor the smell of fresh bread one final time. Their plan for the day was simple: wander, take photos, and linger over every sight they hadn't yet seen. They strolled along the River Liffey, pausing to watch the swans glide gracefully across the water. Mavis insisted on taking dozens of pictures, directing Wilbur and Maude into awkward, playful poses by the bridges. Next came Merrion Square, the colorful Georgian doors lining the streets like candy wrappers. Mavis paused in front of a bright blue door. "This one's perfect. I can see Opal smiling if she were here." She snapped a photo of the three of them leaning against it, laughing at their silly expressions.

Lunch was at a small, tucked-away bistro where they indulged in hearty bowls of Irish stew. Mavis twirled her fork with flair, declaring, "I could live here on stew alone." Wilbur sampled everything cautiously, muttering, "I could maybe survive on stew, if there's Guinness on the side."

After lunch, they wandered into a quiet park,

where Mavis suddenly crouched down near a patch of clover. "Let's see if we can find one more sign of magic."

Wilbur raised an eyebrow. "A leprechaun sighting already counts, you know."

Mavis ignored him and pointed to a tiny, moss-covered stone that looked almost like a door. "Maybe a tiny friend lives here," she giggled.

"I'll pretend I see it. Magic or not," Maude whispered to Wilbur.

They spent the rest of the afternoon meandering through shops and taking in the streets one last time. Mavis bought a few postcards, Wilbur grabbed a tiny Celtic charm for Emily, and Maude bought chocolate. "You can never have too much chocolate!"

By late afternoon, it was time to return to the hotel, gather their luggage, and take a taxi to the airport. The drive through Dublin felt familiar now, yet fleeting, like a dream they weren't quite ready to leave. At the airport, they checked their bags and lingered by the large windows overlooking the tarmac. Mavis clutched the little leprechaun coin in her hand, turning it over again and again. "I can't believe we did it," she said softly. "We saw everything, ate everything, and laughed so much, all thanks to Opal. She would have loved this." Mavis rested her head on Wilbur's shoulder. "And we did it together. That's what matters most."

"I admit this trip was pretty fantastic. Even with the walking, the rain, and the leprechaun," he smiled.

Mavis laughed, "Especially the leprechaun!"

They watched as planes took off into the gray sky, their reflections mingling with the rain-spattered windows. The magic of Dublin in the cobblestones, the music, the warmth, the little pockets of whimsy lingered around them. "This has been wonderful," Wilbur nodded. "But I'm ready to get back home to Rhinestone. I miss Emily something fierce."

"I have a feeling you'll be back around these parts before you know it. Once Emily retires, y'all will be world travelers," Mavis smiled.

"Retires?" Wilbur chuckled. "I think she's got a few more years before she's willing to let someone else take over. I'm real proud of her, I tell you what. But I admit, I would love to come back here with her one day."

Finally, it was time to board. As they walked toward the gate, Mavis slipped the coin into her journal. "A little piece of magic to bring home," she whispered.

Maude and Wilbur followed, smiling, knowing this trip would live in their hearts forever. Dublin had been the perfect ending to their wild European adventure, a city of music, laughter, and just enough magic to make them believe in leprechauns. As they settled into their seats and the plane began to taxi, Mavis looked out the window one last time, watching the city shrink below them. She exhaled with a contented sigh. "Until next time, Dublin," she whispered.

Chapter Twenty-Two

Wilbur, Maude, and Mavis slept for an entire day once they returned to Rhinestone. Wilbur felt like he would never be able to catch up on the sleep that he missed. "Time wasn't meant to be crossed so much during one trip," he explained to Emily over coffee one morning.

"You better get used to it," Emily laughed. "That old bucket list still has quite a few adventures left on it."

"I'm sitting the next trip out," Wilbur said. "I don't know that I trust those two in Mexico, but I can't get on another plane anytime soon. My back is still trying to sort itself out."

"They'll be crossing off four or so different items on the list though. Are you sure you're ok missing that?" Emily asked. She had missed Wilbur so much during his absence, but she also knew how important honoring Opal was to him.

"I've got a laundry list of things I put off for those two weeks that will just grow longer if I don't start tackling them now," Wilbur nodded. "They aren't leaving til November, but still, it'll take me that long for my body to catch up. I'm getting old," he chuckled. "I missed you too much to go anywhere else right now."

"Bear and I missed you, too! I think you've still

got some good miles left on you," Emily grinned.

Meanwhile at Magnolia Manor, Mavis had never been so grateful for a Friday. The week had felt long, and she'd been looking forward to her evening with Mac like a teenager counting down to homecoming. She smoothed her blouse in the mirror one more time before heading out the door, telling herself she wasn't nervous, just excited. Mac was waiting outside her house, leaning against his car with that relaxed smile she'd come to like so much. He straightened when he saw her, opening the passenger door like a gentleman. "You look beautiful," he said simply.

Mavis felt a flush rise in her cheeks. She wasn't used to compliments like that, not ones that sounded so sincere. "And you look quite handsome yourself. Now where are you taking me this time?" she blushed.

"You'll see," Mac teased, his eyes twinkling. "I wanted something a little different tonight."

The something different turned out to be a small Italian bistro tucked away on a quiet street in Junction. The place had twinkling lights strung across the patio and a faint scent of basil in the air. "Mac," Mavis said as he pulled out her chair, "you didn't have to go all out."

"It's not all out," he said with a grin. "This is just right. Cozy, good food, and no distractions so I can actually look at you across the table without a marching band going by."

She laughed, shaking her head. "You do know how to charm a woman."

They settled into easy conversation. Mac told

her about his latest accounting clients, sprinkling his stories with a self-deprecating humor that always made her laugh. Mavis shared more of her trip to Europe and all of the amazing things they had experienced. By the time their plates arrived, her chicken piccata, his lasagna, they were laughing so much the waiter lingered nearby just to smile at them. After dinner, they shared a tiramisu. Mavis dabbed her fork into the cocoa powder on the plate, then looked up to find Mac watching her with a seriousness that surprised her. "What?" she asked, suddenly self-conscious.

"I like you, Mavis," he said. "I mean, I really like you. You make me laugh. You make me think. And I'd, well, call me old fashioned, but I'd like to meet your family."

Mavis froze, fork halfway to her mouth. Her heart did a little flip; half thrill, half panic. Meeting her family wasn't a casual step. Wilbur could be gruff and protective, especially after her entanglement with Earl. She didn't have any parents for him to meet, but Wilbur, Emily, and Maude were the center of her world. They were her circle, her people, and introducing Mac meant letting him into that particular circle. Mac already knew how much those three meant to her. She had already told Mac all about her parents, half-sisters, and being raised by her grandparents. She had told him how Wilbur had entered her life when she was six years old and how he was the closest person to her. She took a breath, setting her fork down carefully. "That's a big step."

"I know," Mac said gently. "But I think it's

important. They're important to you, so they're important to me." The sincerity in his tone melted her hesitation. She studied his kind eyes, the steady way he held her gaze.

"All right," she said at last, her voice soft but sure. "I'll introduce you. But don't say I didn't warn you. They can be a lot. I've been through a lot, and they know that. I haven't always made the best decisions."

"I'm ready. Not a worry in the world over here. I can take it," Mac smiled.

"Ha!" Mavis laughed, shaking her head. "You just wait, Mac. You just wait."

After dinner, he drove her home, the evening air soft and fragrant with honeysuckle. They lingered at her porch, neither in a hurry to end the night. "You sure about this?" Mavis asked one more time, teasing but a little nervous still.

"Absolutely," Mac said. "I want to know them, Mavis. I want them to know me." Mavis smiled and went to hug his neck, but he kissed her goodnight instead. His lips were soft and gentle. Mavis thought maybe, just maybe, she'd been waiting her whole life for someone like him.

The next morning, Mavis sat at Emily's kitchen table with a mug of tea clasped in her hands. She'd barely slept at all. She kept tossing and turning; Mac's request had played over and over in her mind like a record on repeat. Finally, she decided to confide in her sister-in-law first. Emily was steady, sensible, and, most importantly, far less intimidating than Wilbur.

"So," Mavis began, stirring her tea though she

hadn't added sugar. "Mac asked if he could meet the family."

Emily's face lit up instantly. "Oh, Mavis, that's wonderful!"

"Is it?" Mavis chewed her lip. "It feels like a big step."

"It is a big step," Emily agreed, reaching across the table to squeeze her hand. "But it's the right step. You wouldn't even be considering it if you didn't feel serious about him."

Mavis gave a small, guilty smile. "I do like him. A lot."

Emily laughed. "I've seen the way you come back from your dates grinning like a schoolgirl. Don't think you've been subtle." Mavis swatted her with the dish towel, but her blush betrayed her.

Just then, Wilbur ambled in, drawn by the smell of coffee. He poured himself a cup and raised a brow at the two of them. "What's going on? You two look like cats who swallowed the canary."

Emily opened her mouth to answer, but Mavis jumped in. "Nothing! Just, just talking."

Wilbur took a long sip, unimpressed. "Talking, huh? The kind of talking that has you blushing like you're sixteen again? Oh Lord, I can't go through that again," he chuckled.

"Fine. If you must know, Mac wants to meet you all," Mavis groaned.

The mug paused halfway to Wilbur's lips. His eyes narrowed and he faked a pretty good impression of an Italian mobster. "Mac. Wants to meet. The family."

"Yes," Mavis said firmly, though her palms were damp.

Wilbur set the mug down and pursed his lips. "Well, I suppose that means I'll have to sharpen my questions," he shrugged.

"Questions?" Mavis stammered.

"Of course," he said, crossing his arms. "Man wants to court my sister, he's going to answer for it. What's his credit score? Does he pay his taxes on time? Does he know the difference between a socket wrench and a crescent wrench?"

Mavis rolled her eyes. "Wilbur, he's an accountant. I think he's got the taxes covered."

"All the more reason to make sure he's not creative with numbers," Wilbur shot back.

Emily smothered a laugh behind her hand and shook her head. "It'll be fine, Mavis. Wilbur will be on his best behavior."

Later that afternoon, Maude dropped by Magnolia Manor. She didn't bother to wait for Mavis to open the door; she had her own key. "What's this about an inquisition tomorrow evening?" she asked, lowering herself into a chair in Mavis' kitchen.

"Not an inquisition," Mavis said quickly. "Just dinner. I'm introducing Mackenzie to everyone." She wasn't sure why she had said his full first name, but it felt right to start on a more professional level with Maude. She had thought that Wilbur would be the tough one, but something in Maude's tone said otherwise.

"Well, well. I was beginning to think you were hiding him out of shame," Maude said matter-offactly.

"I was not hiding him!" Mavis blushed.

"Oh, don't get yourself in a twist," Maude said, waving a hand. "If the man has any sense, he'll find us charming. If he doesn't, well, better we scare him off now before you waste more lipstick."

"Oh God," Mavis muttered.

Mavis awoke the following morning in a flutter. She had planned to make beef pot roast, rice, roasted carrots, and dinner rolls. Emily volunteered to bring the dessert, her grandmother's homemade apple cobbler. Maude had volunteered to bring the ice cream. It was shaping up to be a good evening. After stressing out for over an hour about what to wear, Mavis settled on black jeans and a Halloween sweater. Halloween was at the end of the month and it was one of her favorite holidays. Emily and Wilbur arrived promptly at five o'clock. Mac was set to arrive around six, which gave Emily some time to try and settle Mavis' nerves.

"Wilbur has promised to be good," Emily assured her. "Right, Wil?"

"Sure, sure," Wilbur nodded with a twinkle in his eye. "As long as he answers correctly, everything should be fine. As long as he's not Earl's clone, I'll be fine."

Mavis blushed and shook her head defiantly. "Not at all similar. No worries there." There was a sudden abrupt knock on the door and Mavis gasped. "Oh my, he's early. The food's not ready."

"Unless Maude picked him up on the way, I don't think he's here," Wilbur said as he walked towards the front door.

"Why is Maude knocking? She usually just blows on in," Emily laughed. Wilbur shrugged and hurried to open the door. Maude had her hands full of bags and photo albums that were stacked higher than her head. Wilbur grabbed the stack of books and held the door as Maude ambled in.

"What in the world is all that?" Mavis asked. Her eyes had grown to the size of saucers.

"History," Maude explained. "And ice cream. I brought enough for us all."

Emily carefully put the four gallons of ice cream in Ruby's old deep freezer in the mud room. Maude had made sure that no one would go without vanilla, chocolate, or butter pecan ice cream tonight.

Wilbur set the table and watched as Maude shuffled over to the stove to check on Emily's cobbler that was wrapped in foil. It was still warm to the touch. "How does the living room look? I don't want anything to look too messy," Mavis fretted.

"You know what's not messy? A background check!" Wilbur announced.

"Wilbur!" Mavis groaned.

"You know, I think I'm going to enjoy this dinner immensely," Maude smirked. She joined Emily and Wilbur at the table and together they waited for the guest of honor to arrive.

As the grandfather clock in the front foyer struck six o'clock, Mavis gulped. A car had appeared in the driveway. Mac arrived right on time, holding a bouquet of bright daisies. Mavis' heart leapt at the sight of him. "You didn't have to bring anything," she said, smiling as she opened the front door.

"I wanted to," he replied warmly, handing the flowers to her.

"So this is the fellow," Wilbur said, voice low as Mavis led Mac into the kitchen, "who thinks he can date my sister."

Mac straightened. "Yes, sir, I'm Mac. I've heard a lot about you." He shook Wilbur's hand and grinned broadly.

"And you'll hear more," Wilbur replied, narrowing his eyes in mock suspicion. "Do you work hard? Pay your taxes? Know the difference between a crescent wrench and..."

"Wilbur," Mavis interjected sharply, "he's an accountant. He pays taxes and can tinker with tools. Now hush." Wilbur returned Mac's grin and sat down next to his wife at the table.

Emily greeted him with her warm, easy smile. "Welcome. So nice to finally meet you."

"Thank you," Mac said politely, giving her a small bow. "And please, call me Mac."

"Mac? Like a Big Mac from McDonalds?" Maude huffed. She shook her head. "I ain't calling him Big Mac. That sounds inappropriate."

Mac burst into a fit of laughter. "I like her!" he howled.

"You like me? There's your first mistake. I'm too old for you and you're with Mavis. That ain't right. I ain't into that weird stuff some of y'all kids do. I watch the television. I know what's going on," Maude grumbled. Mavis turned a deep shade of red and shook her head. Mac roared in laughter. "Oh Mavis, honey you didn't do her justice in your telling me about her. She is hilarious."

"Well, I am that," Maude nodded.

Emily chuckled. "See, Mavis? Even Maude approves."

"Approve is a strong word," Maude said dryly. "But I'm curious, and that's worth something."

"That sounds like a point in my favor," Mac winked at Mavis.

"Let's hope he's as charming as he looks. Or at least has the stamina to endure us," Maude shrugged.

Mac chuckled, nodding politely. "I'm up for the challenge."

Dinner began with polite conversation. Emily asked about his work and family, which he answered with care and good humor. Mavis relaxed a little as she saw him engage naturally, laughing at Emily's gentle teasing about office life. Wilbur started with light-hearted questions, then gradually edged into more pointed territory. "So, Mac, do you have a plan for taking care of Mavis? You know, down the line?"

Mac smiled without hesitation. "I want to be someone she can count on. I want to make her life easier, happier, and full of laughter."

Wilbur leaned back, scrutinizing him for a beat. "Hmm. Bold words."

"I mean every word," Mac said steadily.

Mavis blinked at him, touched by his sincerity. She hadn't expected a line like that in the middle of Wilbur's interrogation.

"Not bad. Not bad at all. Maybe there's hope for him yet," Maude snorted.

By dessert, everyone was laughing freely. Mac had survived Wilbur's questioning, Maude's pointed jokes, and even Emily's gentle prodding. Mavis dished out the apple cobbler and Wilbur ladened scoops of vanilla ice cream on top of each portion. "Thanks, Wilbur," Mac nodded. "I can see why Mavis speaks to highly of you, highly of you all. Thank you for agreeing to meet me."

Wilbur, pretending to scrutinize, actually gave a subtle nod. "You're acceptable," he muttered.

Mavis nearly choked on her laughter. Maude clapped Mac on the back. "Congratulations, son. You survived the family gauntlet. That's an achievement."

After dinner, Mac helped clear the table and then excused himself to the restroom. Mavis showed him the half bathroom off the kitchen and joined her family in the living room. Wilbur finally admitted, with a rare softening, "He's all right. Seems steady. Not bad for someone dating my sister."

Maude grinned. "I told you. He's got potential. Let's hope he's not perfect, wouldn't want to scare anyone off." She shushed them all as Mac walked into the living room and joined Mavis on the couch. "Well, I must be going," Maude announced. "Wilbur, Emily? Y'all can help me to my car and we'll leave these two to talk all about how wonderful we are."

Mac stood up and shook Wilbur's hand again. He hugged Maude and Emily and watched as

Mavis held the front door open for them to leave. When they were gone, Mavis returned to the living room and leaned against Mac on the couch. "I'm glad you met them," she said quietly.

"I'm glad, too," he said, squeezing her hand. "Your family's a reflection of you. And I like them all, which means I like you even more."

Chapter Twenty-Three

The air at Magnolia Manor carried that unmistakable October sharpness, cool enough to make Mavis pull her sweater a little tighter as she led Mac across the front lawn. Leaves swirled down from the oaks in russet and gold, gathering against the fence posts. A pumpkin sat on nearly every step along the front porch. She had gotten a good deal on them down at the Piggly Wiggly. "It's always prettiest here in the fall," Mavis said, glancing back at him. "Everything feels alive, even when it's about to sleep."

Mac smiled, his hands tucked in his jacket pockets. "It feels like one of those picture-perfect postcards. All you need is a scarecrow and a wagon of hay."

"I love a fall hayride!" Mavis agreed, laughing. "It's been a while since I've been on one. I remember going to the corn mazes as a kid and trick-or-treating downtown. I still love Halloween so much." She motioned for him to follow. "Come on. I want you to meet someone special."

She took him toward the pond, its surface glinting in the afternoon light. A few ducks floated lazily, quacking at one another, but it wasn't them Mavis was after. She knelt at the bank, rapped her knuckles on the small wooden dock, and gave a sharp whistle. At first, nothing stirred. Then a dark shadow rose from the depths, slow but deliberate, until a broad whiskered head broke the surface. Mac stepped back. "Good Lord! That thing's the size of a small whale."

"Mac, meet Clive," Mavis beamed.

"Clive?" Mac coughed.

"My catfish," she said proudly. "Wilbur caught him a few years ago and I just couldn't pass him up. He's so beautiful, and boy is he smart! Wilbur near about threw a fit when I refused to let him fry Clivey up." She crouched closer, remembering. "He was flopping around in the bucket, fighting for his life, and something in me just couldn't stand the thought of eating him. So I dumped him into the aquarium in the dining room, Big Mama's aquarium. Floor-to-ceiling, filled with tropical fish."

Mac raised an eyebrow. "Let me guess. Clive didn't exactly get along with his new neighbors?"

"Not a one of them survived," Mavis sighed. "He ate them all and grew so big Wilbur had to lug him down here. He's been king of the pond ever since."

Clive gurgled, opening his cavernous mouth as if to say hello. Mac crouched beside her, shaking his head in disbelief. "You've got a catfish for a pet. And here I thought the llamas and barn cats were eccentric."

"Speaking of," Mavis smiled and stood, brushing her hands on her jeans. "Let me show you the rest."

The barn was only a short walk from the pond

close to the Manor, its doors thrown wide. The scent of hay and dust filled the air. As soon as they entered, two solid black cats slinked out from the shadows. "This is Shadow, and this is Onyx," Mavis grinned. Shadow wove his way in between Mac's legs, but Onyx hissed and ran away. "They keep the barn mouse-free," Mavis explained. "Shadow is just such a love!"

Mac bent down, scratching behind the purring cat's ears. "Guess he likes a man who knows tax forms and spreadsheets."

From the pasture behind the barn came a trio of hums and snorts. Winnie, Clementine, and Morgan, the llamas, ambled to the fence. Clem nudged her nose against the rails, Morgan chewed lazily, and Winnie flicked her ears with suspicion. "I'm so glad I rescued them after the fair's petting zoo shut down," Mavis said. "They were going to be auctioned off, and I couldn't let them go to just anybody. They've been here ever since."

Mac reached out a tentative hand, stroking Clem's thick coat. "You've got llamas, barn cats, and a giant catfish. You're like the Noah's Ark of the county."

"Don't tempt me. If a kangaroo ever shows up on the courthouse steps, I might just bring it home," Mavis giggled. They lingered at the fence, the llamas snuffling curiously, while the late afternoon sun dipped lower. The talk shifted naturally toward the season.

"So," Mac asked, "what are your Halloween plans?"

Mavis's eyes twinkled. "Last year we all went

over and handed out candy with Opal. I didn't know it would be our last time. Emily and Wilbur are going to a Halloween party at Emily's office. She's got him dressing up like some superhero and she's being one, too. I can't keep all those heroes straight anymore. I don't want Maude to be alone, so I'll just go over and hand out candy with her, I think. What about you?"

"I was thinking you and I could dress up and maybe go to a Halloween event. Maybe one with a hayride, a corn maze, and a silly haunted house. We could even bring Maude with us. I know those festivals have the best food," Mac explained.

"Oh, Mac! That's a wonderful idea. I don't know that Maude will do a haunted house, but everything else is up her alley. You sure you don't mind? We could always go another day and be with her on Halloween or?" Mavis began.

"I like your family, Mavis," Mac said gently. "They make you happy and that makes me happy. Why don't you call her up and see if she's agreeable, and if so, I'll pick you both up on Halloween and we'll go to dinner, the festival, and have a good old time."

"What do we dress up as?" Mavis exclaimed.

"What are you thinking?" he asked. He was game for any crazy idea she came up with.

She tilted her head thoughtfully. "Maybe something bold. Cleopatra, perhaps."

Mac smiled. "Then I suppose I'll have to be Caesar. Or at least bring the toga." They walked back toward the house, laughter between them like leaves caught on the wind.

Across the property, at the edge of the woods, Wilbur was working steadily behind his cabin. His hammer struck rhythmically, the beginnings of a new screened-in porch taking shape against the back wall. Sawdust clung to his shirt and the brim of his cap, but he welcomed the mess. He paused, looking past the porch frame toward the clearing where he had staked out a rectangle of ground. That space would hold the greenhouse. He could already picture the glass panes glinting in the sun, and the rows of benches inside lined with Opal's plants. Her ferns. Her orchids. The potted rosemary she'd tended with such care. "Don't worry, Opal," he murmured, wiping his brow. "They'll have a good home." The thought steadied him. Building wasn't just work, it was a way to keep her close. Every board nailed down, every joint fitted, felt like stitching her memory into the walls around him. As the last light slipped through the trees, he set his hammer aside and stood back to survey the porch's skeleton frame. It wasn't much yet, but it was something to hold onto. And in the distance, drifting faintly across the fields, came Mavis's unbridled laughter. Wilbur smiled to himself, then got back to work.

One week later, Emily sent Mavis a photo of her and Wilbur dressed as superheroes at her office Halloween party. Mavis laughed at how happy Wilbur looked in his blue spandex suit with a matching Emily next to him. She had been thrilled when Wilbur began dating Emily and subsequently married her. He deserved all the happiness in the world and she was so happy he had found it in Emily who quickly became one of her own best friends, along with Mona.

Mavis smiled at her reflection in the mirror. She had invited Mona to come along with them to the festival, but she had plans with Harry, Tamara, and a man she had started seeing casually. They were going to an all-night Halloween horror movie showing in Montgomery. Mavis wasn't quite up for that, but the two promised to get together soon. Mavis adjusted the golden headpiece nestled in her hair and took a step back from the mirror in the hallway. Her Cleopatra costume shimmered in the light, the white gown cinched with a beaded belt, gold bangles stacked on her wrists, and eyeliner dramatic enough to stop traffic. Outside, the crunch of tires on gravel drew her to the window. A moment later, Mac appeared on the porch, wearing a white toga that looked suspiciously like a sheet stolen off his bed. His makeshift laurel wreath sat crooked on his head, one leaf dangling in front of his eye. Mavis burst out laughing as she opened the door. "Caesar, you look like you robbed a linen closet," she giggled.

Mac tugged the wreath straight and gave a dramatic bow. "All hail Cleopatra, ruler of the Manor. I come bearing my chariot."

"You look ridiculous," Mavis grinned, sweeping her arm like royalty. "But I approve."

He eyed her up and down, not even pretending to hide his admiration. "You don't look ridiculous at all. You look dangerous. Rome doesn't stand a chance."

Mavis flushed, but she tossed her hair like a

queen would. "Good answer."

They linked arms and headed toward the truck, Cleopatra's train trailing in the gravel. "Now," Mac said as he opened her door, "we just have to pick up Maude."

Maude's house was decorated with a modest string of orange lights across the porch railing and a plastic skeleton that looked more tired than frightening. When she opened the door, the sight of her nearly undid both Mavis and Mac. She wore jeans, comfortable sneakers, and a black sweater with a bright orange pumpkin stitched across the chest; no makeup, no hat, no accessories, just the pumpkin signifying it was Halloween. "This is as festive as I get," she announced, hands on hips. "And don't you dare try to make me into some Cleopatra sidekick. I'm here for food and people-watching, and that's it."

Mavis bit her lip, trying not to laugh. "It's perfect. You're the Pumpkin Queen."

"Pumpkin Queen, my foot!" Maude snatched her handbag off the hall table and stepped onto the porch. "If anyone asks, I'm dressed as a woman with good sense."

Mac, valiantly keeping a straight face, gave a courtly bow. "Your Majesty, Pumpkin Queen, your chariot awaits."

"Don't butter me up, Caesar," Maude said, though a smile tugged at her lips as she climbed into the truck. "You two look like you fell out of a costume catalog. I look like I fell out of the clearance rack at Walmart." As Mac started the truck and pointed it toward Junction, Mavis leaned back with a grin. The night was just getting started, and already Maude was in rare form.

The Junction Pizza Parlor was the kind of place that always smelled like melted cheese and garlic bread sticks, but on Halloween night, it had taken on a whole new life. Orange and purple string lights crisscrossed the ceiling, fake cobwebs dangled in every corner, and the servers wore plastic vampire teeth that made their speech sound garbled. Mac held the door for the ladies, Cleopatra sweeping in with regal poise while the Pumpkin Queen marched in like she was on a mission. The hostess, a teenager in cat ears, gave them a wide-eyed grin. "Uh, table for three?" she asked.

"Yes, darling," Maude said, patting the girl's arm. "Somewhere I don't have to hear sticky-fingered children shrieking."

They were led to a red vinyl booth near the back. The place buzzed with families in costumes. Tiny princesses ran between tables, a gaggle of teenage boys dressed as rock stars wolfed down breadsticks, and a couple in their seventies were decked out as Frankenstein's monster and his Bride. Mac slid in on one side of the booth, Mavis beside him, while Maude claimed the opposite seat, her handbag plopped in front of her like a shield. "Alright," she said, flipping open the menu. "Let's get this over with."

The waitress appeared, a cheerful girl dressed as a witch. Her hat flopped to the side every time she moved. "Happy Halloween! What can I get y'all started with?"

"Large pepperoni," Mac said eagerly. "And

whatever else these two queens want."

Maude pointed her straw at him like it was a weapon. "Smart man. He's learning."

"Let's add an order of garlic bread and a salad for the table," Mavis smiled.

The waitress jotted it down with a laugh. "Anything to drink?"

"Sweet tea for me," Mavis said.

"Root beer," Mac added.

"Coffee. Black as night," Maude said.

Their drinks arrived quickly, clinking onto the table. The sweet tea was ice cold, the root beer foamy, and Maude's coffee steamed like a cauldron. "Now that's more like it," Maude said, taking a long sip. The server set the salad down with bowls for each of them. "Pizza's being made and your garlic bread will be just a few more minutes."

While they waited for the pizza and bread, Mavis people-watched with delight. A toddler dressed as a tiny Dracula toddled passed by and tripped over his cape, rescued at the last second by his mom. A group of high schoolers in matching skeleton onesies attempted to balance breadsticks on their noses. Mac nudged her shoulder. "You're grinning like a kid."

"It's Halloween," she said. "It's the one night you can be anyone you want."

"Yeah?" Mac tilted his head. "And you wanted to be Cleopatra?"

"Obviously. Who doesn't want to rule Egypt for a night?" Mavis smirked playfully.

Just then the pizza arrived, steaming and glorious. Maude wasted no time. She slid two slices onto her plate, and dug in. "Now this," she declared with her mouth full, "is why I came."

The meal was loud, messy, and perfect. Maude kept up a steady commentary about the costumes around them while Mac and Mavis tried not to choke on their laughter. By the time the check came, Maude leaned back with a satisfied sigh. "Alright, I'm full enough to tolerate a festival. But if someone hands me a caramel apple, I'm not responsible for the dental bill."

Mac slid out of the booth and offered his hand to Mavis. "Ready, Queen of the Nile?"

She slipped her hand into his, smiling. "Lead the way, Caesar."

Maude grabbed her handbag and stood. "And the Pumpkin Queen follows behind, wondering how she got roped into this nonsense."

The three of them stepped out into the crisp October night, the sounds of the Junction Halloween Festival drifting across the square. The Junction town square looked like it had been plucked straight out of a Halloween postcard. Strings of orange bulbs looped between lampposts, every shop window painted with ghosts and bats, and the smell of kettle corn, funnel cakes, and fried dough floating on the crisp October air. A local bluegrass band played near the courthouse steps, their fiddles and banjos competing with the squeals of kids darting from booth to booth. Mac parked along the side street and the trio joined the flow of festival-goers. Mavis' Cleopatra gown shimmered under the streetlights as she clutched her golden train in one hand. Maude, sweater pumpkin bright against the crowd, trudged behind them like a woman resigned to her fate. "Smells like heaven," Maude announced, inhaling deeply.

"Corn maze," Mac said, nodding toward a field on the edge of the square where towering stalks of corn loomed. A hand-painted sign read 'Enter if You Dare!' in dripping red letters.

Maude squinted at it. "That doesn't say corn maze. That says emergency room."

"Come on," Mavis teased, tugging Maude's hand. "You'll love it."

"I'll tolerate it," Maude corrected, but she followed anyway.

At the maze entrance, a teenage boy in zombie makeup handed them a wrinkled map. "Good luck finding your way out," he said in his best spooky voice.

Maude snatched the paper. "If I get lost in here, young man, I'm suing."

Mac led the way down the first path, confidently turning left, then right, then left again. "It's all about strategy," he declared.

"Strategy, huh?" Mavis said, eyeing him. "Or wild guessing?"

"Instinct," he said, puffing out his chest.

Ten minutes later, they hit their third dead end. "Your instinct is broken," Maude announced, arms crossed.

"Just warming up," Mac insisted, spinning on his heel.

As they retraced their steps, a group of kids in werewolf masks jumped out from behind the stalks with a chorus of howls. Mavis shrieked and laughed, clutching Mac's toga sleeve. Maude, however, didn't flinch. She peered over her glasses at the kids and said flatly, "If you scare me, I drop my coffee on you." The boys snickered and scampered away. "See?" Maude said. "They know better than to mess with the Pumpkin Queen."

Mac tried another turn, swore under his breath when it led to another dead end, and finally gave in to checking the map. "Looks like we need to backtrack two rows," he admitted.

"Told you," Maude said smugly. "Women always end up doing the navigation. Cleopatra, give him the map." Mavis giggled and took it. "Fine, but if we wander in circles all night, you're buying me a caramel apple."

They pressed deeper into the maze. The corn rustled like whispers all around them, the air cool against their cheeks. At one point, Mac tripped on a stray root and nearly went down face-first into the dirt.

"Caesar down!" Mavis gasped.

He righted himself quickly, brushing off his toga. "Didn't see that."

"Oh, we saw it," Maude said, dry as bone.

When they finally stumbled out of the exit nearly forty minutes later, Mavis threw her arms up like she'd won a marathon. "Victory!"

Mac wiped his brow dramatically. "We conquered the maze," he wheezed.

Maude followed behind, unimpressed. "If that's conquering, I'd hate to see losing." She glanced back at the rows of corn. "I should've stayed out here with the kettle corn booth. At least they don't get lost." Mavis looped her arm through hers. "Admit it. You had fun."

"I admit nothing," Maude replied, but her mouth twitched at the corners as they rejoined the glow of the festival lights.

By the time they spotted the wagon at the edge of the wooded square, the night had grown sharper, the moon bright against a sweep of stars. A tractor idled near a line of hay bales stacked on a wooden wagon, the smell of cut straw strong enough to make Maude wrinkle her nose. "Lovely," she muttered. "I always dreamed of spending my golden years sitting on itchy hay that smells like barn animals."

Mavis nudged her. "It's tradition! You can't have Halloween without a hayride."

"You absolutely can. In fact, most sensible people do," Maude countered.

Mac offered his hand to help both women up. The wagon was already half-full of kids in costumes bouncing with excitement, teenagers clutching glow sticks, and a couple of parents sipping cider from Styrofoam cups. Mavis perched primly on a bale, careful of her gown. Maude plopped down beside her with a grunt, handbag in her lap like it was going to protect her from whatever lay ahead. The tractor gave a low rumble and lurched forward, pulling them along a dirt path that wound past the pumpkin patch and into the woods. At first, it was peaceful. The night air was crisp, crickets chirped, and a few leaves drifted down like confetti. "This isn't so bad," Maude admitted grudgingly. "Cool breeze, stars overhead. Could almost enjoy this if not for the hay poking my rear end."

A bloodcurdling scream split the air. Half the wagon jumped. Mavis grabbed Mac's arm and Maude let out a holler that could've woken the dead. "What in the hell!" she sputtered, clutching her chest. From the trees burst a man in a hockey mask revving a chainsaw. Sparks flew as the motor rattled. Kids squealed, parents laughed nervously. "Sweet mother of Moses!" Maude cried, scrambling to her feet. "They're trying to kill us!"

"Maude, sit down!" Mavis hissed, tugging at her arm.

But Maude wasn't hearing it. When another figure draped in a torn cloak and wielding a plastic axe lunged out of the shadows, she shrieked again and hurled her handbag at him with surprising force. "Back off, you creep!"

The actor staggered, doubled over in laughter under his mask and handed Maude her purse back. The rest of the wagon erupted too, the kids howling with delight and the teenagers cheered. Mavis was torn between mortification and hysterics. "Better him than me!" Maude snapped, pointing a trembling finger at the cornfield. "You didn't tell me this was haunted!"

"It's Halloween!" Mavis squeaked, laughing so hard tears streamed down her face.

The tractor chugged on, deeper into the woods. More actors appeared as ghosts darting from behind trees, a vampire leapt onto the wagon's railing, and a werewolf crawled out of the brush howling. Each time, Maude screamed, swatted, or tried to fend them off with whatever she could reach. At one point she ripped a piece of hay from the bale and waved it like a sword. "Don't come any closer! I've had a flu shot and I know how to use it!"

Mac nearly fell off the bale, wheezing with laughter. "Maude, they're actors!"

"They're lunatics!" she retorted, batting away a rubber spider dangled in her face. "Somebody call the sheriff!"

By the time the ride looped back toward the pumpkin patch, Maude's hair was sticking up, her sweater stretched crooked, and her face the color of boiled beets. When the tractor finally came to a stop, she all but leapt off the wagon, brushing hay from her jeans with violent swipes. "This," she declared, planting her hands on her hips, "is exactly why I stay home and hand out candy. No chainsaws. No maniacs. Just me, a bowl of Snickers, and peace."

As the three of them walked back toward the glowing square, the music and laughter of the festival washing over them again, Maude shook her head but couldn't quite hide the smile tugging at her face. The streets were quieter as they left Junction behind, the glow of the festival fading in the rear view mirror. Mavis reclined in the passenger seat, Cleopatra's train draped across her lap, while Mac drove with one hand on the wheel. "You two are insane," Maude said, shaking her head. "Absolutely insane. But somehow, somehow it was fun."

Mavis grinned broadly, "See? That's the

Halloween spirit."

"Spirit? I'm haunted," Maude corrected, though her eyes sparkled. "You two dragged me through a horror movie, and now I'm the comedic relief."

Mac glanced at her in the rear view mirror. "Oh, it's very fair. You made the night unforgettable."

Mavis leaned behind her and took Maude's hand. "You were amazing. Honestly, it wouldn't have been the same without the Pumpkin Queen leading the charge."

Maude squeezed her hand, pretending to scowl but unable to hide the grin tugging at her lips. "I'll allow it," she said. "But only because you promised pizza next time, and no haunted anything."

Mavis laughed. "Deal. Next year, something tamer. Maybe just a haunted movie marathon. We'll wear matching pajamas."

"Matching pajamas," Maude repeated, smirking. "We'll see what all happens in a year."

Chapter Twenty-Four

Mavis relished in the fun from Halloween all week. She recounted Maude's pure terror and fight or flight from the haunted hayride with vigor to Emily and Wilbur the next night over cake and coffee at a cafe in town. Mac rushed in after they had already been served, apologizing for running late. He sat down in the empty seat next to Mavis and kissed her cheek. "I hope I didn't miss all the fun!"

"Oh, Mavis was just telling us how Maude almost got kicked out of the festival," Emily chuckled. "I hope she's better behaved in Texas next week."

Talk soon turned to Mavis' upcoming trip to Texas and Mexico to continue the bucket list adventure with Maude. It would just be the two of them this time, which made Wilbur and Emily both worry inwardly. "Oh, Maude's a character, that's for sure," Mac laughed. "I can't wait to hear all about this adventure!"

The plane wheels touched down in San Antonio four days later with a soft bump that made Maude grip the armrest until her knuckles whitened. Mavis, on the other hand, was already craning her neck to peer out the window, her face lit with the glow of anticipation. She had found the best deal on round trip tickets from Montgomery to San Antonio and back for their quick trip.

"Well, we made it, Maude," she said brightly. "Texas! Home of big hair, bigger hats, and a big slice of history."

Maude released her death grip on the armrest and gave her friend a look. "I'm eighty-five, not dead. I know what the Alamo is. Davy Crockett, Jim Bowie, and all those boys. They taught it all back in school."

"Yes, but now you'll see it with your own eyes." Mavis patted her arm.

By the time they checked into their modest downtown hotel and had a quick rest, the sun was beginning to slant low in the sky. The Alamo was only a short walk away, and Mavis insisted they take the scenic route. The plaza outside the Alamo buzzed with the energy of tourists snapping photos, children with ice cream dripping down their hands, and a mariachi band playing on the corner. The limestone mission stood quietly amid it all, its worn façade glowing golden in the evening light. "There it is," Mavis whispered reverently.

Inside, the cool stone walls seemed to hush the outside noise. They joined a guided tour, the young ranger leading them through stories of the famous battle. Mavis leaned forward, hanging on every word, her eyes sparkling like a schoolgirl at story time. When the ranger described the final stand of the defenders, even Maude felt her chest tighten. She glanced sideways at Mavis, who had tears shimmering in her eyes. "History breathes here," Mavis whispered.

"History's a bit stuffy," Maude whispered back, but she squeezed Mavis's hand.

A group of schoolchildren passed by, their teacher urging them to pay attention. One little girl tugged at Maude's sleeve. "Were you alive back then?" she asked innocently.

Maude's eyebrows shot up, but Mavis snorted so loudly she had to cover her mouth. "Not quite, sugar," Maude replied dryly. When the tour ended, the two women stepped back out into the twilight. The plaza was still lively, lanterns beginning to glow along the River Walk just a few blocks away. "I think Opal would've liked it," Maude said quietly.

"I know she would have." Mavis pulled the folded bucket list from her purse, the paper creased and soft from being handled so often. "One down, three to go."

The River Walk awaited them, winding along the San Antonio River with strings of lights twinkling above. They chose a restaurant with outdoor seating, the sound of laughter and mariachi music spilling through the air. A waitress brought baskets of warm chips and salsa, and Mavis ordered chicken enchiladas. "You're not going to try Tex-Mex?" she asked when Maude requested something simple like grilled chicken.

"Not yet," Maude said. "We're saving our tamale moment for Mexico. You'll thank me later when you're not rolling yourself back to the hotel."

Mavis only laughed, already scooping salsa onto a chip. "Suit yourself. But I'm eating like I'm making up for lost time."

The riverboats glided past, their passengers waving as though everyone along the banks were old friends. Maude leaned back in her chair, letting the hum of the city wash over her. For all her complaints, she had to admit it was nice. "You know," she said, after a while, "that ranger did a fine job. It made me feel like I was right there in the middle of it all. I almost wanted to pick up a musket myself."

"If you had, you'd have bossed everyone into line and won the battle outright," Mavis laughed.

"That's probably true," Maude smirked, then grew thoughtful. "It's funny, isn't it? How something that happened so long ago can still make your heart beat a little faster."

"That's the point," Mavis said softly. "That's why we're here." They clinked their glasses of iced tea together. Across the river, the mariachi struck up another tune, lively and bright.

The next morning, Maude shuffled into the hotel lobby clutching her travel mug of coffee like it was holy water. Mavis, of course, was already waiting by the front doors, sunhat perched on her head, guidebook tucked under her arm, and an energy level Maude couldn't decide whether it was inspiring or exhausting. "Rise and shine, Maude! Today we stand beneath a waterfall!" Mavis announced, earning a few curious looks from other guests.

"At my age, I stand beneath a shower and that's excitement enough," Maude muttered.

Mavis ignored the grumble and shepherded

Maude toward the rental car. "I found just the place, Hamilton Pool Preserve. It's not too far, and there's a gentle trail down. Nothing you can't handle. Trust me," Mavis said, starting the car with more confidence than she usually had when driving in big cities. "This one's worth it."

The drive out of San Antonio unfolded like a quilt of rolling fields, scrubby oaks, and limestone bluffs. Maude dozed in the passenger seat, waking only when Mavis let out little gasps of delight at the scenery. When they arrived at the preserve, the ranger at the entrance handed them a map and warned about the steep steps down to the pool. Maude narrowed her eyes at Mavis. "Steep steps?"

"Details, details," Mavis said breezily, grabbing her walking stick from the trunk. "We'll go slow."

Slow turned out to be the operative word. The stone path wound downward through cedar trees, sunlight dappling the ground. Every few minutes, Maude stopped to catch her breath, pretending she was admiring the scenery. "You all right?" Mavis asked, steadying her elbow.

"I'm fine. Just making sure I don't miss anything. You never know when you'll see a squirrel worth remembering," Maude heaved.

At last, the path opened into a breathtaking sight: a jade-green pool nestled beneath a limestone overhang, with a waterfall spilling in a sparkling curtain from above. The sound of rushing water filled the air, mingling with the chatter of families already wading at the edges. Mavis gasped, clasping her hands together. "Oh, Maude, look! Isn't it magnificent?"

Maude's eyes softened. She'd seen her share of pretty places in her long life, but something about the way the sunlight danced in the spray and the way the cliff curved protectively overhead struck her as magnificent. "Well," she said slowly, "I suppose it's not bad."

They found a spot where the rocks were flat enough to sit and remove their shoes. Mavis tugged hers off eagerly, rolling up her pants to wade in. "Come on," she urged, holding out a hand. "We have to stand underneath it. That's the whole point!"

Maude raised an eyebrow. "You expect me to go stand under falling water on purpose? At my age, most people are worried about catching a chill, and not catching pneumonia for fun."

"Opal put it on the list," Mavis said simply, and that was that.

With a sigh that sounded more dramatic than she meant it to, Maude allowed herself to be helped across the slippery rocks. The water was cool around her ankles, shocking but refreshing in the Texas heat. Step by cautious step, they made their way toward the cascade. The closer they came, the louder the roar. Mist clung to their faces, dampening their hair. Finally, they stepped into the curtain of falling water. For an instant, the world disappeared into white noise and spray. Mavis let out a joyful laugh, tilting her face up into the downpour. "We're doing it, Maude! We're really here!"

Maude clutched Mavis's arm, startled at first, then slowly began to laugh, too. The water plastered her hair to her head and dripped down her glasses, but she didn't care. It was ridiculous, it was uncomfortable, and it was utterly glorious. "You've officially lost your mind," Maude sputtered between chuckles. "And so have I!"

When they finally stumbled back to the dry rocks, dripping like two bedraggled hens, they collapsed in a fit of giggles. A young couple nearby snapped their picture and offered to send it to them. Mavis beamed at the photo on the phone screen. "Look at us, Maude. We look like wild women! Double trouble."

"More like two drowned rats," Maude said, but her smile betrayed her.

"That's two down," Mavis said softly.

Maude chewed thoughtfully, gazing out at the pool. "You know, Mavis, that was fun. Messy, silly fun. I'd almost forgotten what that felt like."

"That's the magic of a bucket list," Mavis said, nudging her shoulder. "You do the things you always talked about but never quite got around to, and sometimes they turn out better than you imagined. Now let's drag our soggy selves back to the car and get back to the hotel. Once we shower and change clothes, I want some more chips and salsa."

The day of the hot air balloon ride began before dawn the next morning. Mavis was practically humming with excitement as she bustled about the hotel room, checking her camera battery for the third time. Maude, on the other hand, sat on the edge of her bed staring at the laces of her sneakers as though tying them was a matter of life and death. "Mavis," she said finally, "remind me why in the world anyone would voluntarily climb into a wicker basket and dangle beneath a giant balloon propelled by fire to be blown around by the wind?"

"Because it's magical," Mavis replied without hesitation. "You'll see the world from a whole new perspective. It'll be like floating in a dream."

"Or like plummeting to my death," Maude muttered, but she tied her shoes anyway. "Same as when Opal jumped from that perfectly good airplane."

"She said it was the time she felt the most alive!" Mavis exclaimed.

"It would have killed me," Maude shuddered.

The balloon company's launch site was a wide-open field outside of the city. As they arrived, the horizon was just beginning to lighten, painting the sky with faint streaks of lavender and peach. Several crews were already at work spreading out vast swaths of fabric across the grass, fans roaring as they inflated the balloons with air. Maude stopped in her tracks, clutching her cardigan closed against the cool morning air. "Good Lord," she whispered. "They're enormous."

Mavis's eyes sparkled. "Aren't they beautiful? Like giant sleeping butterflies waiting to take flight."

"They look like dirty laundry someone forgot to fold," Maude said, but her voice was quieter now, touched with awe.

Their pilot, a genial man named Carl with a bushy mustache, helped them into the basket once the balloon was upright. Maude gripped the edge so tightly her knuckles turned white. "This doesn't look sturdy enough to hold groceries, much less two grown women," she hissed.

"Trust me, it's perfectly safe," Carl said with practiced calm.

Mavis placed a reassuring hand on her friend's arm. "Just breathe, Maude. Think of it as a picnic basket for adventure." Before Maude could retort, the burners roared to life, sending a plume of fire into the balloon above. The ground began to slip away beneath them, slowly at first, then with surprising swiftness.

"Oh Lord, oh Lord, oh Lord," Maude chanted under her breath, eyes glued to the receding earth. Mavis, meanwhile, leaned over the edge with unconstrained delight. "Look, Maude! We're flying!"

The air was crisp, cool, and startlingly quiet, broken only by the occasional whoosh of the burners. They drifted over patchwork fields and winding rivers, the world unfolding beneath them like a living map. Mavis pointed out shapes in the clouds while Maude shook her head but smiled all the same. At one point, Carl produced a small bottle of sparkling cider and two plastic cups. "It's tradition," he said. "Every first flight ends with a toast."

Mavis eagerly accepted her cup, clinking it against Maude's. "To Opal," she said softly.

"To Opal," Maude echoed, her voice catching.

They sipped the cider as the balloon drifted gently downward, eventually settling back to earth in a wide meadow. Back on solid ground, Maude wobbled a little as they climbed out of the basket. "My legs forgot what it feels like to stand still," she muttered, though she couldn't hide the rosy glow on her cheeks.

Mavis looked at her with unabashed pride. "See? You did it. You braved the skies."

"I did it," Maude said slowly, as if trying the words on for size. Then a grin broke across her face, rare and dazzling. "And I didn't scream once."

"Not out loud, anyway," Mavis teased. "That's three down! Let's go handle number four!"

It wasn't necessarily safe to drive across the border to Mexico, but Mavis was determined to cross this item off the list. Crossing into Mexico felt to Maude like stepping into a different rhythm of life. The streets of the small border town bustled with vendors calling out their wares, the scent of roasted corn and spices hanging in the warm air, children darting between stalls with laughter that carried on the breeze. They planned to only spend a few minutes eating a tamale or two, then jumping back in the car to travel back to San Antonio. It was one of the craziest things they would ever do.

As soon as they found a small Mexican woman who had tamales, Mavis handed over a stack of dollar bills and hid the warm masa dough wrapped in a corn husk in some paper towels. Once she was back to the car, she handed Maude one of the wrapped tamales and reached behind the seat for two bottles of water she had brought with her. Maude unwrapped hers reverently, as though opening a gift. Inside was a mound of soft masa filled with spicy shredded pork. "Just try it," Mavis urged.

Maude bit a tiny piece of the masa off with her front teeth and paused mid-chew, her eyebrows lifting. "Not bad," Maude nodded. Mavis swallowed her tamale rather quickly, then drained half her bottle of water. "Ok, let's get out of here."

By the time they returned to San Antonio, the afternoon was beginning to turn to evening. Mavis once again craved Mexican food, so they made their way down to the cozy restaurant from the first night on the river. Once the waiter took their orders and disappeared to the kitchen, Maude cleared her throat. "You know, Mavis, when you first started all this, I thought you'd lost your marbles dragging me all over creation for a piece of paper."

"And now?" Mavis asked softly.

"And now," Maude's voice trembled, but her eyes were steady. "Now I think it's the best thing we've ever done." Mavis squeezed her hand, her own eyes shining. "Me too."

Chapter Twenty-Five

The Tuesday night book club was already in full swing when Mavis slid into her chair beside Mac, her arms loaded down with a tote bag and a travel mug of hot cider. The backroom at the library smelled faintly of cinnamon and the candles Eleanor had lit. She claimed the flickering light set the mood for intellectual discussion. Tonight's victim was a gloomy little novel Mavis had struggled to finish. Eleanor tapped her hardback like a preacher slapping a Bible. "The vines represent constraint," Eleanor said. "Our inability to escape the patterns of our childhood. It's all very allegorical."

Mavis stifled a yawn. She hadn't found the vines allegorical at all. To her, they'd just been creepy vines that needed pruning shears. She glanced sideways at Mac, who was sitting with his usual quiet attentiveness, one broad arm stretched along the back of her chair. His profile looked almost regal in the candlelight, though the amusement tugging at the corner of his mouth suggested he wasn't taking Eleanor's sermon any more seriously than Mavis was. The thought slipped out before Mavis could stop it. "You know what? I think I'm going to write a book," she announced. Her voice carried more than she intended. Eleanor paused mid-rant, blinking as if someone had interrupted her on live television.

"Excuse me?" Eleanor said.

A few other members glanced their way, but most seemed relieved to have a break in the lecture. Mavis felt her cheeks warm. "I mean, not right this second, but someday soon. I've got plenty of stories. Might as well write them down."

Mac leaned toward her, his lips brushing her ear. "What kind of book are we talking? Thriller? Romance? Cookbook? Tell me it's not a thinly veiled murder mystery where poor Eleanor here winds up in the compost heap."

Mavis stifled a laugh and whispered back, "Don't tempt me. But no, something more personal. My family has decades worth of stories." Her throat caught at the thought of Ruby and Opal, memories of Wilbur came to be a part of the family, her trials with Earl, and all of the moments in between. "I don't know yet," she continued. "It just hit me."

Mac's smile softened, his voice pitched low so only she could hear. "I think you'd be good at that. You've got stories spilling out of you every five minutes."

"That's not a bad thing, is it?" she asked quickly.

"Not at all. I happen to like listening," he smiled.

Eleanor cleared her throat loudly. "While I appreciate the enthusiasm, perhaps we could return to discussing the actual book at hand?"

Mavis shot her a sunny smile. "Of course. The

vines are very allegorical. Truly fascinating."

Satisfied, Eleanor resumed, though a few members were still eyeing Mavis curiously. Mac gave her hand a discreet squeeze under the table, and she leaned into him, feeling uncharacteristically pleased with herself. When the meeting finally wrapped, Mac helped Mavis gather her things. They strolled toward her car, the gravel crunching beneath their feet. The evening was quiet, save for the hum of crickets. Mavis slipped her hand into Mac's, the gesture easy now, though it still made her stomach flutter.

She glanced at him, her voice softening. "Mac, can I ask you something? We've been seeing each other steady for months now, right? Just us?"

He slowed, turning toward her. "That's how I've seen it, yes. Why?"

"I just realized we never officially said we were exclusive. And here I am at book club labeling myself a wannabe author, and it got me to thinking about labels in other areas of my life." She tried to sound casual, but her heart thudded against her ribs.

Mac's brow furrowed slightly, then he smiled in that patient, grounding way of his. "Mavis, I don't need a label to know I only want to be with you, but if you want official, then yes. We're exclusive. I thought that was already settled," he explained.

Relief bubbled through her, mixed with a pinch of triumph. She nodded like she'd just signed a contract. "Good. That clears that up. Now, when I publish my book under a pen name, I don't want you telling anyone you know who it is."

Mac laughed, squeezing her hand. "Guess I'll take my chances."

They decided to walk instead of driving straight home, meandering down the sidewalk that edged the sleepy downtown square. Storefronts were dark except for the bakery, which always left its neon sign announcing fresh donuts buzzing long past closing time. "You know what? You're right, Mavis. We should do this the right way. Will you be my girlfriend? My one and only true love girlfriend who's going to write the next bestseller?" Mac asked.

Mavis' heart skipped a few beats as she turned to look at Mac whose smiling face was illuminated underneath the closest street light. "Yes, why yes I will." She leaned over and kissed him on the lips which made him chuckle.

"Alright, writer," Mac said, grinning at her. "What's the first chapter about?"

"Easy," she said. "I don't know yet, but it's something to think about."

Mac stopped, gently tugging her around to face him. "It's going to be amazing, whatever it is. When you tell stories, you make people feel like they were there. That's a gift, Mavis."

Her throat tightened. "You really think so?"

"I know so," he nodded. The sincerity in his voice nearly undid her. She had to look away before she got teary right there on the sidewalk. They reached the little park at the end of the square and sat on a bench beneath the lamppost. The light cast a warm halo, catching the silver threads starting in Mac's hair. Mavis tucked her legs up and turned toward him, her excitement rekindled. She rested her head on his shoulder, letting the comfort of his presence settle her racing mind. They sat in companionable silence, the kind that came easy with Mac. Around them, the town slept, but Mavis felt wide awake, her heart buzzing with ideas and the thought of Mac Potter who may have just admitted that he was in love with her. For once, she wasn't afraid. Deciding to write a book and deciding she and Mac were official all felt right; like the first chapter of something she couldn't wait to keep writing.

By the time Mac walked her back to her car, the night air had grown crisp. He kissed her softly, lingering just long enough for her to forget about Eleanor and allegorical vines and whatever the next book assigned for book club was going to be. As she drove home, Mavis caught herself grinning. She was going to write that book. And hopefully, just maybe, more and more chapters would include Mac.

As Thanksgiving neared, plans began to hatch. Mavis would once again host Thanksgiving at Magnolia Manor with her family and friends. It was an event she looked forward to all year long. She counted down the days until everyone would be seated around her table. Thanksgiving morning soon dawned crisp and clear across the sprawling grounds of Magnolia Manor. Mavis stood in her kitchen in a flour-dusted apron, humming to herself as she checked her list for the tenth time. The ham was already in the oven, the stuffing had been assembled in a large porcelain dish, and two saucepans bubbled away on the stove. She loved the idea of a potluck, but she knew she would always be the one who made the mashed potatoes and creamy macaroni and cheese.

The old house felt alive with the holiday. The dining room table had been stretched to its full length, polished until it gleamed, then draped with a linen cloth embroidered with magnolia blossoms. Mavis had set out her best dishes and stemware, each place marked with a little handwritten card. She tucked sprigs of rosemary and magnolia leaves into the napkin rings for a touch of freshness. Magnolia Manor had always been a place for gathering, and Thanksgiving was the holiday that reminded her most sharply of her grandmother who used to orchestrate feasts in this very room. "Clive," she murmured, glancing toward the path to the pond outside the kitchen window where her giant catfish lurked. "If only you could smell what's happening in here, you'd be jealous."

She chuckled at her own joke, stirred the gravy base, then checked her watch. The turkey would be arriving with Wilbur soon, along with Emily and her cakes. Maude would bring her sweet potato casserole later in the morning. And then, of course, there was Mac. Her heart gave a little flip at the thought. Mac was coming, and he was bringing cranberry sauce and rolls. Mavis bit her lip, grinning despite herself. It had been years since she felt this fluttery about a holiday guest.

The grandfather clock in the hall chimed nine. Soon the house would be full of footsteps, voices, laughter, and the clatter of serving dishes. Mavis lit the candles on the sideboard and stood back to admire the room, savoring the brief moment of peace before the joyful chaos began. The sound of a truck pulling into the gravel drive broke the morning quiet. Mavis wiped her hands on her apron and hurried to the front door just as Wilbur swung out of his pickup. He carried the turkey in a heavy roasting pan covered with foil, the smell wafting through the cold air like a promise. "Happy Thanksgiving, Mavis!" he called, grinning under his ball cap. Behind him, Emily climbed out, balancing three cake boxes like precious cargo. Her cheeks were flushed from the chill, her hair tucked neatly into a scarf. "Mavis, you're going to need a second dessert table," Emily teased as she swept into the foyer. "I've got chocolate fudge cake, strawberry, and a lemon layer. I couldn't decide, so I made all three."

Mavis laughed. "Lord have mercy, Emily, you'll spoil us all."

"Whatever doesn't get eaten can go to my grandmother's tomorrow with my family. Remember you're welcome to come, too," Emily said.

"I would love to, but Maude and I are leaving for Alaska on Saturday and I haven't even begun to pack. I can't believe the bucket list is almost over!" Mavis sighed.

Inside the kitchen, Wilbur set down the turkey with a thud. "Now, don't you go messing with it," he warned. "She's been basted every half hour on the dot. Crisped up just right."

Mavis patted his arm. "I wouldn't dare interfere," she laughed.

Moments later, Maude arrived, tottering up the porch steps in her good coat with a casserole dish cradled in her arms. The smell of sweet potatoes, brown sugar, and toasted marshmallows filled the entryway before she even spoke. "Step aside, children," Maude declared, pushing through with the confidence of someone who knew her dish was indispensable. "This casserole could win prizes. I don't trust a single one of you to carry it."

"Happy Thanksgiving to you too, Maude," Wilbur drawled with a hearty laugh as she set the dish carefully on the counter and took off her gloves. "Mavis, your table looks like something out of a magazine. You've outdone yourself again," Maude congratulated her.

Mavis glanced up at the clock near the stove and directed Wilbur to begin peeling the potatoes. Emily helped her mix the three cheese blend into the cooked noodle mixture and then placed the pan in the oven to brown. She darted a glance toward the window and saw Mac's vehicle pulling up the drive. A swirl of nerves and excitement fluttered in her chest. She practically flew to the door to meet him. Wilbur and Emily shared a knowing smile.

The front door creaked open, and Mac, tall and broad-shouldered, wearing a nice sweater that made him look both polished and a little bashful, entered. He carried two brown paper bags carefully, one tucked under each arm. "Happy Thanksgiving," he said, his smile warm.

"Mac!" Mavis hurried forward. "Come on in. You found us all mid-chaos, but that's how it always goes."

"I wouldn't expect anything less," he said, handing her one bag. "Here's the cranberry sauce, creamed corn, and dinner rolls," he added, lifting the second bag. "Still warm."

"Come sit, Mac. Coffee? Or would you rather help me wrangle gravy?" Mavis asked.

"Gravy sounds like something I can handle," he said, earning a laugh from the whole room. Mavis caught his eye as he moved toward the stove, and for just a moment, everything felt exactly right.

By late morning, Magnolia Manor was humming. The kitchen counters were covered in dishes, the oven full, and the stovetop crowded. The house smelled of roasting meat, melted butter, sweet potatoes, and cinnamon. Just when Mavis thought she might lose track of which dish was due for stirring, the doorbell chimed. "I'll get it," she said quickly, slipping off her apron and smoothing her hair.

When she opened the door, Harry stood there with his arms full of four pie tins stacked precariously and wrapped in foil. His wife, Tamara, hovered behind him with a steadying hand on his elbow, while Mona marched up the steps with her trusty green bean casserole in a quilted carrier bag. "Happy Thanksgiving!" Harry boomed, his grin as wide as ever. "I hope y'all are hungry, because I brought enough pie to feed an army."

Mavis ushered them inside, hurrying to take one of the pies before Harry dropped the lot.

"What've we got this year?"

"Pumpkin, pecan, sweet potato, and apple," he announced proudly, setting them on the kitchen counter with a sigh of relief. "Piemaking is such a simple art, though each one a masterpiece, if I do say so myself."

Tamara shook her head with a fond smile. "Don't let him fool you. He's been up since five fussing over crusts like they were newborn babies."

"Hey now," Harry said, mock-offended. "You can't rush art."

Meanwhile, Mona swept into the kitchen like she owned the place, setting her green bean casserole down with a thump. "Made it the same way I always do, but it's still the best one you'll ever eat. Y'all better leave room on your plates."

"You say that every year," Wilbur smirked.

"Because it's true every year," Mona shot back, planting her hands on her hips. The kitchen filled with laughter as coats were hung and greetings exchanged. Mac and Harry clasped hands in an easy familiarity, old friends reconnecting without missing a beat. "Look at you," Harry said, giving Mac a hearty slap on the back. "I hardly recognize you outside of those spreadsheets or fishing waders."

"And I hardly recognize you without a diner apron or a fishing pole," Mac chuckled. "Oh, don't remind me," Mona cut in. "You two nearly worked me to death back then. I still don't know how we ran that place without losing our minds."

"But we did," Harry said, a note of pride in his

voice. "And now it's in good hands. Those sisters running the Starlight Café are making it their own."

Mavis, listening from the stove, smiled. She'd eaten at the café more than once since the sisters had taken over, and while it was different, it still carried echoes of Harry and Mona's diner days. Seeing Harry, Tamara, and Mona here now felt like carrying those memories forward into something new.

"Alright, alright," Maude said, shooing everyone toward the living room. "If we all keep standing around this kitchen, Mavis'll never get anything finished. Go on, out with you. Food will be ready soon enough."

"Bossy as ever," Mona muttered, but she let herself be herded out, linking arms with Emily as they disappeared into the next room.

Mac lingered behind, steadying the gravy with Mavis as the others settled into a rhythm. She glanced at him gratefully, their hands brushing as they reached for the same ladle. When the final dishes were pulled from the oven and the last spoonful of gravy whisked smooth, Mavis declared it was time. She rang the little brass bell that had belonged to her grandmother, the one she always used for holidays. Its bright chime carried through Magnolia Manor, drawing everyone to the kitchen to assemble. Platters and bowls lined the counters in a parade of colors and aromas. Wilbur's golden-brown turkey, Mavis's glossy ham, Maude's marshmallow-topped sweet potatoes, Mona's casserole with its crunchy onion topping, Mac's neat basket of dinner rolls, all were placed alongside Emily's cakes and Harry's homemade pies.

"Before we dive in," Mavis said, raising her voice just enough to quiet the chatter, "I want to say thank you. Every year, this day reminds me how blessed I am. Not for the food, though Lord knows it looks good, but for all of you. Family and friends, old and new, I'm grateful you're here."

There was a murmur of agreement and smiles all around. "Alright," Wilbur said, clearing his throat. "Before we all get sentimental, let's carve this bird." He lifted the carving knife with the authority of a man who took poultry seriously. Mavis gestured to the ham near Mac with a teasing smile. "Think you're up for the job?"

"I'll try not to embarrass myself," Mac laughed nervously.

"Just keep the slices thick," Harry advised. "Thin ham is an abomination."

The room erupted in chuckles as Mac made his first careful cut. He wasn't graceful, but he was steady, and soon neat slices fanned across the platter. Mavis leaned over and whispered, "Perfect."

"Mercy," Mona said, fanning herself as she looked at all the food. "I don't know where to start."

"You just dive in," Wilbur instructed. "A little bit of this, a little bit of that. Oh, and a lot of this right here." He scooped a large spoonful of Maude's sweet potato casserole onto his plate and grinned.

Everyone filled their plates high with food and made their way into the connecting dining room. The dining room table glowed under the beautiful lighting fixture Wilbur had installed for Ruby almost ten years ago. No one ever ate in the formal dining room unless it was a big occasion like the holidays. Harry leaned back, patting his stomach. "I'll tell you what, Wilbur, this turkey is something else. Juicy all the way through. What's your secret?"

"Patience," Wilbur said proudly. "And a good basting brush."

"That man treats poultry like it's royalty," Emily teased, cutting into her slice of turkey.

Mona chimed in, "Well, don't think I didn't notice half the casserole's gone already. Y'all can thank me later."

Laughter rolled around the table. The food was plentiful, the conversation lively, and Mavis soaked it all in like sunlight. She caught Mac looking at her once or twice, his expression soft, as if he was just as grateful to be here as she was to have him. By the time second helpings had been offered and accepted, plates sat empty, and everyone leaned back in their chairs with groans of satisfaction. "I don't know how I'm supposed to make room for dessert," Tamara said, shaking her head.

"You'll find a way," Harry promised, already rising to slice the pies. Emily followed suit to slice her two cakes, their glossy frostings gleaming under the kitchen lights. "Alright," Harry said, slicing into the pumpkin first. "Let's see some loyalty here."

"Cut me a sliver of pecan," Mona said quickly. "Sliver, I said, not a plank. Don't you dare."

"You'll get what I give you," Harry shot back, though he obeyed his twin sister.

Emily's lemon cake was soon devoured, while Tamara swooned over the chocolate fudge Mavis had made the night before. Maude insisted she couldn't possibly eat another bite, then proceeded to clean her plate of two pieces of pie.

"Coffee, anyone?" Mavis asked, rising to her feet.

A chorus of agreement answered her. She disappeared to the kitchen and returned with a silver tray, cups rattling, and the rich aroma of brewed coffee filling the room. By then, conversation had shifted into stories of old Thanksgivings at the diner, mishaps in kitchens past, and the year Maude had set the turkey aflame after stuffing it full of popcorn kernels.

Later, with plates scraped clean and only crumbs left on the platters, the group migrated to the living room. The fire was lit, crackling warmly as everyone sank into armchairs and couches. Tamara and Emily folded blankets across laps, while Mona claimed the corner seat nearest the heat. Mavis settled beside Mac, who handed her a steaming mug. Their shoulders brushed, and she felt a quiet contentment wash over her. Around her, the voices of family and friends rose and fell, familiar and comforting as the ticking of the grandfather clock. Harry leaned back, balancing his coffee on his knee. "I'll say this," he mused, "there's nowhere else I'd rather be today. Good food and even better company. We've done well."

"Amen to that," Mavis agreed. She caught Mac's eye, and he gave her a smile that said he felt that he belonged here, that this was the continuation of something magical. Outside, the November afternoon deepened. Inside, the house glowed with warmth, filled with the happy exhaustion that only came after a day of feasting and fellowship.

Chapter Twenty-Six

Saturday morning at Magnolia Manor was buzzing with a kind of energy that only comes when two women are about to chase the Northern Lights and go whale-watching in Alaska. Maude was darting around the guest room, tossing scarves, hats, and gloves onto the bed with the sort of precision that somehow always ended in chaos. She had agreed to stay over at the Manor the night before their trek to appease Mavis' rushed timeline.

"Our flight doesn't leave for six hours, Mavis!" she exclaimed, holding a fuzzy hat aloft like a victory flag.

Mavis, perched on the bed with a travel guide spread across her knees, gave her a look. "Six hours is plenty of time if we don't forget anything important. Thermal socks, your camera, chargers, gloves. Did I mention gloves?"

"I have gloves!" Maude shot back, shoving two mismatched pairs at her. "See? Adventure ready."

"Adventure ready," Mavis muttered under her breath, shaking her head but smiling. "Well, it's not just gloves and socks. We're about to witness auroras so bright they'll make your jaw drop, Maude. And whales swimming gracefully in icy waters. I've got goosebumps just thinking about it."

By eight o'clock, after a whirlwind of packing, double-checking boarding passes, and frantic coffee-drinking, the car was loaded, and they were off toward Hartsfield-Jackson Airport in Atlanta.

"You remember we have to connect in Seattle, right?" Mavis asked as she navigated Atlanta traffic a few hours later. "Seattle first, then Alaska Airlines to get where we're going."

Maude's eyes gleamed. "I know. But that's part of the adventure! Imagine us on the plane, hot cocoa in hand, peering out the window as the auroras glow green and purple across the sky."

Mavis laughed. "Don't forget your camera, or you'll be stuck with memories and no proof."

Airports have a way of testing patience, and Hartsfield-Jackson was no exception. Crowds surged past them, dragging oversized luggage and herding children like tiny, confused cattle. Somehow, they navigated check-in, TSA lines, and coffee stands without losing anything or each other.

"Did you check your bags?" Mavis asked, eyes darting around.

"Yes," Maude replied, taking a sip of coffee and spilling a little on her scarf. "I may have done a celebratory spin at the counter after the agent said it was fine."

Mavis rolled her eyes but couldn't hide a grin. "You're going to get us kicked off the plane if you do that here."

Once seated, both women pressed their faces to the airplane windows. Below, Atlanta shrank into a mosaic of roads, rooftops, and tiny moving cars. "Look at that," Mavis said, her voice soft. She could spend hours looking out the window and never lose excitement.

Maude leaned over her, snapping photos. "I just hope the auroras are as magical as the pictures. I don't want to be disappointed."

Mavis patted her arm. "You won't be. Alaska doesn't do anything half ass," she nodded knowingly.

They had plenty of time to meet their connecting flight to Anchorage. They picked up chicken tenders and fries and ate their meal happily at the gate while they waited to board. The flight was just under four hours long. They rushed to make their last flight of the day to Fairbanks, their ultimate destination. After an hour flight, Fairbanks greeted them with a biting chill that made their cheeks rosy and noses numb. Snow crunched under their boots, trees sparkled with frost, and the low, amber sunlight made the town look like a postcard from a winter wonderland. Their home for the night was a resort near a hot spring that was rustic but cozy, with panoramic views of the northern sky. After quickly unpacking, they layered up and ventured outside, hearts thumping in anticipation.

"I see a flicker!" Maude gasped.

Mavis followed her gaze. The sky was beginning to glow, faint greens swirling like paint across the dark canvas above. The aurora ignited in full force, green and purple ribbons twisting, spinning, and dancing overhead. "It's alive,"

Maude whispered, camera clicking furiously.

Mavis laughed softly, tears pricking at her eyes. "Northern Light can officially be checked off the list." They wandered outside for an hour sipping hot chocolate, laughing at their frozen fingers, and marveling at the spectacle above. When they finally retreated indoors, exhaustion mingled with euphoria.

The next morning, a light dusting of snow covered the grounds. Mavis insisted on taking a short morning aurora walk before leaving Fairbanks. Maude went along, secretly amused, watching Mavis slip and skid across icy patches while trying to capture the perfect photo. "Careful," Maude warned. "You might end up face-first in the snow."

"I'll risk it for the perfect shot!" Mavis declared, tumbling but catching herself with a dramatic flair. "Do you think anyone will notice if I melt into a snow angel mid-walk?"

Maude couldn't help but laugh, shaking her head. "Only you could turn aurora viewing into slapstick comedy." After breakfast, they flew to Juneau, the landscape below transforming from snow-capped mountains to winding fjords and icy rivers. The scenery was breathtaking, every glance out the window another postcard waiting to happen. Their hotel room was small, but refreshing. They decided to walk around the street and visit the quaint shops up and down the lane.

As the evening progressed, Mavis and Maude slipped into the warmth of a small Alaskan restaurant just as the evening air turned sharp outside. The windows were fogged from the contrast of the cold and the heat within, and the place smelled richly of grilled salmon, butter, and fresh bread. A friendly waitress in a flannel shirt led them to a booth near the window, where they could still see the last threads of daylight stretching across the snow-covered street. Maude rubbed her hands together to chase off the chill, while Mavis immediately opened the menu with a decisive little snap. "I think we ought to try the halibut," Mavis said, peering at the options over her reading glasses. "If we came all this way, we're not ordering chicken."

Maude laughed, still studying the specials scrawled on a chalkboard. She was tempted by the king crab legs, piled high and served with melted butter, though she wasn't sure how much of a mess she'd make in such a nice restaurant. When the food arrived, it was a feast of flaky halibut, roasted vegetables glistening with oil, and thick slices of sourdough bread that steamed when they tore them open. The crab legs came too, a gleaming mound that Maude gamely tackled with the nutcracker tool, sending a bit of shell flying onto the tablecloth. Mavis chuckled and reached across with a napkin, dabbing at the butter on Maude's sleeve. They ate slowly, savoring each bite, talking in easy rhythm about the trip so far, the bucket list they were working through, and what adventure tomorrow might hold. Outside, the northern night deepened, but inside the little restaurant, the two women felt warm, full, and content.

The charter boat left the dock in a morning mist the following day, the air crisp and filled with the smell of saltwater. With cups of steaming coffee in hand, they scanned the horizon for any sign of life beneath the waves. "Do you see that?" Mavis suddenly cried, pointing.

A humpback whale breached, its massive body arcing gracefully before splashing back into the water. Maude squealed, nearly spilling her coffee. "Oh my gosh! Look at that!" she laughed. "It's enormous!"

More whales surfaced nearby, including a pod whose sleek black fins cut through the water. Curious sea otters floated along the boat's side, eyes bright and playful. "I don't think any photo could capture this," Mavis said, snapping pictures anyway. "You just have to be here feeling it. Wow!"

The wind whipped at their hair, the water sprayed their faces, and every breach felt like a gift. By the time they returned to shore, their cheeks were pink, their fingers pruned, and their hearts full. That evening, in the cozy hotel room, Mavis and Maude reflected on their whirlwind adventure. "We experienced the lights," Mavis said, tapping her notebook. "And today the whales. I still can't believe we did it."

Outside, snow fell softly, blanketing the town in a quiet stillness. Somewhere above, the aurora continued its endless dance, a reminder that the world was full of wonders waiting to be seen, and adventures yet to come. Maude clinked her cup to Mavis's. "To the next item on the list."

"We don't have much more," Mavis said. There

was a hint of sadness in her voice.

"Remind me what's left," Maude instructed.

"She wanted to visit all fifty states, and then the final one says she wanted to throw a dart at a map and visit wherever it landed," Mavis read the list.

"What kind of map?" Maude asked.

"It doesn't say," Mavis shrugged.

"Well, the kind of map matters. A map of the whole world or a map of the United States? A map of Alabama or a map that shows every baseball stadium or gas station? Every map is different," Maude rambled.

Mavis nodded and grinned behind her notebook. Maybe letting Maude choose which map to use would be the perfect finale for this bucket list adventure. "Before we get to that one, how do we know which states are left exactly?" Mavis asked. "I have a list of states I know she went to, but I don't know what all she did to be perfectly honest. She was a woman of mystery."

"That she was indeed," Maude nodded. "Let's see the list of states you've got so far." Mavis handed her the notebook that had a list of states that Mavis was sure Opal had been to. Maude began to write in a fury. "I have a little confession," Maude said. Mavis' eyes widened and she waited for Maude to continue. "I have Opal's diary, well, diaries. She kept quite the account of her life. I know what states she has left."

"Maude!" Mavis gasped. "How long have you had them?"

"Opal gave them to me a few weeks before

she died. I swear she knew she wasn't going to come out of the hospital," Maude sighed. "It was a big old box of books and I've been reading them nonstop. You know I'm not much of a reader, but Mavis, I tell you, Opal was the most fascinating person this side of heaven."

Tears filled Mavis' eyes and she nodded. "I'm glad you have them. That is so special, Maude."

Maude nodded and took a second to answer. "She hasn't been to Wisconsin or Minnesota. Nothing ever interested me about those places, but maybe I should have traveled more."

"Now you can," Mavis smiled gently. "Hey, I have an idea. Let's go. Let's change our flight tomorrow and just go. Spontaneous just like Opal would have done.

"I don't even know what there is to see in those two states," Maude said.

"I don't either, but we can research it real quick. The internet is great for these kinds of questions," Mavis exclaimed.

For the next hour, Mavis sat on the bed with a cup of coffee cooling in her hands as she tried to learn what she could about Minnesota and Wisconsin. Maude shuffled through a stack of boarding passes, her reading glasses perched at the end of her nose. They were supposed to be flying back to Atlanta in the morning and then driving back to Rhinestone. With a grin, Mavis announced that she had texted Wilbur and Emily their new idea, and surprisingly, they were both pleased with the idea. Wilbur loved a plan and a schedule, but he agreed that Opal was indeed one for spontaneity, and it was a fun way to continue to honor her. "So it's settled. We'll swing through Minnesota, then pop right over to Wisconsin. Quick and tidy."

Maude laughed, tapping the now old boarding passes against the table like a judge's gavel. "Lord help us, but I think that's exactly what we should do."

They were both up early the next morning and made their way to the airline desk attendant at the airport who raised an eyebrow when the two women marched up, determination written all over their faces. Mavis did most of the talking, her charm sweet as molasses, while Maude stood behind her, nodding like an accomplice. "We just need a little change of plans," Mavis explained. "Instead of Atlanta, could you please send us to Minneapolis first? And then Madison after that?"

The attendant blinked. "You want to reroute your flight to Minnesota and then Wisconsin?"

"That's right," Mavis said with a smile that could melt an iceberg. "We're on a mission."

It took a bit of typing, some re-routing fees, and a sympathetic ear, but by the end of it, the boarding passes in their hands were proof that the two spontaneous women had two new states waiting ahead. As they walked away from the desk, Mavis tucked the new passes into her purse and whispered, "Opal's probably up there shaking her head at us right now."

"Maybe," Maude said, looping her arm through Mavis's. "But I bet she's grinning while she does it. I'm just glad she didn't have something like sneak on a plane on that list. Hell, she probably already did that."

They landed in Minneapolis under gray skies and brisk air. Maude immediately noticed the friendliness of the people, every stranger offering a smile or a helpful tip about what to see with only one day in town. They wandered through the Mall of America for the novelty of it, dragging their suitcases behind them, laughing at the roller coaster that zipped past shoppers and stopping at a little café for hot dish, because, as one chatty server insisted, "You can't say you've been to Minnesota until you've had hot dish."

Mavis tried it, then pushed her bowl toward Maude. "Wilbur could eat three of these I bet. I wonder if I could make this back home," she said, laughing at the cheesy, potato-topped casserole.

That night, they found a quiet spot by the water and stood together, watching the city lights dance on the dark ripples. Mavis pulled a small notebook from her bag, the one where she had kept track of every bucket list item. With a dramatic flourish, she drew a checkmark next to "Minnesota."

"One more," she whispered.

The next morning, they crossed into Wisconsin on a short flight that felt more like a bus ride. The landscape changed quickly into rolling farmland, red barns, and little towns with names they couldn't quite pronounce. They stopped at a cheese shop on the side of the street opposite their hotel, where a cheerful woman in an apron insisted they try samples of every variety. Mavis laughed so hard she nearly cried when Maude's eyes lit up at a sharp cheddar. "Mercy, this is heaven," Maude declared. "I could live on cheese curds and never complain."

They ended their whirlwind day in Madison, standing in front of the gleaming dome of the state capitol building. The sun dipped low, casting a warm glow over the marble steps. Mavis pulled out the notebook again, her hand steady as she placed the final checkmark. "There," she said softly. "All the states. Every last one Opal missed."

Maude slipped her arm around her. "We did it, baby girl. We really did it. Now to celebrate, let's take a nap. Those cheese samples are making me sleepy."

On the flight home the next morning, the women sat side by side, tired but satisfied. Mavis rested her head on the window, thinking about all the places they had seen, all the laughter and tears, and the deep sense of purpose that had carried them through. "It's like we carried her with us the whole way," Mavis murmured.

Maude squeezed her hand. "Because we did," she nodded. "Only one thing left. I think we should wait a bit for that one. Maybe for New Years or something."

"What a great idea," Mavis nodded. She had plans to visit her sisters in Denver the weekend before Christmas, but she was looking forward to the next two weeks where she could decorate the Manor for Christmas. She hadn't even begun her Christmas shopping either. She was well behind where she normally liked to be ahead as the first week of December approached.

Chapter Twenty-Seven

Wilbur and Emily were waiting on the porch of Magnolia Manor when Mavis pulled onto the property later that afternoon. She had already dropped Maude off at her house. Wilbur helped her unload her suitcase and Emily hugged her tightly. "We missed you!" Emily said.

"I missed y'all, too!" Mavis said. "All this plane hopping has me exhausted. I think I could sleep for two days straight."

"Have you eaten?" Wilbur asked. "If not, I'm thinking of running over to Willie's and picking up some barbecue. Or if you're wanting something else I can get that for supper instead."

"I'm ravenous," Mavis nodded. "Anything sounds good. Oh! One day next week I'm going to make y'all hot dish, it's something we had up there and it was delicious!" She launched into a description that both Emily and Wilbur agreed sounded delicious. "We'll hold you to it," Emily smiled.

Mavis stepped inside the Manor and breathed in the familiar scent of home. The scent of her lemongrass cleaner still lingered in the air from when she polished the entry way table before she left. She dropped her coat onto the banister and stretched her arms over her head. "I cannot believe it's almost December. I need to get this place ready for Christmas before I leave for Denver."

Emily glanced over from the kitchen, where she'd already started making sweet tea. "What day are you leaving again?"

"I'll fly out on the eighteenth and come back the twenty-second," Mavis replied, taking off her shoes. "I'll only be gone for a few days. Brandy and her crew will all be there. Oh, and guess what? Sarah is flying in from California, too."

"Well, that'll be a full house," Wilbur chuckled, setting the suitcase and Mavis' bags down in front of the stairs. "All right, why don't I go pick up some supper while y'all catch up."

While Wilbur went to pick up barbecue, Mavis started a load of laundry and then she and Emily wandered up to the attic to pull down the Christmas decorations. They dragged a few boxes full of lights, ornaments, and other holiday decorations down the stairs and into the front room, already envisioning how Magnolia Manor would sparkle once everything was up.

With a mug of spiced tea in hand and holiday music playing softly on the radio, Mavis and Emily fluffed the artificial garland, strung twinkling lights around the stair banister, and hung velvet bows on the doors. The tree, an old but faithful faux spruce stood tall in the corner of the front living room. They strung the lights first, then the ornaments, each one carrying a memory. There was the porcelain dove that Ruby had always loved, the faded red mitten Opal had made during a craft fair one year, and the tiny photo frame ornament with a picture of Mavis and her sisters in matching pajamas from the first time they had met last year. Mavis smiled at it, holding it in her hand for a moment before hanging it near the top.

By the time Wilbur returned with the food, the Manor was beginning to look like a postcard. After they ate pulled pork sandwiches and coleslaw, Wilbur helped string lights outside along the porch, and Emily hung the wreath on the front door, weaving in some fresh magnolia leaves from the tree out front. Later that evening, the three of them stood on the lawn, hands tucked in their coat pockets, admiring the house.

"You outdid yourself this year," Emily said, nudging Mavis with her elbow.

"We sure did," Mavis replied, her breath puffing in the cold air.

"It looks magnificent," Wilbur nodded. "Looks like something out of one of those fancy holiday catalogs."

The next few weeks passed in a blur of holiday bustle. Mavis baked gingerbread cookies for the local fire department and wrapped presents to take with her to Denver. She made time to ferry Maude to her regular appointments, took extra special care of the llamas since she had missed them so much on her travels, and fit in as much time with Mac as possible. It was a busy time of the year for him as he wrapped up the books for the various businesses he worked with as an accountant and bookkeeper, so they made the best of the times when they could get together.

Mac came over the Friday before she left and

picked her up so they could go to dinner and then tackle more of her Christmas shopping list. The sky had already turned dusky with early winter shadows. She slid into the passenger seat with a warm smile, cheeks pink from the cold and anticipation. "Where are we going?" she asked.

"Junction," Max said, glancing at her with a grin. "Figured we'd grab dinner and then knock out some more of your Christmas list."

Dinner was cozy, just the two of them tucked into a booth at a small bistro, the soft hum of conversation around them and snow beginning to gather on the windows outside. Mavis talked about her upcoming trip to Denver, how she wanted all her shopping done before she left in a few days. Mac listened closely, asking questions, laughing in the right places, and ever attentive as he had always been.

After dinner, they wandered through a few shops. Mavis scanned shelves and thoughtfully considered gifts for her family in Denver. She had always been an intentional gift giver, never one to grab the first thing she saw. Mac held the bags and offered opinions when asked, content just to be near her. In one of the quieter moments, as they stepped out into the chilly air again, Mavis glanced over and said, "I still don't know what to get you for Christmas."

He stopped walking and looked at her, seriously but gently. "You want to know what I want most?"

She nodded and took out her notebook to write down his list of wants. "I want to spend every holiday with you," he said, without hesitation. "And I hope you know that."

Mavis's breath caught a little. Her heart, already soft with the season, felt a little fuller. They'd only been dating a few months, but something about it already felt lasting. "I would like that very much," she smiled. She took his hand and led him to the next shop on the street, a quirky little boutique full of handmade trinkets, vintage books, and cozy home goods. Mavis smiled, already sensing a few items that might be perfect for the people on her list.

On the morning of the eighteenth, Mavis stood in the doorway of Magnolia Manor with her suitcase and a travel pillow under one arm. Wilbur honked the horn from the driveway. "Time to roll!" he called out the window.

"Thanks for driving me to the airport!" Mavis said as she buckled her seatbelt in Wilbur's truck.

"That's what family is for," Wilbur smiled in return.

As the truck pulled away, Mavis glanced back once more at the house decked out in twinkling lights and greenery. It looked warm and full of life, even in the quiet. She smiled to herself, already looking forward to coming home.

Wilbur dropped Mavis off at the airport and watched as she headed inside with a pep in her step. She would have just enough time to get herself some breakfast before boarding. After she waved goodbye one more time, Wilbur glanced at his watch and knew that by now Emily would be at work at her office in Junction. She was planning on taking off mid-afternoon for them to finish some of their Christmas shopping together. That meant Wilbur had a finite amount of time to hurry to the stockyards and then meet Mac for lunch before his date with Emily that afternoon. He had quite the busy day ahead of him.

The drive to the stockyards in Junction took him roughly an hour from Montgomery's traffic. The December air was sharp, biting Wilbur's cheeks as he leaned against the rail at the stockyards that housed horses, cows, and various barn cats and dogs. Beyond the fence stood the reason he'd braved the cold, a tall red thoroughbred, strong in the shoulders, with a proud arch to his neck and a keen brightness in his dark eyes. The horse pawed the cold ground, his breath steaming in the winter air. Wilbur felt a tug in his chest. "You'll do just fine," he murmured. "Emily's gonna take one look at you and fall head over heels."

Boot steps crunched on the gravel behind him. Wilbur turned to see Harlan, the sheriff of Rhinestone and his closest friend, making his way across the yard, with his coat collar flipped up against the wind. Harlan's stride had the easy confidence of a man who'd been out in weather rougher than this a hundred times over. "So this is the fella you've been fussin' over," Harlan drawled, stopping beside Wilbur. He hooked his thumbs into his belt and studied the horse with a practiced eye. "He's a fine one."

Wilbur's chest swelled a little with pride. "Retired off the track. They called him Majestic

Echo in his racing days. I reckon Emily'll like the sound of that," Wilbur grinned.

"Majestic Echo," Harlan repeated, rolling the name slow. "Got a ring to it. Suits him."

The horse pricked his ears at the sound, almost as though he recognized himself in the sheriff's voice. Both men chuckled. "Emily's always dreamed of a horse," Wilbur said, his tone softening. "I want to walk her out to the barn on Christmas Eve and he be standing in his stall waiting for her."

"That's a mighty fine gift," Harlan said with an approving nod. "So I'm to play Santa Claus, huh?"

Wilbur chuckled. "Something like that." He glanced back at the horse who had come closer now, blowing warm air against the rails. "I can picture her face already. She'll light up like a Christmas tree."

Harlan clapped him on the shoulder. "Consider it done. I've got the trailer ready to go and I'll haul Majestic Echo out to my pasture. He'll be safe, and she won't have a clue. You just text me when y'all leave that evening and I'll bring him over and slip him in the pen." Wilbur's eyes softened, gratitude plain on his face. "Much obliged, Harlan. You don't know what this means to me."

"Oh, I do," Harlan said, his tone turning warm. "Man only goes to this much trouble when he's head over heels himself. Emily's lucky to have you and you're lucky to have a friend like me." They both laughed as they stood watching Majestic Echo trot along the fence line, his stride still carrying a hint of the racetrack's glory days. After

Echo was loaded in Harlan's trailer, Wilbur shook his friend's hand and jumped back into his own truck. He checked the time and realized he would be cutting it close to make it on time to meet Mac. Wilbur wasn't entirely sure what to make of Mac's invitation. Men didn't usually ask him to lunch unless it was about tractors, property lines, or fishing season. Still, he liked the guy well enough when the four of them got together for coffee or at Thanksgiving. He knew that Mac would be joining them for Christmas as well. He was steady, polite, and clearly smitten with Mavis.

When he pulled into the gravel parking lot at the deli, he spotted Mac already waiting inside at a corner booth, tie loosened, sleeves rolled up like he'd been pacing himself for this moment. Wilbur tipped his cap and slid into the booth. "Alright, Mac. You said you wanted to see me. What's so important you couldn't wait?" he chuckled.

Mac grinned sheepishly. "It's about Mavis."

"Well, I assumed," Wilbur nodded.

They ordered iced teas and the daily special, a ham and cheese melt with chips and a pickle spear. Once the waitress moved off, Mac leaned forward, his tone earnest. "She told me something weeks ago at book club. Said she's always dreamed of writing a book. You probably already know that."

Wilbur's chuckle rumbled low. "Boy, she's been scribbling stories since she could hold a pencil. I think she'd be great at it. She has a lot of stories to tell."

"That doesn't surprise me. She loves reading,

and writing comes naturally to her. Since we met at book club, I wanted to do something more than just say I support her dream. I want to show her," Mac smiled.

Wilbur raised a brow. "So what're you thinking? Journals? A fancy pen?"

"Something lasting. Something that tells her I believe in her," Mac explained. "I found her an antique writing desk. A real writer's desk. Old wood, sturdy, with drawers for all her notes. A space she can claim as her own. She could sit there every morning and feel like she's stepping into her calling."

Wilbur's eyes lit up. "That's perfect. She'd love that. Where did you find it?"

"At the antique store she consults with," Mac grinned sheepishly. "I asked one of the dealers to be on the lookout and he finally found one. He called me last night, but it's in Atlanta. I'm going to head there this afternoon and pick it up. I was hoping I could hide it at your house and maybe you could bring it over on Christmas Eve when Mavis and I get together to open gifts."

"Absolutely. Consider it done," Wilbur smiled. Harlan may be playing Santa for him, but he would play Santa for Mac. This was shaping up to be an exciting Christmas!

Mac's shoulders relaxed as though a weight had been lifted. "Wilbur, that means more than you know. Thank you."

The waitress dropped off their sandwiches and they ate in companionable silence. Wilbur eventually broke it with a grin. "You really do care for her, don't you?"

Mac looked him square in the eye. "I do. She's remarkable, Wilbur. I just want her to feel as supported as she makes everyone else feel."

Wilbur studied him for a long beat, then nodded slowly. "Alright. You get her that desk, she'll know. That's the kind of gift she won't ever forget."

Mac and Wilbur fell into an easy sort of conversation. Wilbur had a feeling that it wouldn't be long until he started seeing a lot more of Mac on a more regular basis. The man was clearly in love! Mac told Wilbur that when he met Mavis at book club in Junction, something had shifted. She was unlike anyone he'd ever known. Her love of books matched his own, but it was her zest for life and her deep care for the people around her that caught him off guard. For the first time, he found himself imagining a future built not just on balance sheets and solitary dinners, but on shared dreams and laughter echoing through hallways.

Chapter Twenty-Eight

Magnolia Manor glowed brightly on Christmas Eve. The grand old house sat in stillness under a light dusting of frost, the white trim glistening in the glow of icicle lights that Wilbur had strung along the porch railings. The evergreen wreath on the front door was fat with magnolia leaves and a velvet red bow, and every window flickered with the golden warmth of lamps inside.

In the living room, the tree stood tall and full, its ornaments a mixture of heirlooms and new finds. Shiny red balls caught the firelight, glass icicles shimmered, and tucked between them were little trinkets with stories like the angel made of straw from Mavis' childhood, a pair of porcelain doves from Maude, and a new ornament Mac had gifted her earlier in December: a Magnolia blossom carved in wood. The house smelled of cinnamon and butter and something savory bubbling away in the oven. The fire in the hearth popped and crackled as though it too wanted to be part of the celebration.

The dining room was dark and waiting for tomorrow, when Wilbur, Emily, and Maude would come to eat Christmas lunch. But tonight, for the first time, Magnolia Manor belonged solely to Mavis and Mac. It was their first Christmas together, just the two of them. Mavis had thought long and hard about that. She loved the bustle of family and the clatter of dishes, but this quiet, this closeness was something she hadn't realized she'd needed until Mac suggested it. Here she was experiencing a Christmas Eve carved out for them alone, a chance to soak in the beginnings of a life they were building together.

"Careful now," Mavis said, sliding a tray of cooled sugar cookies onto the counter. "That snowman's liable to lose his head if you don't hold him steady."

Mac grinned, already reaching for the piping bag of royal icing. "I've done spreadsheets with more fragile numbers than this, I think I can handle a snowman cookie." He drew a careful zigzag of white icing along the snowman's hat brim, his tongue poking slightly from the corner of his mouth as he concentrated. Mavis laughed and set her own piping bag down long enough to sip her hot chocolate. The whipped cream had melted into a froth, dusted with cinnamon.

"You're really something, you know that?" she teased.

"Something good or something questionable?" he asked.

"I haven't decided yet." She tilted her head at the cookie. "But your snowman does have better style than mine."

Mac held up the cookie for inspection. The hat was neat, the scarf a tidy swirl of red icing, and the eyes made from miniature chocolate chips looked somewhat cheerful. Mac placed it gently on the platter and reached for another cookie, the crooked star that Mavis had cut out without noticing the dough had stretched.

"You'll need all your accounting skills to fix that one," she said. Mac laughed and set to work, turning the lopsided star into something whimsical with looping green lines and dots of silver sugar. When he finished, he slid it across the counter for her approval.

Mavis studied it, then nodded with mock solemnity. "I'll allow it."

Their laughter mingled with the Christmas music playing faintly from the old record player in the corner. Bing Crosby crooned about a white Christmas, and Mavis felt that cozy contentment seep all the way through her. The kitchen, the cookies, the warmth of the oven, and Mac standing there with flour on his sleeve made it all perfect. She reached for another cookie, this one shaped like a tree, and spread green icing with broad, cheerful strokes. "You know," she said softly, "I haven't decorated cookies like this in years."

Mac looked at her gently, holding the cookie he was decorating. "I'm glad we're doing it together then." She gave him a smile that was equal parts gratitude and tenderness. "Me too," she sighed happily.

They worked side by side, the platter slowly filling with trees, stars, snowflakes, bells, and snowmen. Some were perfect, some messy, and all of them bore the mark of laughter and togetherness. When they finally set the last one down, Mavis leaned against the counter and took a long sip of hot chocolate. "Lasagna should be ready in about half an hour," she said. "And the garlic bread."

Mac rubbed his stomach dramatically. "Best Christmas Eve dinner I've ever had lined up."

"Well, it's not traditional, but it's ours," Mavis laughed.

When Mavis turned to tidy up the counter, Mac slipped his phone from his pocket. He tapped quickly, keeping his body angled so she wouldn't see. He sent Wilbur a quick text asking him if he was still on track to deliver the desk tonight. Wilbur fired back immediately and let him know that the desk would be delivered within the hour with a bow on top, courtesy of Emily. They were headed to Harry and Tamara's afterward and would make sure they were quiet. Mac smiled to himself, relief settling over him. He looked across the kitchen at Mavis who was rinsing mixing bowls at the sink. Her dark hair was caught in the warm glow of the light above. She was humming along with Bing Crosby, her shoulders swaying just slightly. Sliding his phone back into his pocket, Mac straightened and reached for the dish towel to help dry. Mavis glanced over her shoulder, smiling. "You don't have to help."

"I want to," he said, and he meant it. Together they worked in easy rhythm, the kitchen slowly returning to order. The cookies waited proudly on their platter, the lasagna bubbled happily in the oven, and the fire in the next room promised warmth for the night ahead. And though Mavis didn't know it, the barn was about to hold its own secret surprise wrapped in a sheet and topped with a red bow.

The timer on the stove went off and the lasagna came out bubbling, cheese browned just at the edges, filling the kitchen with a mouthwatering scent. Mavis placed it carefully on the trivet in the center of the small breakfast table, which she had set earlier with green plaid napkins, simple white dishes, and two red candles flickering in brass holders. The loaf of garlic bread joined it, wrapped in foil but already sending out the intoxicating smell of butter and herbs.

They served themselves generous portions, the first forkfuls met with appreciative silence. The sauce was rich, the pasta tender, and the cheese perfectly gooey. The garlic bread was crisp at the edges, soft inside, with butter soaking into each bite. "This," Mac declared after swallowing, "is better than any Christmas Eve feast I've ever had."

"Well, then I'll take that as a compliment," she blushed.

The conversation meandered easily, punctuated by laughter and second helpings. Outside, frost clung to the windows, but inside the candles burned low, the plates emptied, and the room glowed with an intimacy that only grew stronger as the evening unfolded. When the last dish was rinsed and set aside, Mavis caught Mac's hand before he could reach for another. "No more work tonight," she said firmly. "We've got presents waiting by the fire."

In the living room, the tree sparkled, the fire

crackled, and the scent of pine and cinnamon mingled in the air. A quilt was draped across the couch, and a platter of cookies sat on the coffee table, waiting to be nibbled. Mavis tucked herself into the corner of the couch, her legs folded under her, while Mac sat close beside her. She reached under the tree and pulled out a small, square box wrapped in gold paper with a crimson bow. "This one's for you," she said, her eyes alight. "And you have to open it first."

He untied the bow slowly, as though savoring the moment, and peeled back the paper. The lid of the velvet box lifted to reveal the luxury watch, gleaming in stainless steel with a deep blue dial that caught the firelight. For a long moment, Mac simply stared. His throat felt tight, his fingers hovering just above it as though he was afraid to touch. "Mavis," he whispered. "This is incredible. This is too much."

"Shh," she interrupted softly, taking his hand and lifting the watch out of its box. "Hold still." She fastened it around his wrist herself, her fingers brushing his skin. "I wanted you to have something that lasts. Something that marks this moment, this Christmas. Our first and hopefully not the last."

Mac leaned over and kissed her forehead, lingering just long enough for her to close her eyes and breathe him in. When he pulled back, he reached under the tree for a package of his own. It was small, slim, wrapped in simple brown paper tied with twine. "It's not much compared to what you just gave me," he admitted, handing it to her.

"But I thought, well, you'll see."

Mavis tore the paper gently, revealing a leather-bound journal, the kind with soft, pliable pages that begged to be written on. Her initials were embossed in gold on the cover. "I know you're serious about writing," he said. "I thought maybe this could be a start."

"It's perfect," she said again, her voice hushed with emotion.

"Come on. I've got one more thing to show you," he smiled. His eyes twinkled with mischief as he stood up and held out his hand. As curiosity tugged at her, Mavis set the journal carefully on the coffee table and took his hand. He pulled her to her feet and, still holding on, led her toward the back door. She blinked in surprise when the cold night air greeted her. "Mac! It's freezing out here!" She slid her feet into her boots that were by the back door and wrapped her shawl tighter around her shoulders, her breath puffing white in the frosty air.

"Just a short walk," he promised, guiding her down the steps and across the yard. The stars overhead glittered sharp and clear. Mavis tilted her head, suspicion dawning. "What are we doing in the barn on Christmas Eve?"

"You'll see," Mac whispered as he pushed the door open.

The interior was dim, smelling of hay and old wood, but at the center of the floor, bathed in the golden glow of the overhead light, sat something covered with a white sheet. A huge red bow gleamed on top. Mavis stopped in her tracks.

"Mac, what is this?"

He squeezed her hand. "Go ahead. See for yourself," he said.

Her heart thudded as she stepped forward. The sheet whispered as she lifted it away, revealing the dark gleam of polished wood. An antique writing desk stood before her, its lines elegant, its surface broad enough to hold stacks of paper and a lamp. The drawers were carved with delicate details, the kind of craftsmanship that whispered of another era. It looked as though it had always belonged here at the Manor. Mavis' hand flew to her mouth. "Oh, oh, Mac!"

He watched her closely, his chest tightening with emotion at her reaction. "Do you like it?" he asked.

Tears shimmered in her eyes as she ran her hand across the desk's smooth surface. "Like it? I love it! It's beautiful. It's perfect." She turned toward him, laughing through the tears.

"Wilbur and Emily helped me bring it over earlier. I wanted you to have a place to keep that journal and all the ones that'll come after," he grinned.

She pressed her palm against the wood again, as if to ground herself. "It looks like it was made for Magnolia Manor."

"That's what I thought when I saw it. A house like this deserves a piece like that. And you," Mac reached out, brushing a strand of hair from her cheek. "You deserve a space that's just yours. To dream, to write, and to remember."

He held her close, breathing in the faint scent

of cinnamon that still clung to her hair from the kitchen. Over her shoulder, he looked at the desk again, and a quiet satisfaction filled him. She traced the curve of his jaw with her fingertips, then looked back at the desk, her smile tender. They stood there for a while longer, just the two of them in the barn with the stars peeking through the cracks in the roof, the desk gleaming like treasure between them. "Be thinking about where you'd like to put it. Wilbur said he would help me bring it inside tomorrow," Mac explained.

"I have the perfect spot in mind," Mavis nodded. They covered it back with the sheet and walked merrily back to the Manor after Mavis locked the barn door. "Best Christmas ever," Mavis smiled as she squeezed Mac's hand back on the couch.

They sat for a while longer, opening the smaller gifts like scarves, books, and other little tokens chosen with care. After the last scraps of wrapping paper had been tossed into the basket and the gifts arranged neatly on the coffee table, the living room settled into a new kind of quiet. The tree's twinkling lights reflected in the glass panes of the windows, and the fire burned lower, its embers glowing warmly. Mac leaned back against the couch, one arm draped lazily across the back. The watch on his wrist caught the light each time the flames flickered, and he found himself glancing at it more than once, not to check the time, but simply because it anchored him in the moment. Mavis curled beside him under the quilt, the leather journal resting on her lap. Her fingers traced absentminded circles on its cover. "What's on your mind?" Mac asked softly.

She hesitated before answering. "I was just thinking about Big Mama and Big Daddy, and Opal, too. About how much they loved Christmas. They would've loved you."

His chest warmed at that. "That means a lot, Mavis."

"Big Mama always said Christmas wasn't about the food or the presents. It was about the people, the memories, and the traditions you build. I didn't really understand that when I was younger." Mavis glanced at him with a small smile. "But now I do."

Mac reached for her hand, squeezing it gently. "I'm glad we're starting our own tradition then. Even if it involves lasagna instead of a Christmas ham."

She laughed, the sound bright and clear. "Lasagna might just become our thing."

He leaned down and brushed a kiss against her temple. "Then lasagna it is," he agreed.

"So," she said, tilting her head toward the television that was playing It's a Wonderful Life. "Shall we start this over or pick something else?" Mac rubbed his chin in exaggerated thought. "Do we have Die Hard?"

Mavis swatted his arm with the quilt, laughing. "Absolutely not."

"Come on, it's a Christmas movie!" he chuckled.

"It is not," Mavis laughed.

He chuckled, relenting. "All right, all right.

How about starting It's a Wonderful Life again? I haven't seen it since I was a kid."

"That's perfect," Mavis agreed. She slipped off the couch to grab the remote and restarted the film. The movie began, black-and-white scenes flickering across the screen. They watched as George Bailey dreamed, struggled, and eventually realized just how many lives he had touched. About halfway through, Mavis reached for a cookie from the platter. She broke it in half and handed the larger piece to Mac. "Here. Your snowman won't survive the night," she laughed.

He grinned as he accepted it. "Proof of my decorating skills," he winked.

By the time Clarence got his wings, Mavis was leaning against Mac's chest, her breathing slow and steady. "Sleepy?" he murmured.

"A little," she admitted, though her eyes remained open, fixed on the screen. When the credits rolled, Mavis stretched, setting the empty cookie plate aside. "That was nice," she said softly.

"It was," Mac nodded.

She stood, gathering the quilt around her shoulders. "I'm going to blow out the candles. You get the fire?"

"Yes, ma'am," he nodded. They moved about the room in quiet partnership, snuffing out flames and tidying up. When at last the living room was dark except for the glow of the tree lights, they stood side by side, taking it all in. "Beautiful, isn't it?" Mavis whispered.

"The most beautiful," Mac agreed, but he wasn't looking at the tree. Hand in hand they climbed the stairs. In the hallway, the shadows stretched long, and the Manor creaked softly as though it too were settling into slumber. At her bedroom door, Mavis paused. "Merry Christmas, Mac," she whispered.

Chapter Twenty-Nine

Christmas morning at Magnolia Manor arrived softly, wrapped in a quiet frost on the windows and porch swing. The old house seemed to hum with contentment, its windows glowing faintly in the pale winter sun. The tree still sparkled in the living room, the ornaments catching bits of morning light and scattering them across the floor like confetti. Mavis pulled on her slippers, wrapped her robe around her shoulders, and walked downstairs towards the kitchen. The smell of coffee hit her before she rounded the corner. Mac was leaning against the kitchen counter with a mug in hand. He looked up at her with that slow, easy smile she adored. "Good morning. Merry Christmas," he smiled.

"Merry Christmas," she echoed, her voice still husky with sleep.

He poured her a cup of strong coffee, and she took it gratefully, the warmth seeping into her hands. On the counter sat a white paper box from the bakery in town that they had picked up the day before. "The perfect Christmas morning breakfast," she said, opening the box to reveal an assortment of donuts dusted with powdered sugar, drizzled with glaze, and some with festive red and green sprinkles.

"Wouldn't be Christmas morning without them," Mac said. "Though I do love a good donut any morning."

They carried their coffee and donuts to the small breakfast table where they sat in the golden morning light, savoring the sweetness and the quiet. Mavis felt a flutter in her chest. Last night had been magic; baking cookies, exchanging their first gifts, and Mac staying the night. She reached across the table and squeezed his hand. "This might be my favorite Christmas already."

"We haven't even made it to lunch yet," Mac teased, though his eyes softened.

"Doesn't matter," she said. "It's already perfect."

"Well, we haven't tried on our matching sweaters yet, so it's only bound to get better," Mac grinned. Mavis hadn't been sure if Mac would wear a giant Christmas sweater that matched the one in her closet or not, but when she gave it to him last week, he seemed overjoyed. After their donuts and coffee had long since disappeared, they changed into their matching sweaters and giggled like teenagers. Mavis appreciated Mac's silliness and he adored her wish to make new traditions.

By late morning, the crunch of tires on gravel signaled company. Mavis set her newly refilled mug aside and hurried to the window. "Wilbur and Emily are here!" she called.

Mac rose to open the door, letting in a burst of cold air and laughter. Emily barreled inside first, cheeks rosy, eyes bright. She didn't even wait to remove her coat before blurting out, "You will not believe what Wilbur gave me last night!"

Mavis laughed at her energy. "What? Tell me!" Even though she already knew. She had been bursting at the bits to tell Emily what Wilbur had been working on behind the scenes, but she had kept the surprise a secret.

"A horse!" Emily squealed, bouncing on her toes. "An honest-to-goodness horse, Mavis. I've always wanted one, and he actually did it."

Mavis gasped, pulling her into a hug. "That's wonderful!" She winked at Wilbur over Emily's shoulder and watched him grin.

"We've got space already sorted," Emily said, practically glowing. "It's like he knew exactly what would make me the happiest woman alive. I already am, but this keeps the streak rolling."

Wilbur followed her in more slowly, carrying a couple of wrapped gifts under his arm. He gave a sheepish grin, scratching at his jaw. "Didn't think she'd be quite this excited over an old racehorse."

"Didn't think?" Emily gave him a playful swat. "You've ruined every Christmas gift I'll ever get after this. Nothing can top a horse."

"That's a hard one to beat, Wilbur," Mac chuckled. He leaned closer to Wilbur and whispered, "Thanks for bringing the desk over last night. She loved it. I will need help taking it upstairs later if you don't mind."

"Absolutely!" Wilbur agreed. He turned back towards the ladies and grinned. "Just wait until you see what she gave me. She doesn't let a man have his moment."

Emily returned his grin and hugged him

tightly. "It was a great idea," Mavis nodded. She had been privy to both of their gifts and had kept them both a secret, even from Mac.

"What was it?" Mac asked curiously.

Mavis laughed and ushered them all to the living room where the tree glittered. "Well, come sit down and tell us everything. We've got a little time before Maude gets here and we need to start cooking."

Emily didn't waste a second after they all settled around the fireplace in the living room. "A saltwater aquarium," Emily said proudly, bouncing on the edge of the sofa. "Five hundred gallons. The one here at the Manor is gorgeous and he's practically an expert in running this one. He's always wanted one of his own, and now he's finally getting it, only a much smaller version. But the same coral reef, colorful fish, the works."

"It's really incredible," Wilbur nodded. "I can't wait to have it installed in the new year."

"Do you like it?" Emily asked eagerly.

"Like it?" His voice was thick with emotion. "I love it. You know me better than I know myself sometimes." Emily leaned against him and smiled." We both know each other so well," she affirmed.

Wilbur laughed, pressing a kiss to her forehead. "We'll call it even."

Mavis sat back, her heartwarming at the sight. This was the good stuff in life. They filled the rest of the morning sipping coffee and eating more donuts recounting their gifts. Once Mavis was sure her hair was perfect, Emily posed Mavis and

Mac on the porch of Magnolia Manor and took photos. They swapped cameras and Mavis then took pictures of Emily and Wilbur. "Sibling photo next!" Emily directed. She took the camera back from Mavis and snapped a few quick pictures of Wilbur and Mavis who both made silly faces.

An hour later, Mac and Wilbur were out by the barn getting ready to move Mavis' writing desk inside to Jameson's old office. Emily and Mavis were stirring pots and pans in the kitchen getting ready for their big Christmas dinner of homemade bread, ham, mashed potatoes, wild rice, green beans, and Emily's homemade chocolate fudge cake. "I think I hear Maude," Mavis said as she looked out the window. When she opened the door a few minutes later, Maude swept in with all the energy of a snowstorm, her arms laden with packages. "Well, don't just stand there gawking, help an old woman before I topple over!" Maude shrieked.

Emily quickly relieved her of a heavy bag, while Mavis took a few of the wrapped gifts. "You're not old," Mavis said.

"Ha!" Maude scoffed, but her eyes twinkled. "Older than you, at least. Now, where's my chair? I need to thaw out before I freeze solid." She settled into her favorite armchair by the fire, rubbing her hands together. "Much better. Now, let's get to it. I may be old but I still know how to make mashed potatoes."

Mavis and Emily followed Maude into the warm kitchen and together they worked on the various sides while Wilbur and Mac carried the antique desk inside. Once it was in the place Mavis had designated, she admired it again in its full splendor. "I love it so much," she smiled.

When the meal was ready, Wilbur set the dining room table with Ruby's fine Christmas plates. They all gathered around to fill their plates as they traded jokes and stories. Wilbur told the tale of trying to surprise Emily with the horse without her catching on, and how he'd nearly been caught sneaking around the barn re-framing a new stall. Emily countered with the chaos of arranging a five-hundred-gallon aquarium measurement without Wilbur noticing.

Laughter filled the Manor, spilling into every corner, softening the edges of the holiday without Opal and so many who had passed long before their time. Their loved ones may not have been there in person, but their presence lingered. Mavis looked around the table, her chest tightening with gratitude. "This," she thought, "is what Christmas is supposed to be."

After lunch, they lingered by the fire sipping coffee and nibbling at cookies and thick slices of Emily's rich chocolate cake. The tree glowed with gifts piled around it, laughter still echoing in the rafters. Mavis leaned against Mac's shoulder with her eyes half-closed. He kissed her temple, and as the snow began to fall lightly outside, Magnolia Manor seemed to hum with contentment again, holding them all safe and close. The fire snapped cheerfully as Maude reached into her bag and pulled out the first package, wrapped neatly in gold paper with a crimson ribbon. She held it out to Mavis. "I thought you'd appreciate this," Maude announced.

Mavis untied the bow carefully, her fingers delicate as she peeled back the paper. Inside, she found an envelope and a neatly stacked bundle of faux leather-bound books. She blinked, her breath catching as she recognized the looping script on the covers. "Open the envelope first," Maude instructed.

"Season tickets to the theater?" she murmured, smiling. "Maude, that's amazing," she grinned. She held up the theatre brochure and immediately noticed some incredible shows that were coming up. She put the brochure and tickets back in the envelope and then turned her attention to the books in the tissue paper. "And these, are these?" Mavis ran her fingers over the books and held back tears.

"Opal's diaries," Maude confirmed softly. "I thought you might keep them safe. You'll find her voice in there, plain as day. She wanted them read. She wanted them remembered. Do with them what you want. I've read them all, hell, I was there for most all of it."

Mavis clutched them to her chest, her eyes stinging with tears. "Thank you, Maude. This, this means the world to me." Mac rested a hand on her shoulder, squeezing gently. He knew without words how much it meant.

"Now, for you," Maude said to Wilbur, passing him a flat, square book. "Something I've been working on ever since I found it."

Wilbur opened the package, and his face

stilled. It was a scrapbook, the pages carefully filled with his mother's old newspaper articles, stories, features, interviews; each one paired with photographs from the paper, yellowed but carefully preserved. Wilbur's eyes lingered on the familiar bylines. "How did you get these?"

"Opal did," Maude said softly. "Opal had them tucked away for years. She had been tracking them down and I think she planned to give them to you when she was sure she had found them all, so I thought you should have them. It's a reminder of where you came from, and of the woman who birthed you and loved you fiercely before you became ours."

He closed the book with trembling hands, then walked over to Maude and wrapped her in a bear-hug. "Thank you," he whispered quietly. After he settled back in his place next to Emily, Maude reached for a box tied with green ribbon and slid it toward Emily. Emily tore into the wrapping and gasped. Inside lay carefully wrapped bundles of Christmas ornaments, garlands, and figurines. She lifted one out an old glass Santa with painted cheeks. "These were Opal's," Maude explained, her tone gentle. "She adored Christmas. I thought you might carry on the tradition."

Emily's eyes shone as she hugged the box to her chest. "Oh, I will. I'll use them every year, Maude. I'll keep her spirit alive in every light and ornament."

The room was quiet for a moment, the gifts carrying the weight of memory and love. "Well Mac, I went the sentimental route this year,"

Maude said. "I know you never met Opal, but I think she would have liked you. There's two season tickets in Mavis' envelope, and I think you should accompany Mavis girl over to the theatre if that's something y'all agree on."

"Yes ma'am," Mac grinned. "I'd accompany her anywhere she'll have me." Mavis sniffled, laughed softly, and said, "Well, we'd better keep going before I turn into a puddle." She leaned forward, her eyes twinkling as she handed Wilbur a slim envelope. "You're hard to shop for, but I think you'll like this."

Wilbur slid the papers out and let out a low whistle. "Fruit trees? Figs, peaches, lemon, apples! Mavis!"

"For the greenhouse," she explained. "Something that'll grow, something that'll last."

"Perfect," Wilbur said with a grin. "Thank you, Mavis."

"Alright, Maude," Mavis said as she handed over a thick scrapbook bound with ribbon and overflowing with photos, maps, and notes. "It's the story of our adventures with Opal's bucket list," she said, her voice gentle. "Every stop, every laugh, every picture I could find. I wanted you to have it. And when we finish the very last item on the list, I'll add that adventure to the book."

Maude's hands trembled as she flipped through the first few pages showing snapshots of them walking in Yellowstone, another of their tattoos in Nashville, the scone recipe from London, and many more. She pressed her lips together, fighting tears. "Oh, Mavis. This is priceless. Absolutely priceless."

"And you," Mavis said with a smile to Emily, "I may have known about Wilbur's surprise."

Emily gasped, clutching her chest. "You sneaky thing!"

"Only because we knew how much you'd love it," Mavis smiled. "Here, open this!" She handed Emily a gift bag that contained a monogrammed bridle and lead rope for Emily's precious racehorse, Echo.

Emily hugged her tightly. "I love this more than I can say. Now it's our turn!"

She stepped forward, carrying a large, carefully wrapped package and set it in Mavis' lap with a grin. Mavis peeled back the wrapping to reveal a polished vintage record player, its brass fittings gleaming, its wood gleaming like new. Beneath it, stacked neatly, was a collection of signed records. She gasped, her hand flying to her mouth.

"These are," Her eyes widened as she recognized the signatures. "The Lake Street Dive collection? Signed?"

Emily winked. "We may have called in a favor or two."

Mavis laughed through her tears, hugging the stack to her chest. "You all know me too well. This is incredible. Absolutely incredible."

"And we couldn't forget you," Emily smiled at Maude. "I told Wilbur how much you loved our adventure at the car park, so this only made sense."

Maude opened the envelope Emily handed her and gasped. "A luxury car experience? Track time? You're letting me loose on a racetrack?"

"Absolutely," Wilbur said with a grin. "We figured it was about time you had some more speed in your life at a place where it's legal and there aren't any of Mavis' rosebushes or mailboxes in the way."

Maude threw her head back and laughed. "Well, I'll be the terror of the track, that's for sure!"

Chapter Thirty

As the new year rolled in, Opal's eighty-fifth birthday loomed like a quiet landmark on the calendar. The holidays were barely behind them, the echoes of laughter and clinking glasses still lingered in the corners of Magnolia Manor, but in Opal's old house the mood was different.

The house already looked emptier than it ever had in all the years they had known it. The familiar floral couch was gone, carted off by a neighbor boy with a pickup truck. The walls, once cluttered with framed photographs, now stood bare and exposed, revealing spots of paint that hadn't seen daylight in decades. Boxes were stacked neatly down the hallway, each labeled for their new destination of various charities and giveaway spots. The kitchen had an unfamiliar echo when anyone spoke, as though the house had already resigned itself to loneliness.

Now, on that pale, empty wall where the couch had once lived, Wilbur and Mavis were fighting with a world map. It was larger than either of them had realized when Maude had ordered it online, rolled up in a cardboard tube like a secret. Unfurled, it spanned nearly the entire wall, its edges curling stubbornly despite Wilbur's careful efforts with painter's tape.

"Hold that corner higher," Wilbur grunted, stretching his arm and pressing the tape into place. His glasses had slid down his nose, and sweat beaded along his brow despite the January chill. Mavis squinted up at the map, one hand braced on her hip. "Higher? If it goes any higher, Wilbur, we'll need a ladder. Maude's not going to hit the top of the world. She'll be lucky if she hits the paper at all."

Wilbur chuckled, the sound warming the otherwise hollow room. "You underestimate her. I've seen Maude play darts over the years. She's better than you think. Question is, where will she aim?"

"I thought she was going to choose a map of Alabama there for a minute," Mavis said, laughing softly. "Or maybe the United States, but the world?" She gestured grandly at the vast paper oceans, the tiny scatterings of islands, the bold names of faraway capitals. "I didn't expect this. Oh, Wilbur, what if she throws the dart and it lands on the ceiling?"

Wilbur adjusted his glasses, giving her a sidelong look. "That'd be a neat trick. Maybe we'd have to book a flight to the moon."

The thought made Mavis laugh harder, though her laughter cracked at the edges. "It just seems risky, that's all. The whole wide world to choose from." Her voice softened. "It feels so final, doesn't it?"

Wilbur heard what she didn't quite say. She wasn't just talking about the map. She was talking about the house, about the way everything here smelled faintly of lavender sachets and lemon polish, about the way the floor creaked in exactly the same spots it had for close to fifty years. She was talking about Opal herself, and how strange it felt to plan new adventures when the one who had always dreamed them up wasn't here to go. He pressed another strip of tape into place and stepped back. The map stretched across the wall now, its wrinkles smoothed, its continents spread wide and ready. It was as though the entire world had been crammed into Opal's living room, waiting for Maude's hand to choose their fate. Wilbur dusted his palms against his jeans. "There. Straight enough?"

Mavis tilted her head. "Crooked as Maude's sense of humor, but I suppose it'll do." She softened, her gaze roaming the map. "Look at it, Wilbur. All those places. Do you think Opal ever dreamed of seeing everywhere there ever was?"

"She dreamed of them all," Wilbur said simply. "But Opal was just as happy in Rhinestone. You know that."

"Yes," Mavis's lips curved into a small smile. "That was her gift, wasn't it? Making wherever she was feel like the grandest place on earth." They stood in silence for a moment, side by side, gazing at the world map pinned to the wall of a house that was almost no longer theirs.

"I just keep telling myself this is a good idea," Mavis murmured, almost to herself. Wilbur glanced at her. He knew she meant the sale of the house, the letting go, the moving on. He nodded once, steady. "It is. It's time."

But both of them knew that tonight wasn't about boxes or real estate. Tonight was about one last memory stitched into these walls before they said goodbye. The creak of the front steps was the only warning they got before Maude swept into the house as though she were making an entrance on a stage. The door flew open, cold January air following her inside like a companion. "Ladies and gentleman," Mavis declared, "your dart-throwing champion has arrived."

Maude was holding the dart in one hand like it was a royal scepter. In her other arm, she carried a paper bag from the Piggly Wiggly that looked suspiciously like it might contain snacks. A silk scarf was knotted dramatically under her chin, though she wasn't wearing it for warmth; Maude had decided to dress the part for such a dramatic event. She had clearly taken a page out of Opal's book. Wilbur raised his brows but said nothing, simply watching her with that half-smile he reserved for Maude's antics.

"Well, don't you look ready," Mavis said, folding her arms.

Maude set the bag on the kitchen counter with a flourish and marched into the living room. When she spotted the map, she gasped and clutched her chest. "Oh, look at it! The whole world, right here in Opal's house."

"Your idea," Wilbur reminded her. "Don't act surprised."

"I didn't realize it would feel so official, or so big," Maude said. She inspected the map and frowned slightly.

"What's wrong?" Mavis asked. "Just imagine wherever this dart lands, that's where we'll go. Spain! Brazil! Morocco!" She spun on her heel to face them, eyes glittering. "Are you ready for this?"

"As ready as I'll ever be," Maude said.

Mavis patted her arm and said, "Ok, then we're ready. Though Wilbur's worried about windows and eyeballs." Wilbur went to object, but Mavis' laughter made him laugh it off.

"Don't be ridiculous," Maude waved off. "I've been throwing darts since before you were born, Wilbur." She pulled the scarf from around her head and gestured for Wilbur to tie it around her eyes. "If I'm going to be blindfolded, it ought to be with something of hers. Feels right, don't you think?"

Mavis swallowed past the lump in her throat and nodded. "Yes. It does."

Wilbur tied the scarf around Maude's eyes, careful not to make it too tight. For a moment, the living room went quiet except for the faint crinkle of the map on the wall. The scarf, faintly scented with lavender and time, transformed the room. The laughter and bravado faded, replaced with something steadier, almost sacred. "How do I look?" Maude asked into the silence.

"Like a queen about to conquer the world," Mavis announced, smiling even as her eyes shone. She snapped a picture of Maude in her blindfold and steadied herself for what was about to come. Would they be going to Fiji, New Zealand, Argentina, or perhaps San Diego?

"That's more like it," Maude said with a grin, adjusting her stance. "Well then, hand me my weapon." Wilbur placed the dart carefully in her hand. "Don't skewer me," he teased.

"Don't tempt me," she shot back, but her fingers curled around the dart with surprising steadiness. The living room felt different now, charged, as if the old house itself was holding its breath. The map loomed on the wall, its bright blues and greens a doorway to every possibility they could imagine. "All right," Wilbur said, stepping back a safe distance. "Let's keep this simple. Take a few steps forward, aim straight, and throw. Easy as pie."

Maude raised the dart as though she were in a parade. "Should I spin around to make it more official?" Maude asked.

"Absolutely not," Wilbur said firmly. "You'd trip over a box and break your hip."

"Scaredy-cat," Maude teased, wagging the dart in his direction.

"Put that thing down before you accidentally throw it at me," he said, stepping back again.

Mavis crossed her arms, her expression amused. "I like the idea of spinning her just a little. Adds drama."

"Adds a trip to the emergency room," Wilbur countered.

Maude sighed loudly, as though she'd been denied the greatest joy of her life. "Fine. But if I hit somewhere boring, I'll know it's because you didn't let me spin."

"Somewhere boring?" Mavis gasped in mock horror. "The world is wide and wonderful, Maude! There is no boring."

"Have you ever been to Des Moines?" Maude deadpanned.

Wilbur couldn't help but laugh at that one. "Just throw the dart," he encouraged.

Maude adjusted her stance, rolling her shoulders back like an athlete about to compete in the Olympics. "This is more than just a dart toss, you know. This is a moment. We'll remember this forever."

"We'd remember it quicker if you'd just do it," Wilbur muttered.

"Wilbur," Mavis scolded gently. "Let her have her moment."

Maude tilted her chin up, blindfolded eyes toward the ceiling. "For Opal," she said, her voice suddenly serious. The room quieted. "And for us and our one last grand adventure."

Something about the way she said it made the air thicken. Even Wilbur fell silent. Mavis felt a lump in her throat. She thought of Opal, her laughter, her endless lists of places she wanted to see, the way she'd made even a trip to the grocery store feel like an outing. This dart wasn't just about them. It was about her, too. What if this was the last grand adventure they had with Maude, the last of the Stone Sisters? Mavis nor Wilbur wanted to think about that any time soon.

Maude took a deep breath. Then, just as quickly, the solemnity broke. "Now, tell me, is the map straight? Because if I end up in the Arctic Ocean because Wilbur can't tape straight, I'll never forgive him."

"It's fine," Mavis assured her.

"It's a little crooked," Wilbur admitted.

Maude stamped her foot. "If I end up in Antarctica, I'm blaming you both."

Mavis laughed, partly from nerves. "Imagine us bundled up like penguins, sipping hot cocoa in igloos. Maybe it wouldn't be so bad."

"Penguins don't live in the Arctic," Wilbur corrected automatically.

"See?" Maude said triumphantly, pointing the dart in his direction again. "He's already preparing excuses."

Wilbur held up his hands in surrender. "All right, all right. No more talk. Just throw it, but not at me."

Maude straightened again, adjusting her grip on the dart. The room seemed to narrow until it was just her, the map, and fate waiting to reveal itself. Mavis realized she was holding her breath. "Here goes nothing," Maude whispered. Maude lifted her arm, the dart glinting faintly in the overhead light. For a long moment, she didn't move. The house held its breath with her, the silence broken only by the faint tick of the old mantel clock in the hall that Wilbur planned to take home with him that afternoon. Maude's knuckles whitened around the dart, her elbow bent just so, her wrist flicking slightly as though testing the air. Mavis held her breath. The world seemed to shrink until there was nothing but the distance between her friend's hand and the great map on the wall. With a sharp, clean motion, Maude let the dart fly. It sailed across the room in a brief flash of silver. For the smallest heartbeat, time itself seemed to pause, all their futures suspended in midair. Then came the sound: a crisp, satisfying thwack.

None of them moved. None of them spoke. They simply stared at the map, at the small bit of steel embedded in paper continents, too reverent to step forward and see where fate had taken them. For a long moment, none of them dared to move. The dart sat snug against the map, its little feathered tail trembling slightly as though it too were catching its breath. Mavis' hands had folded at her waist, fingers knotted together so tightly that her knuckles had gone white. She stared at the map from across the room, her throat tightening.

"Well?" Maude whispered. She was still wearing the blindfold. Mavis gingerly removed it from her face and together they stared at Wilbur who took that to be his invitation to reveal the location. His feet had already started moving to carry him across the room. Each step echoed off the empty wood floor, amplifying the silence. He slowed as he reached the wall, his broad shoulders blocking their view.

"Well?" Maude said again, louder this time. "Don't just stand there like a scarecrow. Tell us where it landed."

But Wilbur didn't speak. He leaned forward, his nose almost brushing the map, as though he couldn't quite believe what he was seeing. "Wilbur?" Mavis' voice had a tremor in it now.

Finally, he turned, slowly, his face a mixture of astonishment. "You're not going to believe this," he said quietly.

Mavis' breath caught. Maude tilted her head.

"Where?" they both asked.

Wilbur stepped aside, motioning toward the map. "See for yourself."

Together, Mavis and Maude moved forward, their eyes scanning the sprawling paper continents and oceans until they found the dart. It hadn't landed on Paris or Rome or some faraway island. It hadn't even strayed to the glitter of New York City or the sweep of the Pacific. It had landed in Alabama right on the dot where Rhinestone sat, almost invisible on the map, but there, nonetheless. Mavis' hand flew to her mouth. "Oh my stars," she gasped.

"That can't be right," Maude blinked, her lips parting.

"It's right," Wilbur said, his voice low.

"But the whole world," Maude whispered, shaking her head. "The whole wide world and it chose Rhinestone?"

"It seems so," Wilbur breathed. He looked at the dart as though it had become something sacred.

Mavis pressed her palms against her cheeks, tears prickling at the corners of her eyes. "It's, oh, it's perfect. Don't you see? It ends where it began. It's so poetic. "

"Of all the places," Wilbur nodded.

They stood there in silence for a long time, each of them caught in their own flood of memories. The church picnics, the dusty football fields, the small-town parades with crepe-paper floats. The grocery store where Opal always knew the cashier's name. The sidewalks they'd walked as children, barefoot in the summer heat. Rhinestone wasn't just a pinprick on the map. It was everything that had shaped them, the soil beneath their roots. And somehow, fate, or perhaps Opal's steady hand guiding them still, had brought them back to it. Mavis was the first to speak again, her voice breaking softly. "She would love this. You know she would. She'd be laughing that great big laugh of hers, saying we don't have to travel far to find what matters most."

Wilbur finally stepped forward, gently pulling the dart free from the map. He held it for a moment, staring down at the tiny hole it had left in the paper, as though it were a marker carved into their story. Then he set it carefully on the mantel. "Well," he said, clearing his throat. "Looks like we've got ourselves a destination."

Mavis laughed again, this time through her tears. "Home," she whispered.

"Home," Maude repeated, still staring at the tiny dot that had sealed their fate.

Chapter Thirty-One

The morning sun filtered softly through the branches of the magnolia tree, scattering golden light across the lawn of Magnolia Manor. The house stood timeless, its white columns a silent witness to the decades of stories lived and shared here. For Mavis, Maude, and Wilbur, stepping onto the familiar grounds felt like stepping into memory itself. They had come to do something tender. The last item on the bucket list would soon be crossed off by releasing some more of Opal's ashes in the place where so much time had been treasured.

Wilbur carried the small pouch of ashes carefully. His eyes held the weight of years and a tenderness that seemed almost boyish today. The woods of Magnolia Manor was where he had first seen Opal by the creek in the fall of 1985. He was a young boy then and nearly forty years later he could still see her as if it were yesterday: the young woman with laughter in her eyes bending down to scoop a pebble from the water as if it were treasure.

Mavis walked beside him, her arm looped through his as though to steady them both. She was quieter than usual, letting the crunch of the wooded path under their shoes fill the silence. Maude followed, her face set with a kind of determined serenity, though every so often her lips pressed tightly together, betraying the ache she carried in her heart. They came to the creek, where the water gurgled softly, carrying with it fallen leaves and the faint scent of moss. Pine and oak tree branches stretched overhead, draping them in a canopy of memory.

"This was it," Wilbur said, his voice low, reverent. "Right here. She was standing by that rock." He pointed to a smooth, flat stone along the bank. "She told me the water made her feel like time slowed down. That day, I believed her. It felt like time did stop. You sure you're ready?"

Maude stepped closer. "We've said a lot of goodbyes already. But this one feels like we're putting her back where she belongs." She reached out and laid her hand gently on the pouch, and Mavis followed. For a moment, the three of them stood linked together, holding not just ashes, but decades of love, friendship, and laughter as a breeze stirred through the trees.

Wilbur crouched by the creek and tilted the pouch, letting a fine stream of ash slip into the current. The water carried it gently downstream, swirling it into the bends and ripples. He thought of her laugh and the way she could brighten a room with nothing more than her smirk. "She loved it here," Maude said, her tone steady but tender.

Mavis stood a step back and thought of all the adventures they'd had with the bucket list that was now checked off, and the way Opal had insisted life was meant to be lived with gusto. "We finished the list for you, Opal," she whispered.

"Every last thing."

For a while, they were quiet, listening to the creek, the rustle of leaves, the distant calls of birds in the trees. Wilbur looked at them both, his eyes shining. "Full circle," he said simply. They stood together by the creek, three souls bound by loss and love, knowing that while they had let go of Opal in the physical sense, she would never truly leave them. Magnolia Manor, Rhinestone, the creek, the salon, every memory, every laugh, every lesson still lingered, stitched into the fabric of who they had become. As the sun climbed higher, the three of them turned toward the Manor, the house standing proud and familiar against the sky. "I guess it's getting to be that time," Maude said. Mac and Emily would be getting off work soon and they all planned to meet one last time at Opal's house to say their goodbyes to the home.

Opal's home had sold in just two weeks. A young couple had fallen in love with it the moment they stepped inside, and none of them were surprised. Opal's home, just like Opal herself, had always known how to welcome people, even strangers, into its heart. Still, knowing it was in good hands didn't make the goodbye easier. Mavis stood at the top of the steps, her coat buttoned against the chill. She let her gloved fingers trace the railing, feeling the grooves worn smooth by decades of hands before hers. A thin wind stirred the porch swing, setting it to a slow, empty sway. Behind her, the screen door creaked open and Maude stepped out onto the porch.

Down the drive came the sound of Wilbur's

truck, the tires crunching on the gravel. Emily hopped out first, her scarf wrapped tight against the cold, a flash of color against the muted day. She waved, her smile bright despite the sting of winter air and melancholy. Wilbur followed, moving slower, his eyes on the house, his breath caught somewhere between pride and sorrow. "Feels odd seeing it this way," Wilbur said as he climbed the steps, pausing to rest his hand on the porch rail. "Like she might come storming out the door, asking me to help her load up the buckets from the garden." His chuckle was soft, edged with ache. He could remember the first time he saw Opal Tyler hunched over a pair of buckets in the woods of Magnolia Manor searching for clay, roots, and gems. He had watched her many times before she caught him hiding in the bushes from his abusive father who lived on the other side of the woods. She may not have been the woman to give him life, but she immediately breathed new life into him at twelve years old. She would always be the spark that changed the direction of his life.

Mac arrived last, balancing a bakery box against one hip. The smell of cinnamon drifted out when he set it on the porch step. "Evening," he said finally, his voice carrying a kind of reverence. He eased into one of the rocking chairs. For a moment, the porch held only the soft sounds of rocking chairs and the faint whistle of wind through the tree branches. The stillness pressed in, not empty but full of memory, of the life that had passed across these boards.

Emily broke the silence first. "You know,

when I first came here, I was so nervous, but Opal had a way of folding you in, even when she made a fuss. Sitting on this porch, I felt part of something bigger than myself," she smiled.

"She made room for everybody. There was never a day I doubted she loved me," Wilbur agreed.

Mavis rocked gently in her chair, the boards beneath her creaking with their familiar rhythm. "If these boards could speak, they'd tell the story of all of us." The wind stirred again, rattling the bare branches of the trees out front. Somewhere in the distance, a crow called. The day was closing in, winter shadows stretching long across the yard. It was Wilbur who spoke what they all felt. "Hard thing, letting go," he said, his voice gravelly. "But maybe that's the proof it mattered." The words lingered there, carried by the winter air, sinking into the porch boards like a final benediction.

"I still remember the summer Opal convinced me we should paint this porch ourselves," Maude announced. A chuckle slipped out before she could stop it. "We ended up splattered head to toe with white paint, arguing the whole way about whether we'd made it worse than before. By the time Wilbur came by to check on us, the porch looked like a patchwork quilt." The wind rustled through the branches, a reminder of the season. The porch seemed to lean closer, as though the house itself was listening. They sat together for a long while sharing stories about the eighty plus years of Opal Tyler. Each memory wove itself into the night like threads in a quilt, patching together something whole out of the pieces they carried.

The stories wound down slowly, like embers in a fire, until only the quiet hum of insects and the creak of rocking chairs filled the air. The winter dusk had thickened around them, the porch light casting a warm halo that stretched across the worn boards. Mavis shifted in her chair, her heart beating just a little faster than usual. She had carried the weight of her decision for days, waiting for the right moment to speak. Tonight, on this porch where so much life had happened, felt like the only place to share it. She sat forward, folding her hands in her lap. "I've been thinking," she began, her voice carrying steady in the cool night. "I've been thinking about all these memories we've shared tonight about Opal and about this house. Well, about how much life has been lived here, and how much it's shaped all of us."

The others turned toward her, their faces softened by the golden porch light. She took a breath. "I don't want it to end. The house may be passing on, but the stories, all of our stories don't have to stay locked up in our hearts. Opal left behind her diaries. Every last one of them are filled with her thoughts, her charm, her prayers, her disappointments, her joys. I've been reading through them, and I," Mavis hesitated, her throat tightening. "I feel like she left them for me, for all of us. Maybe even for the world. I want her and everyone who has gone before to always be remembered, now and forever."

Maude's head tilted, her eyes narrowing slightly, though not unkindly. "What are you saying, Mavis?"

Mavis pressed her palms together, gathering courage. "I want to write them into books. Not just one, but a whole series. A series that tells the story of Opal, you, and Big Mama. Stories of all of us, even you, Emily, and you, Mac." The words hung in the air like frost, delicate but powerful.

"Mavis, that's beautiful. You're the only one who could do it," Emily smiled. Wilbur leaned back in his chair. He rubbed his chin thoughtfully, then gave a slow nod. "Opal always said you had a way with words. I reckon she knew you'd find a use for those diaries someday."

Mavis felt a warmth spread through her chest, a flicker of relief. Still, there was one more piece to share, though she wasn't sure how they would take it. "I'd want to write under a pen name," she said quietly. "Not because I'm ashamed, but because I want the focus to be on the stories, not on me. If I do this, it's not about me. It's about all of us and everything we've been through together."

Maude pursed her lips, studying her with a long, penetrating gaze. Then, with a sigh, she reached across the table and squeezed Mavis' hand. "If anyone's going to tell our story, it should be you. And if you want to hide behind some fancy pen name, I suppose that's your business." Her expression softened, the edges of her mouth quirking upward. "But don't you dare do it alone. You'll need someone to keep the facts straight, make sure you don't gloss over the hard parts."

Mavis blinked, her throat tightening again, but this time with gratitude. "You mean?"

"I mean I'll help you," Maude sat back, folding her arms. "Lord knows I've got plenty of memories rattling around up here, and I'll be sure to remind you of the ones you forgot or don't know about."

Emily laughed through the thickness in her voice. "Oh, this is going to be something. I can see it already. Readers everywhere falling in love with Opal the way we did." Wilbur chuckled low in his chest. "Opal would be proud. So would Big Mama and Big Daddy."

Mavis let out a shaky breath, realizing only now how much she'd needed their blessing. She had told Mac about her ideas the night before, and he had been more than supportive. She had a feeling her family would be just as happy for her. Her shoulders loosened, and the night air felt lighter. "Thank you," she whispered. "I promise I'll honor it all."

When the last of the coffee was gone and the pastries reduced to crumbs, Mavis rose from her chair. She looked at the others, her eyes shining with both resolve and sorrow. "We should walk through her house," she said softly. "One last time."

No one argued. They stood together, their breath puffing in pale clouds against the January night, and stepped toward the front door. The key was still in Maude's pocket, though not for much longer. Tomorrow she would hand it to the young couple who'd bought the home and land that Opal had so carefully adored. The door creaked open on its familiar hinges, the smell of the house rushing out to greet them. The smell of faint lavender, traces of lemon polish, and something deeper, something that belonged only to Opal and her memory. It was the scent of years lived fully, of bread baking and quilts airing, of voices raised in song and prayers whispered. They gathered first in the kitchen, where countless meals had been shared. The room felt oddly bare now, the counters cleared, the cupboards emptied, but echoes remained. Mavis touched the edge of the counter. "I can still see Opal standing up here trying to reach something in the top cupboard. She was always so graceful!"

The group lingered there a moment longer, letting the memories warm them like the phantom heat of an oven long cooled. The dining room came next, the long table now stripped of linens and dishes, but the air still seemed heavy with laughter and the clatter of forks. They stood around the empty table for a while, letting the silence stretch. The living room with its wide windows and faded rugs had hosted everything from quiet evenings with books to boisterous gatherings on stormy nights. Wilbur had taken the giant map down off the wall and rolled it back inside its packaging tube. He wasn't sure where Maude had put it, but he knew she would keep it. Emily glanced back down the hall. "It's strange, isn't it? How a place can feel so full and so empty at the same time."

"It's because we carry the fullness now," Mavis nodded.

"It's not goodbye," Maude said at last, her tone firm, as though daring anyone to disagree. "It's just handing over the keys. The life here doesn't end because we're walking out. It goes with us." They stood together in the small entryway bound by memory, by loss, and by love. Then, slowly, they stepped back out onto the porch, the night air wrapping around them once again. The porch felt colder when they stepped back outside, as if the warmth of the house had clung to them and was reluctant to let go. Maude locked the front door one last time and exhaled her frosty breath into the night air. No one hurried to leave, though the cold bit at their cheeks and their breaths hung thick in the air. It was as if the house itself asked them to stay just a little longer, to give it a proper farewell before its new life began.

The old swing creaked as Maude settled into it, pulling her shawl tighter. "Strange, isn't it," she said softly, "how quickly it all happens? One moment we're gathered here for Sunday dinners and birthday cakes, and the next we're here getting ready to hand over the keys."

Emily curled up beside Wilbur on the railing, her mittened hands clasped together. "It doesn't feel like an ending," she said. "Not really. More like the closing of a chapter."

Mac leaned against the post, his steady presence grounding them all. "That's the thing about places like this," he said quietly. "You can sell the land and hand over the keys, but the memories don't leave. They're stitched into you."

No one spoke as they walked down the steps and onto the gravel drive. Their breaths puffed white in the air, their footsteps crunching in rhythm. At the edge of the yard, Mavis turned for one last look. The house, dark now, seemed to breathe in the stillness. Mavis felt Opal's presence there as a blessing. She whispered into the night, "Thank you." Then she turned back to her family, and together they walked on, carrying the stories with them.

Acknowledgments

I would never have been able to finish this book, or any of the others, without the love and support of my family and friends. This installment in the series was a tough one to write, due to it being the final one. I never imagined it would become what it has become over the years.

Thank you Between Friends Publishing who was once Southern Willow Publishing; you've been the biggest blessing from the beginning. The Rhinestone gang is forever grateful for our partnership.

About the Author

Wanda Jennings writes books about family, lifelong friendships, and the adventures that come with living in a small town! Her books have received starred reviews online and in print, as well as standing ovations and sellout shows during the performance run of Color Me Crazy at Warner Robins Little Theatre. Her first book, Dirty Laundry, received the 2021 Georgia Independent Author Award for Literary Fiction.

Before she started writing comedic fiction, Wanda received a degree in English Literature from Troy University in Alabama. Wanda is represented by Between Friends Publishing, formerly known as Southern Willow Publishing. Wanda loves to cook and enjoys reading poetry on her front porch. When Wanda isn't writing the Magnolia Manor series, she can be found planning her next adventure or in her garden with her honeybees.

Email: magnoliamanorseries@gmail.com
Facebook: facebook.com/MagnoliaManorBookSeries
Instagram: MagnoliaManorSeries